WHEN LIFE GIVES YOU LEGENDS

LUNA RYDER

AUTHOR'S NOTE

I love a big adventure, but I have a pretty short attention span. Perhaps it's down to my neurodivergent brain or perhaps that's just the way things are in this digital age.

Either way, I didn't want my need for perpetual amusement to stop me from slaying monsters, facing down bad guys, and saving the world. And that's why I wrote *When Life Gives You Legends*.

As an avid reader, I love for the high points to just keep coming and never stop. I don't want to sit through a five-page description of an old forest, thank you very much. I want to know what's going to happen once our character wanders in!

And hey, maybe you're like me.

If so, you'll find yourself happily at home in the world of Verandel

with the likes of Tilda Quickthatch and her misfit band of chosen family.

I've kept the chapters short and fast-paced—once you get past the first one, that is!—and I've employed a cast of characters that are far more than imaginary. They represent people in my real life, in our real world, doing super awesome, high fantasy things.

This isn't a book to be taken too seriously. It's all about finding yourself and having fun while doing it.

And I hope you will,

1

A new day dawned, and already mistakes had been made.

By me.

Mainly, that I'd lost track of time... Again.

Cursing my own carelessness, I pumped my legs in a frantic blur, but that didn't help to carry me any faster down the cobblestone streets of Briarhaven.

It always seemed that no matter how hard I tried—and believe me, *I tried*—it still took twice as long to get anywhere. That's just how things worked when you stood hardly a smidge over three feet tall.

I tried my best. Really, I did.

But I had a way of losing track of people, things, and especially time. In that moment, I felt like a silly little fly drowning in a puddle of mead after drinking its fill. At least the fly had a good excuse for its dilemma.

As for me? Um, I could still make it—if I don't hit any detours, if absolutely everything went perfectly, and if by some beautiful act of divine intervention, I managed to add a few feet to my stumpy leg-span sometime in the next three seconds.

Yeah, none of that was going to happen, but a gal could still hope.

At least I knew my boss wouldn't give me a hard time about my tardiness today. Honestly, he rarely gave anyone a hard time about anything.

Brynlee, though, she was a different story entirely. My sweet elven coworker was counting on me; she was also the last person I'd ever want to let down. The poor thing worked so hard for so little, and she didn't need me making her life any more difficult. Especially not on such an important day.

Gah! Stupid, stupid.

"Evening, Tilda," the local baker was eager to greet me. His words came out just as smooth as the butter he so generously slathered on his breads, but they had no effect on me. Like me, he was a halfling. Unlike me, he thought we should go on a date. And that was so *not* happening.

I didn't even glance his way as I called out, "Oh no,

you don't, Bramble Thistledown! It's not the evening yet. You can wish your own day away, but don't you dare steal time from me."

I tried to lift my feet higher, faster, as I navigated the winding streets of the cozy village I'd called home for nearly a decade now. My breaths came out in ragged huffs as Bramble's throaty chuckle chased after me.

Up ahead, I spotted the village square. It meant I was getting close now. Typically, this spot was a hub of activity at this time of day. But today, it lay empty, save for Ol' Clara sitting on her usual bench by the community flower garden. The elderly gnome gave me a toothless grin and waved her cane in greeting. "Afternoon, Tilda dear! Cutting it a bit close today, aren't we?"

I forced a smile and waved back. *No time, no time.* "You know me. Always living life on the edge!"

Clara just chuckled and shook her head, returning to her people watching even though there were precious few people to watch. That would change come tomorrow as out-of-towners began to flood our small town for the festival, but the brief and sudden surge in our population was a problem for tomorrow. I needed to focus on the problem I had that very minute —the whole being horribly late thing.

Just a little further... I willed my aching legs to

move faster still, ignoring the painful stitch that had now begun to form in my side. Seconds later, I breezed past the apothecary with its strange herbal scents and then the boisterous sounds of the armory. The black-smith's hammer pounded out a steady beat to match my pace.

I rounded another corner and, at last, the Mystic Mug came into view. This wasn't just my place of employment. It was my favorite place in all of Briarhaven. Heck, in all of Verandel too. Whenever I was closed within those four walls, I felt safe. Felt like I could actually be myself. Like nothing mattered, not even time.

And when you're in perpetual hiding, that's a pretty huge deal.

Taking a quick moment to smooth my wrinkled tunic, I peeked in through one of the small porthole-style windows that adorned the building. Didn't look too busy yet, but soon the place would be bustling with life—and I'd be contentedly soaking up every single second of it.

The busier I stayed now, the less I thought about what happened back then. Almost ten years had passed, and it still felt like yesterday.

Maybe that's why I was late so often. I *needed* the numbing thrill of the rush to keep me focused on the present, to keep my mind from wandering back, from wondering what if...

But this wasn't the time to torment myself yet again. No. I needed to get in there and start my shift. After all, that was the whole point of my ridiculous rush through town in the first place.

And so, I approached the thick, weather-worn door to the tavern, readying an apology for Brynlee, especially since I'd promised her just yesterday that I wouldn't be late, that I'd be early even. *Sigh.* When was I going to learn?

At least I was here now. I also knew she would forgive me faster than I could mutter the short two syllables required to give voice to my sorry.

Right before I passed through the threshold, I reached up with both hands and slapped at the empty air. I missed the ornate sign that featured a bold, curly font and a tarnished metal tankard by a good three feet. It didn't even swing in the gentle pre-twilight breeze as it hung from Durgan's old battle maul, stiff as a board, mocking me in the way only an old friend could.

Silly as it may sound, our more vertically blessed patrons had a habit of smacking the tavern sign both on their way in and their way out. Somewhere along the way it became a bit of a running joke that I attempt to do it too, and so I did. The more people kept smiling and laughing, the less they thought of asking any questions. That was a big part of how I'd survived undiscovered for so long.

Maybe one day I'd finally stop worrying. Maybe one day I'd also learn to keep track of time. Those were both big maybes. I knew they'd never happen—not for real—but I still liked to pretend I could be different, better, freer.

"I'm here, I'm here," I cried, moving swiftly toward the long right-angled bar in the corner. They didn't call me *Quick*thatch for nothing. Yeah, I couldn't move as fast as I'd like most of the time. But when I saw Brynlee, it's like some unseen force pushed me toward her.

She appeared unbothered as she ran a rag across the polished wooden top of the counter, her silver hair falling forward to conceal her face. She kept polishing with one hand and used the other to tuck the errant lock behind her pointed ear, focusing intently as if she had all the time in the world.

Heat rose to my cheeks as I unconsciously pushed a strand of my own graying brown and very curly hair behind an ear. All my remaining breath whooshed out of my lungs, and I felt as if I might fall to the floor. I felt the same way each day whenever I first laid eyes upon this particular coworker and friend.

Believe me when I say, everything about Brynlee

Starbrook was sweet, kind, unimposing—the patrons loved her, and so did I. She and the tavern owner, Durgan Stoutbarrel, were the closest thing I had to a family in this town. I only wished I got to see her more, but she worked days at Mystic Mug while I managed the nights.

We were like ships passing in the harbor, or some other such tired metaphor. Yet, no matter what problems life threw at me, Brynlee's smile always gave me the strength to find one of my own. It had been that way ever since she started working at the Mug a couple years back. She just had that warm and fuzzy thing that everyone ate right up. Probably explained why she got better tips than me.

But I wasn't in this business to charm customers or amass great riches. I was simply trying to survive the best I could, and for me, that meant remaining hidden, anonymous. Just another cog in this well-oiled machine with a small-town facade.

I waited, knowing my friend wouldn't stop until her task was done—also knowing that she wouldn't have even begun this task had I shown up on time to relieve her. Slowly, I let my heart rate drop back from the current *bada-bada-bada* back to its more normal *boom-boom-boom*. The comforting warmth of the tavern helped to soothe me, wrapping me in a much-needed embrace. Masoned walls created from small, smooth stones that had once lined the local riverbed stretched high to a single steepled point on the ceiling and a series of heavy wooden beams drew the eye up, somehow making it both cozy and expansive at the exact same time.

I still vividly remember my first time walking into this place almost ten years ago. As a dwarfish tavern, it felt just my size. Since then, Durgan had remodeled to make the establishment more inviting to patrons of all sizes, but back then, the slight, cramped interior had made me feel right at home.

The Mystic Mug was different now, but I'd grown and changed right alongside it.

I no longer felt as small as I looked, but I still found it very necessary to hide my past. Small towns were always big on drama, just not normally the world-ending variety. Durgan knew a bit about what I'd once been, but even he'd been entrusted with precious little—and Brynlee less still. I worried she'd no longer like me if she learned of the scrapes I'd gotten myself into during my adventuring days, of the decisions that had been necessary in order to survive.

Her friendship meant too much to me to ruin it by being the wrong type of friend, or the wrong type of person. And so, I hid my secrets to keep all of us safe, but also to make sure I remained relatively happy.

And my sweet elven colleague was a huge part of that continued happiness.

Brynlee's elbow grease now had the countertop shining as if by magic, though she swore up and down she didn't have a single drop of the stuff running through her veins. I rubbed my palm across it, feeling the grooves and knots in the wood, letting the physical sensation ground me back in the present moment.

Brynlee hummed a quick beat and tossed the used rag into the bucket, finally acknowledging my arrival. "I was beginning to think I'd have to send out a wing scout to track you down." She made light, but I could tell my tardiness had upset her. It upset me too.

"I'm sorry. I wish I had a better excuse, but I just lost track of time. Anyway, you need to get going. So, go. Go!" I grabbed the discarded rag and shooed her out from behind the bar, playfully threatening with a small snap of the damp cloth.

My over-the-top gesture made her giggle. All seemed to be forgiven, though I doubted Brynlee could ever truly be angry to begin with. She glanced at the custom-crafted clock hanging above the narrow stone fireplace that stretched up through the ceiling in the opposite corner of our establishment—a gift from an artisan who was better at putting beer in his belly than gold toward his tab.

"I can still make it," Brynlee sang, rushing toward the door without a single glance back my way. That was okay. She needed to get gone, not stay here and chat idly with me.

"Tell that kid of yours to break an arm!" I called after her. Sure, the expression was to break a leg, but in my experience, it was always better to break an arm. Your opponent couldn't run away if you broke their leg, but take out the arm and they could no longer fire a bow at you, throw a knife... or a flaming sack of crap. I found maiming from the top-down made for the safest and more surefire escape.

Truth be told, I'd broken many of both types of limb in my time—not my own, mind you—but my adventuring days had long since passed. I did love hearing about the exploits of Brynlee's teenaged daughter, Calina, though. Gave me a bit of vicarious satisfaction, reminded me of the old days. Or at least all the best parts of them.

That child had a wanderlust I found quite relatable and couldn't help but admire, even though I hated the trouble it caused her mother.

Because while Brynlee craved a good and simple life, Calina longed for something much greater. I had no doubts she'd one day depart for good and break her poor, sweet mother's heart. If that ever happened, I'd be here to pick up the pieces and see what we might build from them.

For now, though, Calina remained here in Briarhaven, and tonight she had a bit part in the local academy's stage adaptation of *Legends of Yore*. The play was a bit dated for my taste, but small towns had never been the cultural centers of the world. Most of the time the only good stuff we got was whatever stuff hadn't been bought up by the other towns along the merchant routes—or we were left with the things so cliché and overdone that no one else wanted them anymore. *Legends of Yore* fit into the latter category.

Calina was none too happy about getting overlooked for the starring role, but Brynlee was elated that the required afterschool practice gave her child something to do, something that would hopefully keep that little miscreant out of trouble.

Oh, sweet divinity, I used to love finding trouble.

Well, you know what they say. *Trouble has a way of coming to those who go looking for it.* As I thought these words, I could hear the gruff voice of the city watch commander that had tried for years to set me on the "right path." His efforts had of course proven fruitless.

Oh, if only he could see me now. A common small-town tavern wench. He'd be ecstatic. Half the time I was ecstatic too. For years I'd thought adventuring was the only path for me, but retirement hadn't proven half bad.

I watched Brynlee disappear into the evening dusk, no doubt rushing to get a good seat for Calina's performance. She could move faster than me without even trying most days, her long legs effortlessly gliding across a distance that took me three steps to clear. When she was motivated, she moved like a gazelle, her smooth movement making her almost appear to be flying like leaves before a storm. And as far as I'd observed over the years, absolutely nothing motivated her more than that kid of hers.

I let out a long exhale and turned back to the empty tavern. Just me now. Alone, but only for a little while. Soon this place would be filled to the gills, and I'd be too busy *doing* to worry much about *thinking*.

I took a quick inventory of our spirits and noted down what replenishments we'd soon need to order, then I disappeared into the small kitchen tucked into the back room and chopped a few root vegetables to add to that night's stew. Brynlee had already gotten it started for me. It was meant to be my responsibility, but the whole thing started off when Brynlee had realized the customers had a far easier time getting home safely when we first managed to feed them. They flirted less and tipped better too.

I finished up in the back of the house, listening intently for any slaps on the sign that would signal I needed to return to the bar. But no one had come in yet. Slow night.

My boss Durgan greeted me the moment I returned to the front of the tavern. "Enjoying your last night of freedom?" He settled upon one of the thick dwarven barrels that lined the counter. Each barrel was shaped more like a sphere than a cylinder, bloated fat in the middle. They sported intricate carvings that told of the lands in which they'd been built. The one Durgan sat upon came from a small village situated in a mountain pass, which meant it had been soldered with an impressive brass ring. It was my favorite, and I suspected it was Durgan's too.

His cherry-red beard was done up in a series of intricate braids, with various trinkets tucked into the strands, giving him an odd but jovial appearance. Although now he tended to jingle when he walked. The ridiculousness of his grooming matched his equally larger-than-life personality. Each of his baubles represented something important to him, visual reminders of his former heroics—and each came with a story that he'd told so many times I now had it memorized word-for-word.

I chuffed at his greeting. "Freedom, ha! What are you even talking about? I'm still here, aren't I?"

Durgan let out a hearty chuckle and ran a palm over his bald head. He lost his hair young, I'd been told, which is why he tended to overcompensate with that crazy bedazzled beard of his.

"Who are you kidding? You love it here, prisoner of the month," he snapped back.

I rolled my eyes, grasping for my default response when someone hits too close to home: sarcasm. "You know, most employers call it *employee* of the month, but sure, yeah, let's go with prisoner."

He didn't need me to tell him that he was right. Truly, there was nowhere else I'd rather be. But to hammer home the joke, I made sure to hum an old prison song that the hard labor prisoners would sing while working the quarry. Even though I didn't choose retirement the way Durgan had, that didn't mean I couldn't enjoy it.

Yup, my boss was a retired adventurer—just like me. He used to be a paladin of some sort until one day he decided he'd had enough. Said he'd rather put down roots, to work on building something rather than destroying everything.

"I hear the inns are already reaching capacity." He repositioned himself on the stool and leaned forward to lock eyes with me. "I've asked Pat to clear out some space in our storerooms just in case we can pick up an extra coin or two."

"Good thinking," I responded with a nod. "There's nothing wrong with taking money when people want to give it to you." *After all,* I silently added to myself, *it took a lot of coin to cover the expense of a certain someone's nightly drinking habit.*

"You said that right." He laughed again, as if he'd heard both the part I said aloud and the part I didn't. Then, after a brief pause, he pounded a fist on the counter and rose to his feet. Durgan was tall for a dwarf, but even he could barely see over the gleaming wooden bar top while standing on his feet. Of course, I had already taken up position on the sturdy metal crate that I'd spend all night moving back and forth to ensure I could see any customer who sidled up to ask for a drink.

A resounding slap called to us from the doorway, and my gaze followed the sound just as one of our many regulars made his way inside.

Durgan saw him too and let out a hearty cheer, pumping a plump fist in the air. "Insy, my good lad!

What can Tilda get started for you on this fine evening?"

The newly arrived infernal lifted one well-manicured brow and shrugged. He was a fellow of few phrases, and he made sure every single one of them counted.

At a smidge over seven feet tall, with curling ram's horns sprouting from his forehead and eyes that glowed like hot coals, he cut an imposing figure. But I knew better than to judge a person by their cover. Insy was one of the kindest and gentlest folks I knew. Second only to Brynlee.

"The usual?" I asked with a knowing smile.

"Please," he rumbled in a voice that shook the air like far-off thunder. I nodded and got to work mixing up his favorite drink—a sweet concoction I liked to call Demon's Delight. Insy watched me expectantly as I deftly combined fruit juices and spirits, his tail swishing back and forth in anticipation.

"Make it two, Tilda, and bring them over this way," Durgan shouted, moving toward the fireplace where he knew our infernal guests feel most at home.

He was a boss in name only. More than anything he was the famed mascot of the Mystic Mug. Sure, he owned the place, but he also spent his entire time carousing with the clientele. In fact, half my job was making sure he didn't get too tipsy to find his way home to his partner, Pat, who spent long days working as a blacksmith's apprentice.

Night and day, those two. Still, they made a good pair.

Not unlike Brynlee and me.

Speaking of, Calina must have been just about ready to take the stage by then. I could picture Brynlee gracefully poised in the very front row as she waited for the curtain to rise. She was the peaceful sort, but I had no doubts she'd charmed her way into the very best seat.

She'd do anything for that child of hers. Just like I'd do pretty much anything for her... Provided I didn't lose track of time, that was.

With a fresh zest of citrus fruit, I finished off the pair of cocktails for Durgan and Insy, then moseyed over to the fireplace to hand them off. A muscle in my thigh cramped from the earlier rush through town, and I stumbled forward from the sudden burst of pain. Not a single drop spilled from either glass, though.

Some are born with gifts of brawn or brains, but I'd been bequeathed an unnatural grace. In fact, I could've carried this tray through my dash through town earlier without losing even the slightest bit of the liquid.

Durgan caught my eye, and I could tell he wanted to ask whether I was okay, but he also didn't want to worry our customer, so instead he waited for me to give him a silent signal. If I needed anything, he'd be the first to jump to my rescue.

I appreciated that about him, but a little muscle cramp was the least of my worries. Truly. I tucked my hair behind my right ear to let him know I was fine. Right was good; left meant there was trouble. It was a code we used to update Durgan when needed, but that communication only worked one way given his baldness.

I turned to make my way back to the counter and caught sight of a new arrival.

He hadn't slapped the sign like our regulars did, or I would've heard him enter. Instead, he'd just appeared in the corner of my eye like an apparition. He must have been new around here. It was impossible to tell, since a dark, ragged hood covered more than half of his face, keeping any identifying features obscured beneath.

I floated over to him with as much grace as I could muster and offered my usual greeting. "Welcome to the Mystic Mug. What can I do you for?"

But the strange new arrival didn't make a single movement to acknowledge I'd joined him. He didn't say anything, either. He just sat there being creepy like some kind of ominous cliche.

"Can I get you something to drink?" I tried again, working hard not to let the irritation slip into my voice. "Or eat? We've got a nice, little menu of—"

I stopped short when the cloaked figure wrapped long, ice-cold fingers around my left forearm and clamped down like a spring-locked hunting trap, igniting an old wound I worked hard to keep hidden. A chill shot through me, and that knot of pain in my thigh roared to life again. I twisted and yanked, but my assailant held tight, looming above me even though I stood and he remained seated.

Thank the divine, Durgan appeared when he did, charging forth from his cozy spot at the fireplace as if he were rushing into war. "Unhand her. No one assaults my employees but me!" His voice resonated with an authority that's hard to ignore despite his diminutive stature or his distasteful—and, frankly, untrue—attempt at humor. No one in this town cared more about his staff than old Durgan Stoutbarrel, and that was a fact.

I jerked my arm again, and at last, the unwelcome stranger released his grip. My throbbing arm fell back to my side, and I stood rooted to the spot as the mystery man fled the tavern and faded into the night.

Not even Durgan's shouted demands for an explanation managed to bring him back. And I guess that meant I'd never know who he was or what the heck he wanted with me.

Finally admitting defeat, Durgan gave up on shouting and dropped his voice to a heady whisper. "What was that all about?"

I shrugged, still shaken by the whole thing. I was supposed to be safe here. The fact that I had no idea who that man was or why he'd grabbed me set my heart into a frantic gallop.

I worked hard to add a note of detached humor to my voice. "Probably just an out-of-towner here for the festival. I'd wager he had more than his fair share of ale before finding his way here."

Unfortunately, I didn't believe that at all. Drunks tended to stumble and crash around. Whoever this was had slipped in and out like a living shadow, which couldn't mean anything good.

Have I been found out at last?

No. Impossible.

I chose Briarhaven because this sleepy little town never attracted anyone's attention. Then again, the festival happening in a couple days would bring in outsiders by the bucketful. Stupid Centaurs and their stupid centennial celebration. Why should I care that one-hundred years ago one of their ancestors crossed some great expanse to found our village? Sure, I liked living here, but I'd be a whole lot more impressed by their great feats, if the dudes weren't already half-horse. Their race had literally been built for this kind of thing, which made it hard for me to see the point of celebrating.

Well, at least this wasn't a problem I'd have to deal with again for another hundred years. I just had to get through the next few days unnoticed and unscathed, then things could go back to how they were.

After the run-in with our cloaked friend, I'd have stayed at home and hidden beneath my bedsheets if I weren't so worried about letting Durgan down.

"Just be careful," he said, offering a firm pat on my shoulder. "I can't lose my number-one princess just before the big ball." He winked, knowing full well that his friendly joke would melt right through the icy terror that had frozen me to the spot just moments before.

"Your jokes would have more of an impact if you at least tried to keep them consistent," I said, slipping back into our previous banter with ease. "I mean, am I a princess or a prisoner? Make up your mind already."

"I don't see why you can't be both," he called over his shoulder on his way back toward Insy and the fruity cocktail awaiting him there. Durgan was the princess, and he knew it better than anyone. Still, he'd been the one to save my butt tonight.*

And I simply couldn't let that happen again.

As much as I loved my found family, I knew better than to rely on them. It's why I did my best to keep some distance, to only let my guard down while in the tavern and on the clock.

My problems were my own, and it would kill me if either Durgan or Brynlee ended up paying the price for the many misdeeds of my past.

Must be more careful. Must remain alert. Must stay hidden.

And most importantly must not let anyone down ever again.

---

* If you'd like to read some free bonus content about Durgan's back story, go here.

2

The rest of the evening passed without incident. But the next afternoon? That started off with a bit of a bang.

That day I made it to work just in time. Hustling into the tavern, my eyes grew wide as I spotted the rosy-haired youth sitting at the bar with her arms crossed over her chest and her lower lip pouting out rather dramatically.

"That you, Calina?" I asked with a surprised squeak, even though I knew exactly who I was looking at.

She turned to me with her brows pinched together as if she was about to launch into a breathless harangue about the many injustices that marred her otherwise perfect teenaged existence.

"How'd your play go last night?" I asked before she could hit me with any undue complaints. The girl could fill me in later, outside of her mother's earshot, if she really needed to vent. Though I doubted she would. The two of us weren't close like that, and she knew my loyalties lied with Brynlee, which meant I would most definitely pass on any secrets shared, even if they were in confidence.

"Awful." Calina kicked one pointy-toed shoe at the barrel beside her but didn't offer any more of an explanation than that. Elves, everything about them was pointy—ears, shoes, jewelry, you name it. It was like they were trying to make up for their innate softness any way that they could.

Outside of her appearance though, there was nothing soft about this particular young elf. A fact that raised questions I wasn't willing to ask and risk upsetting her mother.

I wondered, though, how the two of them could be so different despite their shared blood. By the divine, did I wonder.

"What was so awful about it?" I glanced around for Brynlee but didn't see her anywhere nearby. Whatever had Calina so upset was probably also what had landed her at the tavern rather than somewhere she could enjoy the start of the short break from school on her own terms. Yesterday, Durgan had joked that I was his prisoner. Today, Calina really was an unwilling inmate at the Mystic Mug.

The kid let out an aggravated sigh before launching into her harangue. "Tulip Thunderhoof got—"

Brynlee came charging in from the kitchen to interrupt. "Don't you dare talk to her!" Her voice was quiet but firm. "She's grounded."

I raised an eyebrow at that. "Grounded from even talking?"

"Yes. Grounded from talking. In fact, she's grounded from *life.*"

Calina let out a hearty harrumph and glared daggers at her mother. I could relate. I'd been quite the surly ray of sunshine back in my day too.

Of course, I couldn't even remember my mother or whether she'd ever cared for me the way Brynlee loved hers. I'd been forced to live on my own from a very early age; it's part of what made me so tough but also the biggest reason why I so loved this merry, little found family I'd come to call my own.

"Somebody thought it would be a good idea to get that little orc friend of hers to hide backstage and light a magical flame under the leading actress's flank when the cast was taking their final bows last night. The poor dear very understandably panicked and accidentally kicked the whole set over. Which means last night's performance of *Legends of Yore* was *the only* performance. A terrible thing after how hard they all worked. Now, none of our out-of-town guests will be able to enjoy it while they're here."

I stifled a laugh, which drew a scowl from Brynlee but elicited a wicked smile from Calina. If Brynlee and I were bread and butter, Calina and I were bread and bread.

"Sorry," I mumbled, bringing a fist to cover my lips as I poorly masked my huff of laughter as a cough. "Something in the air. Just got me, *um*... So grounded for life, huh?"

"No weren't you listening? It's grounded *from* life." Calina was quick to correct as she rolled her eyes so far back, I briefly wondered if they'd get stuck. She kicked the barrel seat again and let out a long, dramatic sigh. "Sylric save me, this sucks." The child invoked the elven trickster god, much to her mother's deepening exasperation.

"Well, maybe you'll think twice next time before you—"

Calina groaned again and raised her eyes toward the ceiling in a full-on tantrum now. Always interrupting each other, these two were.

Durgan ambled over to our trio. It seemed he was

already a couple more drinks in than usual. He burped and then snarled at us. "That's quite enough."

The creases that lined his forehead whenever he got upset resembled an off-balance ladder. I liked to imagine climbing them as a way of calming myself whenever his ire was turned on me. Durgan was a great friend, but I would wager he made an even more powerful enemy. The bad guys should thank their lucky stars he'd retired when he did.

"The young lass can stay, but only if she *stays* out of the way." He shot a pointed gaze at each of the elves in turn. "There's plenty to do, young'un, if you'd like to offer us a hand. I'll even pay you a bit of gold for the trouble."

Calina scoffed at this suggestion without even turning to look at Durgan. "No. No way."

"Suit yourself, but soon enough, you may not have a choice," Durgan said as he turned to watch somebody new pass through the door.

That would be the musician he'd hired to entertain the masses during the festival days, hoping to outdo the other taverns as the go-to destination in Briarhaven for the delightful mass of tourists. Never mind that, even though it had been heavily renovated over the years, this was still a dwarven establishment and most of the out-of-towners were centaurs, which meant they'd be at least three times too large to comfortably take a seat. Centaurs always needed special accommodations to make their way through the world, and they tended to get them too. I had no doubt, Durgan's partner Pat was already whipping up some special kind of seating rig that would make its grand appearance before the festivities came to an end.

"Be on your best behavior," Durgan hissed from one side of his mouth while the other broke into an enormous grin aimed at the musician working his way toward the small stage we'd set up near the back of the house. The result was off-putting, to say the least. But the fact he could still control his face so expertly seemed to suggest he hadn't yet imbibed that many mugs of mead, after all. Maybe he'd stay sober today. Maybe he'd even lend us a hand if we needed one. Ha!

Durgan realigned the two sides of his face and smacked one of the barrel stools as if he'd just decided something important. "Tilda, you're in charge." An assertive foot stomp was added to the barrel slap, and with that he left us, returning to his task of pretending to be a customer while Brynlee and I did all the work.

We were expecting a lot of business, which is why Brynlee had been asked to work a double shift today. Come tomorrow, we'd both be on double duty, which meant I had to wake up extra early just to make sure I got here in time.

Brynlee went to check on the stew while Calina continued to pout and kick at the bar as I polished our drinkware to a shine.

It wasn't long before a small group of humans charged through the doorway. Not a one of them slapped the sign, which meant they were most likely new here.

Tonight would definitely be full of new faces, as it seemed our regulars had decided to go into hiding tonight. Briarhaven wasn't exactly a touristy town. Most of us liked that our lives were small and unassuming. Heck, that very fact was why I'd settled here in the first place.

The small population of centaurs in Briarhaven didn't care how uncomfortable their celebrations made the rest of us. It seemed they were always finding ways to take up even more space than their hefty posteriors already required. The rapidly approaching centennial celebration, however, was the biggest event yet. At least since I'd arrived ten years back. They'd all been neighing about it for months.

At least it gave the rest of us time to prepare... or hide.

I'd wager most of us would get little sleep, thanks

to a veritable stampede of stomping hooves. But given that the centaurs were the landed gentry of the area, we just had to grin and bear it until the festival reached an end. Life would hopefully go back to normal for all of us afterward. That was a fact I was very much counting on.

The bard-for-hire plucked a few test chords on his honey-colored mandola, an instrument I could only identify after having adventured so many long years with a bard at my side.

Brynlee returned to my side and sighed with pleasure. Her expression went blank as she stared into the distance. Music always did this to her—transported her to another realm, made her disappear into herself far more than usual.

The gentle, swirling melodies, however, made me grit my teeth as they unlocked my most painful memories and my most shameful secret. The music always brought me straight back to him, to Gaaron, my former traveling companion, my partner, my friend, and a true virtuoso of a bard. He'd been a bright spot in this world, but now that light was forever dimmed. And the fault was mine entirely... If I'd been better, smarter, or even just a bit faster, he'd still be alive.

It was my idea that we accept that last quest, and it was my inability to break through a stupid dungeon door that had gotten him killed. I mean, what kind of rogue couldn't pick a simple lock? Even a cleric could manage that half the time.

That's why I'd retired. I no longer had my partner, but what's more, my confidence had died along with Gaaron that day. I'd lost two things that were very important to me and gained two cursed afflictions at the same time.

The magical burn that covered a huge swatch of skin on my left forearm itched as it so often did whenever I thought back to that squalid dungeon-turned-tomb. And I mindlessly tugged at the sleeve of my tunic to make sure it was covered up. I always made sure to keep my wounds hidden so that they didn't raise any eyebrows—or questions.

Calina's gaze narrowed at my arm, curiosity sparking behind her pale lavender eyes. Her lips formed a soft "O," and I could tell a question was coming, one that would most definitely require a well-orchestrated lie from my side.

Durgan was the only one who knew anything about my past. As much as I adored Brynlee, not even she knew the real me. I kept so much hidden.

It was safer for everyone that way.

The newly arrived humans finally made their way over to the bar, and I rushed to their aid, eager to escape the young elf's scrutiny. As a former rogue, I was good at lying, but that didn't mean I liked doing it.

"A round of gin and tonics, my good sir," the human's apparent leader said, leaning over the bar and flashing a haughty smile my way.

Ugh. Humans.

They thought they owned every room they entered, and they were absolutely horrible about learning the ways of other races and cultures. Some of them were okay, but most were just like this centaur's backside standing before me. This was a centaurian celebration, so why were these clowns even here? And why did they insist on being jerks about it?

I looked nothing like a sir, and this guy knew it.

That wasn't the only part that irked me though. Throughout all my many travels, I'd never tasted any concoction more vile than the "Gin and Tonic." Who cared that the fizzy waters of some secluded mountain river made it bubble like a witch's brew and caused it to tickle all the way down? The taste ruined the entire experience. Honestly, that's probably why the human men liked it so much. They loved proving their ruggedness and virility, even when it was only to each other. As for me, I'd gladly take a mug of mead over that swill any day.

One of the other humans caught sight of Brynlee

bustling about on the other side of the bar and sidled up to her. I'd encountered enough humans to know exactly where his mind was, and it wasn't above the waist. Brynlee would never return his attentions, just as I knew she would never return mine. She had one—and only one—love in her life, and that was a torch Brynlee would never extinguish.

I knew nothing about the fellow, other than that he'd left shortly after their child was born. Yes, it seemed we all kept secrets around the Mystic Mug. Of course, Brynlee's ex didn't seem like much of a romantic hero to me, yet somehow my friend still blamed herself for his departure. She was so heartsick, she simply couldn't see the truth.

Personally, I'd never been interested in love.

Friendship, absolutely.

Carnal pleasure, sometimes, though it hadn't been for a long time.

But love? No, no way.

Adventurers weren't meant to form strong bonds outside of their parties. It's what kept us on the road, saw us living to fight another day, embarking upon another quest. Attachments were dangerous. It was bad enough how much I cared for my coworkers. If I actually found myself a mate, I'd be completely and utterly screwed.

It didn't matter that I was retired.

Because I'd be spending the rest of my natural life hiding and hoping that adventure didn't come calling once more, all the while fully knowing that it just might.

I guess that's part of why I let myself like Brynlee as much as I did. She was a safe choice for my private affections because I knew her love would forever belong to someone else. Fixating on our friendship kept me from noticing any of the odd patrons who let their eyes linger on me for just a bit too long or spoke words that came out just a bit too sweet. Bramble Thistledown was my most ardent admirer, true, but he wasn't the only one who'd attempted to wrest me from my near decade of celibacy. Some folks had a thing for halflings, but my race was such a small part of who I was.

If I could keep things from getting too serious around here, it was easier to forget the fear that had practically become a shadow, following my every move, forever and always with no end in sight.

I would never be safe until the one who hunted me was gone and seeing that he'd already managed to live for nigh on a millennium, his sudden and final death probably wouldn't happen anytime soon.

And that meant I'd be here in Briarhaven, at the

Mystic Mug, for the rest of my days. It was okay, though. I liked it here... Most of the time.

The next few days would be busy with the centaurs' festival, which meant I wouldn't have much time to think—and especially not to worry.

Thank the luck keeper for her small graces.

As much as I still detested the arrogant human patrons, I managed to smile as I handed off the round of drinks, I'd just mixed for them. And as soon as they'd turned away, I patted my chest, feeling for the coiled metal that hung between my breasts, laying perfectly hidden beneath my unassuming tunic. The magical scar wasn't the only thing I'd picked up from that last mission of mine—and it wasn't the only thing I needed to make sure remained hidden.

3

The centaurs' centennial celebration officially began the next day. And Durgan had made it very clear that he expected both me and Brynlee to work our hardest from sunup until well past sundown. He and Pat had even taken in a few boarders to snare a little extra coin. Luckily, their home had been built with Pat's half-giant stature in mind. Only the divine and, hopefully, Pat and Durgan themselves knew how *that* particular arrangement worked behind closed doors. Despite the mysteries of their private matters, Pat's grandeur ensured the place was more than large enough to stable a trio of visiting centaurs.

This also meant that the Mystic Mug remained free of any overnight guests, at least for now. I had no doubt that Durgan would agree to take in any latecomers, should they be willing to compensate him handsomely for such hospitality.

That morning, I crept slowly through the darkened streets of pre-dawn Brairhaven. Even after all this time, moving with stealth still felt like second nature. *Don't be seen, don't get caught.* Not even a lack of slumber the previous night could take that skill from me. I could feel the lack of sleep as each blink rubbed like sandpaper across my eyes. But I kept careful watch as I moved ever closer to the Mystic Mug, muscles tense, ready for an ambush around every corner.

It was far too early—so early that it felt like I was still living out yesterday. I'd never been a morning person, a fact I didn't expect to see change in the second half of life. Still, Durgan rarely asked for me to take on extra hours. I could swallow down my cranky asides for these two days to give him the help he needed.

That didn't mean I was happy about it though.

As my weary feet dragged me through the darkened streets, my eyes found their way into every nook and crevice, searching for anything that might prove out of place. The encounter with my cloaked assailant a couple days back still had me on edge, and I now made sure to stay properly alert as I made my way toward the tavern.

I also made sure to be punctual.

But since I'd always been horrible at estimating how long it took to do things, I was now a good twenty minutes early. Neither Durgan nor Brynlee had arrived yet, which meant I was stuck outside until one of them came to help unlock the place. Getting in and out of the Mystic Mug required two keys, each needed to be slotted into the corresponding lock in perfect unison with the other. The keys were identical, which meant any combination of the three of us could do the deed, both to open shop in the morning and to shutter up at night.

I hadn't wanted to start what I already knew would be a tiring day off on the wrong foot by making my friends wait out in the cold for me while I once again struggled to get my legs to move faster than they were willing to go. But now that meant I was stuck out on my own. I could have slept longer or eaten more energizing berries to perk myself up, but no. Time had been a cruel mistress for me once again.

Very few villagers had woken for the day. Not even the sun was up yet.

Which meant it was just me and the empty shadows that taunted me, whispering of dangers yet to be seen. It was a strange sensation, being so physically fatigued while also needing to stay hypervigilant in case there were any signs of trouble.

I hated being alone and exposed like this. Briarhaven was a small, usually safe town, but the out-of-town guests could easily spell trouble—trouble of many varieties. I was usually good at handling myself, but I was usually much more awake.

I blew out the breath I'd been holding back and shook out my hands, trying to work out the knots that had formed from being ready for an attack from every direction. *Must wake up, must limber up, must make it through this day.*

Something shifted a few shops down the block before once again disappearing from my view. My heart began to gallop like a bloody centaur, putting me into fight-or-flight mode yet again. I couldn't exactly leave when I was expected at work, which meant I had to be ready for a fight.

Well, at least I was fully awake now.

I patted the hidden pendant beneath my tunic, then reached into the pocket of my britches and wrapped my fingers around the sheathed dagger that I always kept at the ready.

From the outside, I looked like a simple, small-town halfling, middle-aged and mediocre. No one knew what I was really capable of. And I sincerely hoped that this wasn't the day they'd all find out.

The shadows parted again to reveal something quite large creeping my way. Although creeping was probably the wrong word for it, the movement was more like... lumbering? Graceless but hurried. Strangely, it seemed the person believed they were exercising great stealth, based on how they appeared to be hunched over and often pressed himself flat against shop walls to pause before lurching forward again.

I didn't recognize this person, and they made no attempt to call out to me. Would I soon be under attack?

I swallowed down the lump that had begun to form in my throat and unsheathed my blade. "Durgan? Brynlee?"

The figure stopped his advance and ducked into the alley behind the apothecary. I heard heavy breathing. This wasn't excitement. No, it seemed far more like panic. The monster was more afraid of me than I of it. Good. I could use that to my advantage should I need one.

"I know you're out there. Show yourself!" I had my dagger drawn and brandished before me, gripping it tight with both hands and hoping that it would imply I didn't know how to handle the weapon. I was never bothered by an opponent's underestimation of me, because their lack of confidence in my abilities so often tipped the scales in my favor.

I waited.

Precious seconds ticked by.

At last, the creature showed itself. He summoned a small flame that floated in the air beside him, illuminating a face that was very much chagrinned. A flush of pink lit up his greenish complexion, not even his scraggly facial hair could hide the obvious embarrassment this orcish fellow felt.

"Who are you?" I demanded as I continued to cling to my blade. "What do you want?"

He continued to draw closer with both hands held up in a gesture of surrender. I could now tell that this creature was a half-orc. Despite the full beard, he also appeared to be quite young.

"Are you a friend of Calina's?" I guessed and immediately knew I'd hit the mark.

He closed the final distance between us, snagging his oversized foot on a loose paver and stumbling forward several paces before catching himself. I watched in amusement as he collided with his own spell-flame and hissed from the sudden burst of pain.

As the flame blinked off, I finally realized that this

kid was no threat to me. I tucked the dagger back into its sheath and stuck both into my pocket.

"Ruh-Ruh-Ruh-Rurik." The pink on his cheeks had transformed into a deep mulberry color, the same hue my skin would take on if I spent too many long hours under a harsh sun. I didn't know orcs could change color like a mood crystal, although I'd never met an orc as terribly awkward as this one. Not until that exact moment.

"And you're a friend of Calina's."

He nodded. "Her best friend actually. I mean, she's my only friend. The others at school... they don't like me. And everyone at home, they don't understand me. And I juh-juh-just—" The poor guy stopped speaking and started to bawl big, sploshy tears.

I needed a moment to overcome the strange mismatch of his deep and frightful booming voice and the actual words he was saying. I'd never seen an orc cry. If you'd asked me before now, I'd have said it wasn't possible. My stomach turned, threatening to spill its meager contents on the streets before me. I'd gone from tired to terrified to... whatever this was. Like a whirly ride for children, only this was not in any way fun.

"Hey, kid. Stop! I don't need your life story. I just need to know what you're doing here." Yeah, it might have seemed cruel that I was being so hard on him when he clearly already beat himself up on the regular, but he'd given me a great fright and I needed to get at least a little revenge to maintain my dignity and all that. Besides, I already cared about three people too many. I didn't need any other liabilities, and this half-orc wimp seemed like a pretty enormous liability.

Rurik let out a mighty sniff, then straightened to his full posture, looming several feet over me. Good thing I'd already determined he was not a threat, otherwise my knife would be back out and ready to cut this kid to pieces. "Calina said you might need an extra hand at the tavern, that you'd be willing to pay. I-I-I—" He stopped again as if by taking a moment to gather his thoughts, he'd be able to express them a bit better. Somehow, I doubted that would be the case.

"I need to... Oh!" He stopped speaking again and then lowered himself to a squat, meeting me at eye level. It almost looked as if he were about to take a giant dump right here in front of the tavern. A real classy fellow, this one.

"You get up this instant! Hasn't anyone ever told you that's highly offensive to those of us who aren't quite so vertically blessed? I'm not a child or a small, frightened animal. So stand the fig up." I heaved an enormous sigh, my chest rising and falling like the swell of a stormy ocean. This guy put me on edge, and I didn't like it. Not one bit.

As Rurik struggled to his feet, his eyes met my bosom for a moment, and the blush that had taken up residence on his cheeks now spread to his forehead as well. At this rate, he'd be a giant walking tomato before our brief exchange had ended.

"Goodness, child! I have half a mind to ask if you were raised in a barn!"

"Suh-suh-sorry," he shouted so loud that a couple of lights flickered to life down the street. "This was stupid. I'm stupid. I'll go."

He turned to leave, but I grabbed him by the arm. I couldn't even bring my fingers halfway around his meaty wrist, such was our massive size difference. "You're not going anywhere, young man. You said you wanted some extra work. We could use the help. Heck, I'll even pay you from my own wages, if I have to."

Rurik's eyes lit up as if he were about to cry from sheer gratitude. "Rea-really?"

"Yeah, it's going to be record-breaking busy today, and we could use another humungous set of hands like yours. Wait with me. My boss will be here any minute. You can ask him yourself. Though, lose the stutter. Show some confidence for crying out loud." The truth was I didn't really need the extra help, but I wouldn't mind having an imposing-looking bodyguard in case anything a touch more sinister escaped the shadows.

One look at Rurik's hulking form, and they'd think twice about causing any trouble in the tavern. I just had to find something to keep him busy and looking fierce. The moment they heard him speak or saw him stumble over his own feet, the ruse would be up.

"Ho there, Tilda!" Durgan's merry voice rang out from behind me, and I turned to greet him with a friendly wave. "How is it that you're the first to arrive? You're never the first. And not just because you work the night shift."

"Hardy har har. Get all your jokes out now, because I'm going to be much too busy to deal with your pestering once those doors open to patrons. Speaking of, this is Rurik. He's a friend of Calina's and—"

Rurik raised a finger to interject. "Best friend. I am the best friend of Calina."

"Okay, not really the point." I rolled my eyes and shook my head in disbelief. This kid was beyond awkward. How did Calina put up with him?

I shaped my hand into a fleshy beak and slammed my thumb against my fingers several times in quick succession, making wide eyes at Rurik so he'd understand to clap his yap and let the grown-ups do the talking.

"Anyway, like I was saying, this is Rurik. He wants to help out at the Mug today. Think we can use an extra worker drone?"

Rurik pressed his palms together and lifted his hands in supplication, as if the jovial dwarf before him was some kind of deity and not a day-drunk small-business owner. He licked his lips and then shot his gaze back toward my bosom, narrowing his eyes slightly as he studied me for a moment before quickly ripping his gaze away.

Maybe this was a bad idea. I didn't need some lovesick teenager dawdling after me like a baby drag-onling. But before I could say another word, Durgan responded with his characteristic boom.

"Ho ho, of course he can help! The more, the merrier, I always say. Especially when drink is involved. I can pay you in mead rather than coin."

I sighed heavily and pinched the bridge of my nose. These two were killing me. It was far too early for this degree of nonsense. "He's a child, Durgan. Mead is a no-go. Besides, I happen to know you have a bit of extra coin to spare, so get over yourself and pay the kid what he's worth."

"Well." Durgan puffed out his chest and took a step

forward, his gaze sweeping over Rurik from head to toe. He had to crane his neck at quite an awkward angle to do this. "Then, my lad, come on inside and let us see what you are worth."

He pulled out his key and positioned himself in front of the left lock, and I raced forward to jab my key into the right just in time for us to twist them in perfect harmony—and officially open the Mystic Mug for business that day.

"Come on, kid. I'll show you the ropes." I motioned for our temporary muscle to follow me toward the kitchen. And I didn't even need to look back to make sure he was following, such was the cuh-clunk noise that shook the floorboards with every step he took.

This was going to be a long, long day.

Well, best to get started then.

4

Brynlee turned up nearly half an hour late. It was like we had accidentally switched places that day.

"Ugh, I am so sorry. I'm the worst person in the world. It's okay if you want to hate me forever." Her normally perky features were pinched into a tight frown, like she'd just eaten a citrus-fruit whole. Even stressed, her voice remained a soft lilting soprano, and its sweet melody soothed me to the bones.

I offered her what I hoped was a reassuring smile. "Bryn, relax. I'm late all the time. Besides, we don't even have any customers yet."

"I know. I know. It's just..." Her words drifted away when Rurik lumbered out of the kitchen and stubbed his toe on the edge of the bar. That was at least the third time he'd made the exact same mistake. If I'd had any hopes for his performance, they were all out of the window now.

Brynlee's lips parted and she placed a hand on the counter to steady herself. "Rurik. What are you doing here?"

"Working so that I don't have to." Calina strode confidently into the tavern and pulled up a barrel. "How's it going, Rur?"

"You planned this." A sly smile crept across my face. I was most definitely impressed.

Brynlee, however, was not.

Her pinched features became contorted with the rare show of anger. I hardly recognized her as she scolded her daughter. "So that's why you did everything in your power to make me late today! Are you allergic to an honest day's work? I didn't raise you to be lazy or ungrateful." Brynlee's vocal cadence remained the exact same, despite the clear hostility behind her words.

Calina popped both elbows onto the bar and rested her chin on laced fingers. "And I'm neither of those things, so don't act like I am. Honestly, Mom. Rurik could use the money. Besides he hasn't got anything better to do. Not when you insist on having me holed up in this pit all day."

"That's quite enough, young lady. I have a half a mind to..." We all saw the exact moment she lost her nerve. Brynlee was many things, but a match for her teenaged daughter, she was not. Her face returned to its usual placid expression, and not a moment too soon, as far as I was concerned. I hated seeing her so worked up.

She waved a hand in defeat. "Oh, forget it. We're already running behind, and I simply don't have the energy to fight with you anymore."

Calina beamed. She'd clearly sent Rurik to us and delayed her mother to ensure that Durgan and I would enlist her friend's help before she ever set foot in the Mug and risked having to pitch in herself. Clever child.

"Thank you, Mama. I love you!"

Brynlee just grunted, a strange sound coming from the typically graceful elf.

"I'll keep an eye on her," I promised and gave my friend a firm pat on her hip since I had no hope of reaching her shoulder.

Rurik hovered nearby, apparently awaiting further instructions. I'd set him to work on chopping vegetables and readying a triple-batch of our daily stew. He'd need at least another half an hour to get it all done, so why was he up here bothering me again?

"Is there anything else I can help you with?" His

stutter seemed to be gone now that Calina had arrived. Interesting.

"You're supposed to be preparing the stew."

He brought his hands together and circled his thumbs around each other as he struggled to meet my eye. "Right. But I'm done with that. Do you have anything else I can do?"

"What? You couldn't possibly..." I rushed to the tiny kitchen in the back and ate my words when I saw four pots set to boil, each on one of four magical flames.

Rurik stood behind me and scratched at his elbow. "I thought I'd make extra. In case. And I hope you don't mind, but I thought with a bit of magic, I could get them all to cook in half the time."

I stared at him, flabbergasted. Yes, flabbergasted. That was the only word for it.

"How in Verandel, did you manage to do all this so quick?" I demanded.

He blushed for a moment, but the pink quickly faded back to green. "It was easy. I prepare all kinds of ingredients for my spell work. The flame was the first cantrip I learned. Well, the only one, but it's definitely useful."

I continued to stare, and my chin hung toward my chest. Someone could probably stick a whole fist into my mouth, if they'd wanted to. Such was the degree of my surprise. It felt as if the hinge on my jaw had broken, and I no longer had the proper working mechanism to close it.

"You're surprised because I'm a half-orc."

I nodded dumbly. As much as I hated to admit my biases, every single orc I'd ever met was all smash and go, whether they chose an adventuring life or not. Even their healers didn't do much in the way of magic. It was always chewed roots and mud mixtures applied as poultices and the like. Yet here was a teenager of their kind, crafting potions and producing magical flames.

Rurik cast his eyes toward the ground. His tusks seemed to tremble as he spoke with slow and intentional words. "I always knew I was different. My parents... they don't like that so much. Mom's a human. She and Dad were part of the same all-barbarian raiding party. That's how they met and fell in love, decided to have me to carry on their legacy. Only I want nothing to do with that. I'm not like them. All I want to do is learn the secrets of the universe. Is that too much to ask for a guy like me?"

Oh, boy. I had no idea what to say to all that. Even if Rurik could mix some ingredients together and learn a simple cantrip, I doubted he'd ever be able to master the arcane arts beyond the single spell he'd already taught himself. I wasn't trying to be unfair, but that's just the way things had always been. Could some random kid from some tiny village actually change things for an entire race of creatures?

I didn't know, but Rurik sure seemed to believe it.

I shook my head, still in disbelief but also duly impressed now. "I don't know what the future holds, but if you're going to learn those secrets, you'd better find yourself a good teacher," was all I could manage by way of encouragement.

Outside, the sun was only just beginning to rise. Brynlee's arrival had soothed my fight-or-flight instincts, allowing the sleepiness to creep back in. But we had a big day ahead of us. And frankly, it was still way too early for this steaming heap of dragon dung.

"I know." Rurik broke into an enormous toothy grin that showed his tusks off nicely. "I know," he said again, then turned to leave the kitchen with a confidence I didn't yet recognize in him.

Even though I'd worked twice as many hours that day, the time seemed to fly at triple-speed. Soon the day had come to an end, and Brynlee and I found ourselves working together to update inventory, polish flagons, and close the tavern for the night.

Rurik had ended up surprising me in all the best possible ways that evening. While he avoided speaking to any of the patrons, he still did good, honest work, managing the kitchen, the dishes, and bussing duties, while Brynlee and I took care of everything else.

"You did good work, lad," Durgan said punching the half-orc in his thigh. A well-timed punch was the boss's way of showing he liked someone. Still, that didn't stop Rurik from wincing in pain and looking as if he might burst into tears again.

"Relax, he likes you." I winked at the kid. Sure, he was weird, but he was also kind of growing on me. Good thing he wouldn't be around long. I could already feel my heart getting soft, and that just would not do.

Durgan let out a hearty chuckle, then punched the kid in the opposite thigh to even things out. "Care to help us out again tomorrow?"

"Durgan, that won't be necess—"

Rurik did that quivery happy thing with his tusks again as he smiled. "I'd love to."

"Fantasmic!" The boss man let out a big hiccup, proving he too had been "working" harder than usual that day.

"If you can stay here with the kids, I'll get him home to Pat," Brynlee offered, already grabbing the tipsy dwarf by the shoulder and leading him to the exit.

I nodded and watched them go. Normally, Pat came in to fetch Durgan himself, but he hadn't wanted to leave their house unattended while the two of them housed boarders. I didn't mind keeping an eye on the teens for the next fifteen minutes while Brynlee took her roundtrip journey. In fact, it was better that way. Brynlee was nearly twice my height. Much stronger too. She could handle it if Durgan leaned on her too heavily, whereas I would get flattened into the cobblestones. Besides, when given the choice, I always preferred the safety of the Mug.

The two of us would have another double shift tomorrow to cover the final full day of the celebration, but we expected that most of the out-of-towners would leave early, departing in the early afternoon once the final festivities had wrapped.

The door slammed behind my departing colleagues, then a soft thwap rang out as Brynlee slapped the sign on Durgan's behalf. He laughed and shouted something nonsensical. I had no doubt he'd crash hard once he made it to his bed.

I turned to Rurik. "Okay, so you'll be joining us again tomorrow. But just so you know, we won't need you any more after that. The festival will be over, and things will go back to normal, which means we'll be able to manage ourselves."

"That's okay. I'll already have what I need by then." He winced suddenly and took a step back. "I muh-muh-mean, I'll have enough coin. I don't—"

Calina appeared on the staircase coming down from the lofted storeroom. She'd spent most of the day up there doodling and napping and offering us no help whatsoever. She snorted and shook her head as she jogged down the steps toward us. "Way to play it cool, genius."

"Suh-suh-suh-sorry." Rurik looked as if he were in physical pain. "I know you had it all planned out, and I ruined it with my big mouth."

"Yeah, you've got a big mouth, but that's okay. It's part of what I like about you." The two of them exchanged a smile, Calina's coming first and then Rurik's finally dawning after. "So, what do you reckon? Think I'm right about her?"

They both turned to me. I did not like this one bit.

"I know you're right," Rurik answered, then tapped his chest and dropped his gaze toward my bosom again. "That's definitely not some old family heirloom. It's magic. I can feel it."

"What are you two yammering on about?" I placed

both hands on my hips, wishing more than anything that I was tall enough to cut an imposing figure and stare them into submission. But I was a good liar, and they were just two unruly kids.

I could handle this.

Calina bent forward, her pink wavy hair cascading down between us as she whispered in my ear. "We know who you really are, *what* you really are."

"Did you two get into the spirits while the rest of us weren't looking?" I joked, all the while maintaining a very serious face. "If so, I'm going to have to tell your mother, and considering you're already grounded from life, I bet—"

"You don't scare me, Tilda. As you said, I'm already grounded from life. I've got nothing to lose. But you... *Huh.* What's your little secret worth to you, I wonder?" Her voice set me on edge. Normally, she was glib, a fast and smooth talker, but every now and then her melody would falter, letting loose a jarring note of dissonance.

I gritted my teeth. "I don't know what secrets you think you've found. I'm but a simple woman from a small town. I've got nothing to hide."

Calina stood, returning to her full height, and tilted her chin toward my left arm.

My magical burn ignited with fresh pain as the

young elf called attention to it. No. How could she possibly know?

"I saw it yesterday," she said, even though I knew I hadn't asked that question aloud. "That's when I started putting all the pieces together. You're good at hiding, Tilda, but so am I. And I can keep your secret. Rurik can too. But you need to offer us something in return."

So that was it then. I was really and truly being blackmailed by two socially outcast teens. Is this what all my former glory had amounted to? *Really?*

I kept my teeth clenched and my tongue restrained. Denial wasn't working. Lies weren't working. Not even threats were working here. I'd faced down hundreds of tough opponents in the old days—evil sorcerers, powerful necromancers, brutish fighters—was I really to be outdone by two know-it-all kids?

"What do you want?" I ground out, hardly believing this was real.

Calina smiled again, and it wasn't sweet like her mother's, it was more serpentine, cunning. I'd always thought she took after me, and now I had no doubts.

"Just so we're on the same page," she said after clearing her throat. "Rurik and I know you were an adventurer before. We want to be adventurers too. And you're going to be the one to train us."

"This is outrageous," I hissed. Calina wasn't the only one who could call on the serpent to unnerve her opponents. "You're just two spoiled children. You have absolutely no right to demand anything of me. Especially not something like this."

The girl folded her arms over her chest. "So you don't mind if we tell my mom what we saw? We'll be here tomorrow too, you know. It would only take a heartbeat for me to climb up on the bar and shout all your secrets to the masses."

To prove her point, she climbed onto one of the barrel seats and then leaped onto the bar and did a little tap dance. Her cruel smile made me want to sweep her feet out from under her, but I unfortunately drew the line at violence against children. Me and my infernal ethics.

"Yup, pretty easy, really." Calina squatted down on the bar and locked eyes with me. "But you could prevent this little scene from ever taking stage. All you have to do is help us. Is that really such a bad offer?"

"Fine," I spat at her. "Fine. Have it your way. But that means not a whisper about it to anyone. They can't know I'm training you. The moment someone catches on, the jig is up. You got me?"

"I've most definitely got you." Calina let out a shrill and unsettling laugh as she hopped down from the bar and Rurik rushed to polish it up after her. "And, oh, if your secret really is so important to you, I'd do a better job hiding that dagger you keep tucked into your pocket."

Oh blessed mother, they really had me now, which meant I had no choice but to come out of retirement and take up the mantle of teacher.

5

I avoided the youths as best I could the following day. Not such a difficult feat, considering the Mystic Mug was standing room only for much of the day. At one point, a rowdy group of post-festivity centaurs decided to claim the streets outside our tavern as their new stomping grounds—and demanded we serve them tankard after tankard while they hooted and hollered and yelled lewd remarks at any poor fool who happened to pass by.

It wasn't until Durgan realized they were scaring off would-be customers that he shooed them away by threatening to rip his maul from the dangling sign and then pound them within an inch of their no-good lives that the raucous group finally dispersed. I believe I also heard some little quip about "beating a half-dead half-horse," but I pretended that I didn't.

The last thing we needed was for the town to brand us as an anti-centaur establishment, especially since the centaurs were the ones with all the money around these parts. After all, they'd founded the town a hundred years back, and they'd been darned sure to keep themselves on top in all the years that had followed.

After the incident outside, Durgan did a better job of keeping his wits about him for the rest of the shift, which meant the rest of us didn't have to work quite so hard to make up for his shortcomings. We didn't even have to walk him home to Pat at the end of the night; for once, he was sober enough to get there on his own.

"Tomorrow. Sunrise. The southern bridge out of town," Calina managed to mumble in my ear while her mother was preoccupied with helping Rurik tend to an angry red gash on his finger, a wound he'd presumably acquired while chopping garnishes—but I'd seen the young half-orc at work, and I knew better than to take that explanation at face value.

The whole thing was clearly a set-up. Yes, again.

These two kids were very good at getting their way. They'd proven that the night before, and I knew now that I shouldn't underestimate them—or the lengths they were willing to go to. Heck, Rurik had even physically injured himself to create a diversion. I wonder what else he might do at his elven friend's behest. Wait, his best friend's behest, such a universally dangerous fealty.

I didn't like any of this. Not one bit.

They'd figured out my secret, but only a very small part of it. In truth, they had no idea what they were up against when it came to this old rogue. Rurik and Calina may have been skilled manipulators, but I was the figgin' master.

I'd agreed to their little blackmail scheme for two reasons, and two reasons only. The first was that hitting children was generally looked down upon by the villagers of Briarhaven. The second? I knew I could end the whole thing with a single, carefully crafted disaster.

These kids may have thought they wanted to be adventurers, but they'd both been born and raised in the smallest of small towns. They'd run at the first sign of any real trouble, a fact I would exploit beautifully.

I reached the town's southern bridge just as the sun lit up the mountains rising in the distance. Briarhaven sat on a small corner of an enormous land basin that was slowly being devoured by the crescent-shaped mountain range that circled it. Countless prophets had predicted that one day this range would fold in on itself, assimilating all the land that sat between in its continued climb toward the sky.

Of course, I'd be long dead by then. As would everyone I'd ever cared about, so these prophecies never upset me. Every now and then, some wandering spiritual hack would find their way to our village and stir up a bit of panic with the locals by assigning some random arbitrary date to the upcoming cataclysm. They'd be chased out of town just as quickly as they'd arrived, though, and life would quickly return to normal.

Small towns like Briarhaven worked hard to maintain their smallness. Nobody had the time or patience for anyone who attempted to make our lives bigger than they were meant to be. And especially not for outsiders who came shrieking about our doom and gloom.

Was it possible that the other villagers wouldn't care about my secret past? Yes, not just possible, but likely. They'd known me as the wise-cracking, take-no-

nonsense bar wench for years, and it would take more than a couple whispered rumors to change their perceptions of me. I could have ignored Calina's attempts to blackmail me. Let the runes fall where they may.

Had I only cared about the other villagers' opinions in the most general sense, then I would have called Calina on her nonsense. Ignored it. Moved on with my life as normal.

But more than anything I cared about Brynlee's opinions of me. She would believe Calina's words—and remember me. She would never look at me the same again, if she knew how much I had in common with the one who had broken her heart. I wish I'd known her then, that I'd known him. I'd have broken something of his for what he did to her, and I'd have taken great pleasure in it too.

I'd only been waiting at the bridge for a few moments when the expected company arrived. Even though I struggled to be on time for my shifts at the tavern, entering adventure mode brought the punctuality right out of me.

I spotted Rurik first. He was much larger, and his graceless movements easily caught the eye. "You came." His tusks jutted out in what appeared to be a genuine smile, the rascal.

"And you owe me a bronze piece." Calina foisted a hand toward Rurik while keeping her gaze focused solely on me. Unlike her friend, she moved in sharp and clean lines like a seasoned hunter. "I knew she'd be here. She wouldn't want to do anything to risk upsetting my mom."

If I hadn't known better, I'd have sworn this elvish child sprang forth from my very loins. The two of us were unnervingly similar. I respected her swagger, but I'd still be taking her down.

No one could outmaneuver a master thief, especially not a couple of small-town kids. Yup, I'd have Calina crying for her mama in minutes.

"This way." I charged straight ahead without directly acknowledging either of them. I'd already made it halfway across the bridge by the time Calina caught up and grabbed me by the shoulder, forcing me to stop mid-stride.

"There's a quiet spot near the lake. I figured we could go there to—"

I didn't even let her finish. "You asked me to train you, which means I'm the one in charge here. The lake is too close to town. We could be easily spotted. I have a better, more secluded place in mind."

"Where?" Rurik's voice boomed from a couple paces behind.

I didn't answer his question.

"Where?" Calina echoed. This word was quieter coming from her, but far more commanding. I didn't answer to children, or to blackmailers, or to anyone, really. So I kept quiet.

When I failed to answer either of them, the young elf ran ahead to cut off my path. I spied a makeshift bow and quiver slung across her back as she passed me. It appeared to be of reasonably good quality, and I briefly wondered where she'd acquired it.

She stopped at the narrowest point of the dusty path and stretched her arms and legs wide to create an obstacle. I just ducked under her legs and kept going.

"Tilda, don't you dare ignore us!" she shouted and stamped her foot before chasing after me again. Rurik hung back, apparently content to let his friend handle the entire affair.

"We can't go too far! Rurik and I have to get back in time for morning classes."

I simply shrugged. "You're the one who set the time. Not me."

She growled and huffed after me. "If your plan is to run down the clock, I'm telling you right now, it won't work. Rurik and I are committed to this. You can't scare us away."

It took a mighty effort to hide the smile that crept

across my face. I could most definitely scare them away. Calina was already very clearly unnerved. I had her right where I wanted her.

"Do your best to keep up," I said before darting into the thick underbrush that lined the righthand side of our path. I used my small size and limber movements to cut a path through the lush forest that now surrounded us.

To her credit, Calina kept close in pursuit. Rurik, however, quickly fell behind. His occasional grunts and moans of pain as he tripped over roots and slammed into tree branches told me he was still making progress, albeit much, much slower.

I'd already come out this way last night and found the perfect place. It was the place I was leading them to now.

A thick fog kicked up at our heels as vibrant greenery gave way to monochromatic signs of decay. We'd entered the snag forest. The area had been ravaged by a wildfire many years back and had never managed to recover. The skeletal remains of once proud trees looked almost like bony fingers reaching out from the grave. Now that we no longer moved under a canopy of leaves, the sun shone down in bright, bold beams, mixing with the fog and creating an otherworldly effect.

Our line of sight was limited, making us vulnerable while at the same time offering a bit of privacy and protection from anyone who might be watching.

No one was ever watching though. Not really. I knew it was all in my head, but that didn't exactly help to lessen my anxiety. This place gave me the creeps. The villagers tended to avoid it too, preferring the more welcoming environs to this deteriorating relic of what once was.

That's what made it the perfect place for our first and last training session. I'd prepped the snag forest last night to make sure it had everything I needed—and to add a couple choice props to the scene. I found the first of those props now and paused as if just discovering it.

"What's that?" Calina asked, eyeing the circle of jagged stones at our feet.

I finally turned to address her. "It's a protection ward—or it was. The stones are broken, which means the spell failed."

"What spell? What protection?" Her voice got pitchy, just as I'd hoped. Calina was smart and cunning when she was in charge, but it wasn't all that hard to wrest control from her.

I had her on the hook. Now was the time to reel it in. "I don't know. Magic was never my strong suit. My guess is that it was meant to keep something contained, but whatever that thing was, it broke out."

"Like a monster?"

"Or a demon." I shrugged and bent to drag my finger through the dirt. I gave it a quick sniff, then rubbed my forefinger and thumb together while closing my eyes. "Could be anything, really."

Rurik still hadn't caught up to us. I worried he'd see through my trick in a heartbeat, which meant I had to keep Calina moving. She was clearly the leader of their duo, which meant she was the one I'd have to break if I were to free myself from their blackmail scheme.

"You brought a bow." I reached up and deftly tugged the weapon from her back.

She began to protest, but I cut her off by extending a palm. "Nock me up, if you'd please."

I didn't bother turning to look at her, instead I kept my eyes focused on the distant veil of fog, searching for shapes that could just as easily spell my victory as my doom.

"Please be careful," the girl said softly as she placed an arrow on my palm and then closed my fingers over it. "I made these myself. It took months to get the design right."

Her sudden show of vulnerability was like a dagger

straight to my heart. Calina wasn't goading me on out of boredom or some deep-seated need to rebel. She wanted this. And she'd already committed a generous deal of time to it. Adventuring meant something to her.

"Let's keep going," I said, carefully placing each of my footfalls as we crept through the encroaching fog. Several paces past our location, something moved between the husks of trees.

I stopped and put a hand out in front of Calina to stop her.

Her voice trembled as she asked, "What was that?"

"I don't know." I shrugged and continued forward.

Calina fell a couple paces behind me, already losing her nerve. Since Durgan already knew a bit about what I had been, it wasn't hard to recruit his help. I'd asked Pat to make sure his partner was up early and waiting in the snag forest so we could spook the kids a bit.

Durgan banged against a tree unseen and let out a... well, not a mighty roar... but a roar nonetheless.

Calina flinched behind me, and her breaths quickened to a staccato.

Rurik still wasn't anywhere to be seen. Good, good.

Not so tough now, I thought with a satisfied smirk

that both of them missed. "It could be a monster. Could be a spirit. Or a person. Should we kill it?"

Calina sucked in a sharp breath and shook her head.

"You want to be an adventurer? Well, creating corpses is part of that. Oh, I've killed hundreds in my day. Maybe even thousands. I'll always remember the first life I took. The way he looked me in the eye, begged me not to make his children orphans." I shrugged as if it were nothing, but the memory I was sharing with her now was a real one. That man haunted me to this very day, that much was true. What I didn't tell Calina though was that death had been more than he'd deserved. The man had treated himself to whatever desires he craved, often with violence and rarely with consent. When he'd come for a friend, I'd been quick to rid him of his head.

"But that's how the adventuring life goes. Life ends, and sometimes it will be at your very hands. For my first time taking a life, I'd gone for the tried-and-true throat slit. You know, to make it a quick and merciful death. But the dagger broke off in the guy's neck and he just started gushing blood like I've never seen before or since. It got in my mouth, my eyes... Well, anyway, once I started I couldn't exactly stop. So, I ended up hammering the broken blade in with my bare hand until he lost control of his legs. Then I picked up a dull wooden axe I found nearby and finished him off. Whew. Must've taken at least twenty swings to fully get that head separated from his shoulders, but that's killing for you. Doesn't always go the way you want. You've got to be ready to roll with it or you'll end up dead yourself." I paused and let out a hearty sigh. "Ah, you never forget your first. Are you ready to claim yours?"

I offered to return the weapon, but Calina wrapped her arms around her torso and shook her head, refusing to accept it.

Durgan roared again, and Calina tucked herself into my back, trembling greatly.

I spotted a charred spruce near our fake monster's location and raised the bow.

Calina clung tight to my back as I sent the arrow flying.

I watched as it sunk deep into the dead tree's corpse, hoping that my companion's perception wasn't quite as good as mine. I wanted her to think I'd impaled our monster, that I'd casually and coldly claimed a life amidst the fog.

Durgan let out a keening wail and started making exaggerated death sounds before thudding to the ground. He was overplaying the part, but to our benefit Calina had never witnessed a death before. She seemed to be buying into the theatrics.

"I'll go retrieve the arrow and take stock of our kill. The next one will be yours though." I jogged ahead and left Calina trembling in the clearing.

I found Durgan lying flat on the forest floor with an armored breastplate protecting his heart just in case Calina had actually been willing to both take aim and shoot. I bent and whispered in his ear, "Thanks for the help. Now get out of here."

"We hit him!" I yelled back to the waiting kid. "We hit him, but he still got away. Left a pretty gruesome trail behind him too. Sorry about your arrow!"

I returned to Calina, my face a study in quietly composed resignation.

Rurik finally caught up to us, and he appeared quite spent from the added effort it took to get him here. "What did I miss?" he asked between deep huffs.

I pointed into the fog. "There was a monster. I nicked it with one of Calina's arrows, but he still got away."

"Really? A monster already?" Rurik said between heavy breaths. "But it's still so early in the morning."

"No." The girl startled me by grabbing the bow from my grip, readying an arrow, and immediately firing it toward that same dead spruce where I'd aimed mine. She didn't say a word as she took slow, sure steps into the fog, following the path of her arrow.

Rurik and I kept quiet as we plodded along after her.

Sure enough, she'd sunk her arrow into the same tree that sported mine. She'd hit it a few feet higher, which wasn't as impressive as it would have been had she split my arrow clean down the center but still pretty darned impressive.

Calina gave me a scorching glare before hoisting herself up the tree to retrieve her prize. Once she had it, she dropped straight to the ground, landing on her feet with almost perfect posture, turned, and yanked the arrow I'd embedded from the trunk.

"Nice try, Tilda," she said, handing the bow and both arrows back to me. "I knew you'd try to get out of our deal, but you can't. So it's time you played along, and that means playing fair. No more tricks."

"Why?" I asked, faltering in my plan. I'd been so sure I could outwit this pair of teenagers, but they were quickly proving they could match me pace for pace. Especially the elf. "Why does learning this stuff mean so much to you?"

She dropped her gaze to the dirt and mumbled, "My dad was an adventurer. That's the only thing I know about him. It's the only thing I have left of him."

"Calina, this isn't my place. You need to talk to your mother."

"Don't you think I've tried?" Her sudden shout startled me, as her words reverberated through the dead forest. "She refuses to tell me anything. And she refuses to let me have any part of him. It's not fair."

Rurik put a bulky, green arm over Calina's shoulders as she burst into tears. I was very much out of my comfort zone with this one. Water was the element of the heart, and I had closed mine to the world many, many moons ago.

Brynlee was my dearest friend, and I knew she had her reasons for keeping her child in the dark. But shouldn't Calina get to decide for herself?

I'd been hiding my secret past for nearly ten years. As part of that, I hadn't allowed myself to exercise all the skills I'd finely honed, to think back on all the thrilling adventures or the deep bonds of friendship I'd acquired along the way.

For ten long years, I'd shut away the biggest part of myself. But it only took a fraction of a second for me to open it all back up again.

"Okay," I said, both admitting defeat and wondering if this was really a defeat at all. "I'll train you. Not just because you're blackmailing me, but because I want to do it. I do have one condition though."

Calina looked as if she could hardly breathe. "Anything."

"Cut your mom some slack and stay out of trouble while you're at it. You're her entire world, and she'd be devastated if anything happened to you."

"That's two things," Rurik pointed out. "You said you only had *one* condition."

Calina jabbed him in the ribs as I attempted to restrain an irritated growl.

"It is one condition, you lumbering pine tree. Cutting her mom some slack means not getting into trouble. It means being good, so you don't break her heart."

"I get that, Tilda. I love her just as much as you do. And that's why I need you to train me." Wide lavender eyes set intently upon me pleaded her case. She knew I loved Brynlee. There were so many questions I wanted to ask, but none of them were as important as what Calina said next. "With your help, I know I'll be okay. With your help, I know I can keep that promise."

6

"C'mon, Calina. Let's get out of this depressing forest and find somewhere nicer to start our training." I strode back from whence we came, knowing the young elf would follow me. We didn't have a lot of time before she had to get to school, but we had some.

The half-orc followed along.

I stopped abruptly and turned back to him, raising both palms. "Not so fast, mister."

Of course, the bumbling oaf ran straight into me, knocking me to the craggy forest floor. I used my left forearm to break my fall and the magical burn bubbled up with a fresh wave of pain.

"Gah! I'm so suh-suh-sorr—!"

I sucked air in through my teeth and tried silently

counting to ten. But I only made it to two. I just could not take this kid's yammering for another second longer.

"Cut it," I growled in aggravation, cutting him off mid-stutter as I pulled myself back to my feet. "I've agreed to help Calina, but I haven't agreed to help you. I'm not a magic user, so I don't know the first thing about how to train you. Now, if you wanted to work on refining your skills as a barbarian, then we—"

"No!" he thundered with such clarity of intention that it startled me even more than getting pushed to the ground had. "I will not be a barbarian or a fighter or anything else that values the body over the mind. I may be part orc, but that's not all that I am."

Calina leaned into his bulky frame and craned her neck to look up at her friend before returning her gaze to me. "Rurik and I are a package deal. When we're done with school, we'll be going on the road together. If you really want to keep me safe, then make sure I have a good partner along for the journey. Because one way or another, I'm going, whether or not you and my mom approve."

"And I'm going too," Rurik said with complete certainty as his best friend stood at his side. "I've never belonged in this place. The people are too small."

"Hey!" I cried, stretching to my full height of three

feet and one inch to challenge the guy who hovered near six-and-a-half feet tall and wasn't even done growing yet. "There's nothing wrong with being small."

"Small bodies are one thing. Small minds are another matter, entirely." He sniffed, but I couldn't tell whether it was a mark of disdain or to keep from crying. This kid was a paradox in every sense. I wasn't sure I'd ever figure him out.

"Fine. Whatever. We can try, but I make no guarantees." I turned to get going, but Rurik stopped me before I'd even made it a single pace.

"Wait. Please wait." He reached into his baggy pocket and pulled out a small, leather-bound book, which he placed directly in my hands.

The tome, which appeared much larger in my hands than it had in Rurik's, weighed heavy on my palms. Its cover was made from old leather that had faded around the edges. The binding was uneven with several odd pages sticking out farther than the rest. A sleek black feather poked out from the top, and I used it as a guide to turn to the marked page.

"The magical flame cantrip," I murmured, squinting to read one of the many hand-written notes that had been scrawled into the margins. The script was neat and blocky. Fastidious, even. It had been used to detail adaptations to the base spell, such as: *if cast with eyes half-lidded and focused on the ground, the flame will burn several degrees hotter.*

I read a few more of the added notes, then turned the page. This next spell was for healing an injured party member. So much ink filled the page, I could hardly see the tan of the parchment. A loose leaf had been shoved into the binding containing even more added hand-written directives.

"He's been working on that one for many moons," Calina informed me. "But he still can't get it exactly right."

"I won't be a liability," Rurik promised us both. "I'm ready to work hard. I'm already working hard. I'll be grateful for anything you can teach me, even if that doesn't include magic."

"I'll do what I can, but you should both know... This life you seem so obsessed with, it's not an easy one. Most people choose it because they don't have any other options."

"Why did you then? Clearly, you had other options, or you wouldn't have stopped," Calina pointed out. Rurik may have wielded logic like a pro, but it was she who had a way of seeing right through me.

I saw through her too. Like finding like.

And I suspected if I told her more of my story, she'd be willing to share hers—possibly what she knew of Brynlee's as well.

These two already knew more than I'd wanted anyone to find out ever again. I could offer a few morsels from my upbringing, if it kept them focused on the distant past instead of what happened ten years ago...

"I grew up in Mirathane. Poor as dirt and on my own. Nobody cared about an urchin halfling, which meant I had to find a way to take care of myself. I was small and good at getting where I wanted to go undetected. I had fast, sticky fingers, and a quick mind. So naturally I became a thief. I only stole what I needed to get by... At first."

Calina's pale purple eyes sparkled. "But then you fell in love with it, with the thrill. Am I right?"

"More like I got bored. I needed bigger challenges. Bigger risks, and yes, bigger rewards. One day I picked the wrong pocket and found myself indebted to a terrible man. He threatened and forced me into helping with his enterprise." I gave both kids a pointed look. "That's kind of why I don't take so kindly to being blackmailed now. It's happened before, and I vowed never again."

"Yeah, yeah, but now you want to help us," Calina

argued, rolling her index finger in the air to motion that I should continue my story.

I shrugged as I settled back into the memory. "My new master—Finnian Sly was his name—he had a whole network of novice thieves all around the city, and soon I was one of them. Not just one of them, but the best of them. I got a big head, decided to strike out on my own and to take some of the others with me, which meant leaving the city behind."

"At first there were four of us. Always on the move from village to village seeking bounties and glory. We lost two along the way, not to death but cowardice. Made it hard to trust that the risk of bringing anyone else in could ever pay off, so we didn't. Gaar—My partner and I, we had each other and that was enough. For years that was enough. Until our last heist went terribly, terribly wrong, and he..." My voice cracked, and I stopped speaking. Why was I telling them all this? They'd never asked for my poor, woe-is-me backstory. They just wanted me to show them some battle tricks.

"He died, didn't he?" Calina asked softly as she reached toward my left forearm and pushed the loose bell sleeve up. "And you got that scar."

I yanked my arm away and covered the burn. These two knew a few sparse truths about me now, but

I still wasn't comfortable with even the minor exposure.

"You tangled with someone very powerful. Even more powerful than Finnian Sly," Rurik said thoughtfully. "My little flame could never leave a mark like that."

"Very powerful and very dangerous. Also, very off topic. I'm not going to talk about this again, so don't ask. Either we train together, or we don't, but my history is not up for discussion. Understood?" I shoved the book back at Rurik, and it hit his chest with a light thump.

I began to walk away again, knowing the kids would follow. "Durgan could help you with your magic," I called back over my shoulder. "He was a paladin, you know."

Calina scoffed. "Yeah, except Durgan is too drunk to do anything other than to keep drinking." She had a point.

I shook my head and wracked my brain. "Surely, there are others." This whole push and pull had started to make me dizzy. Yes, I was the one who kept agreeing to help and then changing my mind, but Calina and Rurik were the ones who kept asking for more than I had to give.

I couldn't go back, couldn't relive those memories.

I had a hard enough time keeping them at bay now. What would happen when I was actively revisiting old movements and skills? I'd trained my mind to grow quiet, but suspected my body would betray me once it got a feel of what it had missed for so long.

Rurik's voice came out flat as it pursued me along my path. "In Briarhaven? No, not a chance. Most of the people here haven't stepped so much as a foot out of town, not once in their entire tiny lives. Some have never even been as far as this snag forest. Who could possibly know magic?"

"Then how did you get the book?" I shot back. The book's very existence proved he was wrong. It had to have come from somewhere, especially since Rurik himself had probably never left town either. He complained about the other villagers, but he wasn't any different. He wanted to be, but he wasn't. Not yet.

Calina's voice rose behind me. "I gave it to him. I... I found it in my mom's things. I think it was my father's."

This caused me to stop and turn back toward them. "She doesn't know you have it, does she?"

Calina grinned. "Well, you see, I don't have it. Rurik does. And anyway, I took it like a year ago, so obviously she hasn't noticed it missing. It has to have been my dad's. Do you think he might have been a wizard? Like Rurik?"

"I know even less about your father than you do, so asking me questions is pointless."

"I'm going to find him again. One day. I'm going to find him and bring him home," she told me without the slightest hint of doubt.

"How could you possibly do that? You don't know who he is or what he looks like." I didn't want to be mean, but I also didn't want this girl making herself unrealistic promises. That's how people got hurt. Expecting more than they could ever get. I didn't want that to happen to Brynlee or her daughter. "You don't know whether he used weapons or magic to fight, and you probably don't even know his name, do you?"

"Actually, I do know his name. I found that in Mom's things as well. Sweet Sylric, they wrote each other the sappiest love letters. Dad always signed his off as Gaary."

Tingles rose from my feet and settled right into my gut. My shoulders stiffened. I had to struggle to get my words out and even still they came as a croaked whisper. "What? What did you say?"

"Gaary. It's a stupid name, right? I mean, I'm assuming it's short for something."

It *was* short for something. *Gaaron.*

My former partner, the one who had died due to my ineptitude. I'd come to Briarhaven, because he'd spent so many long nights around the campfire regaling me of tales from his wandering youth. Of all the places he'd roamed before finding me among Finnian Sly's men in Mirathane, Briarhaven had been the one that stuck with him most.

He'd left his heart there, he'd told me. I hadn't realized he'd meant that literally. He hadn't just left memories, but actual flesh and blood people.

I kept my features carefully composed as my mind raced with the flood of long-repressed memories and a fresh wave of anxiety. Yes, this could have been just some stupid coincidence. I knew that, but a part of me doubted it very much.

"Gaary is a strange name for an elf," I mused aloud. Testing.

"Actually, my dad was human," Calina answered right on cue, exactly as I'd feared she would. "I know, I know. I look more elvish, but I'm only half. Like Rurik, that's part of how we became friends. We're both half breeds and proud."

Calina continued chattering away with the occasional grunt of confirmation from her orcish companion, but I'd already journeyed far, far away and ten years back in time.

There, Gaaron and I stood beneath the cliffside lair that would spell our shared doom. Getting there had not been easy. In fact, it had required the use of all our best manipulation skills and tactics. This place could only be reached by magic, and not the kind my partner wielded. We'd had to make a trade, but now we were here.

The terrain had been scarred by some long-forgotten cataclysm, where this parcel of land had been ripped away from the rest of the continent. Scorch marks radiated from the huge gash in the landscape and water spilled over into the abyss left from the tear. Chunks of land still floated haphazardly through the space, seemingly unbothered by the lack of anything around them.

The hand-drawn map the quest giver had entrusted to us had marked a small entrance to the cliffside lair, with a drawing showing the intricate yet brutal architecture that hung over the edge of the cliff, like its owner was taunting the natural world. Taunting us.

We'd already come so far. There would be no going back.

"I'm sure it's far simpler than it looks," my best bard friend forever said with the debonair smile that made every female within fifty grand paces weak at the knees. Only I was immune to his virile charm, it seemed.

"But just in case." He pulled out the pan-flute he kept nestled beneath his tunic on the side opposite his heart

and began to play the melody I knew so well. He was fortifying us for the battle ahead.

Of course, if everything went to plan, there would be no battle to speak of. We just had to get in, grab the arti-fact, and get back out. We'd both been nimble and quick-witted, so we gravitated toward bounties where we relied not on fighting prowess or strength of steel, but on a light touch and a fast escape.

And this bounty came with the largest coin purse we'd ever been offered, many times over.

I took a few deep breaths to make sure my fear didn't seep into my voice. This is just any other quest, I told myself, wishing I could believe it. "Dude's a necro-mancer. That probably means he sleeps during the day. As long as we're quiet—"

Gaaron lowered his instrument and gawked at me. "That's a joke, right? Please tell me you know the differ-ence between a vampire and a necromancer."

I shrugged. Sometimes I told myself little lies to boost my confidence. If we headed into this dungeon expecting the worst, we'd basically guarantee the worst would find us. And personally, I'd rather stay alive than sound smart.

"May the gods have mercy. The pan-flute isn't going to be enough. Clearly, this is a job for the gabblewonky. Erm, please hold."

As Gaaron rummaged through his bag in search of all the oddities he'd need to piece together for his chosen instrument, I shook my head and stared up at the lair embedded in the side of the ominous cliff overhead. I'd never have noticed the dark structure if the quest giver hadn't clearly noted it on our hand-drawn map. But now that I knew where to look it was clear as day.

"Got it," Gaaron shouted gleefully, as I turned back to study him. The gabblewonky was a new instrument of his own invention, one he was constantly tweaking in search of perfection. Whenever he brought it into battle, it caused more problems than it solved—and so I'd created a rule that required it to only be used ahead of facing our foes. Gaaron had agreed but also claimed that he needed to keep practicing; he needed to keep practicing, so that he could get it right.

One day the gabblewonky would be the most coveted music-maker in existence—at least that's what Gaaron swore up and down as he affixed a fanned array of bone pipes to his back, hung a bandolier of bladders from magical creatures across his front, and worked himself into the other parts of the enormous and absurd-looking musical contraption.

He offered me a quick wink before proceeding to play what would become his very last performance...

"Tilda! Tilda! Are you okay?" Calina shook my

shoulders with both hands, rattling my teeth and my brain. "You just completely blanked out for a second there."

"I'm fine," I said, even though that wasn't true. I took a few moments to reorient myself in the present, focusing on the feel of the dirt beneath my feet, the wind against my cheek. All was blessedly calm, and in the here and now, we were safe. But how long could that last?

"The book," I barked and held out my hands. "Let me see it again."

Rurik gave me an odd look as he passed the tome my way. This time I ignored the feathered placeholder and flipped straight to the back cover. More hand-written notes, but this time with swooping, curled letters. It was a script I recognized instantly.

"Those notes are Dad's." Calina stood beside me and traced her finger longingly across the text. "It's a list of ingredients. What kind of potion do you think he was making?"

It wasn't a list of ingredients, but rather compo-nents. He'd tested many different parts as he devel-oped the gabblewonky, claiming that taking bones, bladders, and hairs from specific magical creatures would imbue the instrument with special abilities. This was where he tracked his findings in the old book that he'd kept from his misguided days of attempting to cross-class. Gaaron's career as a wizard had never taken off, but his great love for books kept him from disposing of this tome. He'd kept it for many years. Until he'd left it with Brynlee, apparently to remember him by.

He'd been building that blasted instrument long before the two of us ever took up questing together. This list chronicled his earliest attempts. While we traveled together, he'd kept his log on a simple parchment, folded in half twice. And those notes had been on him when he died, leaving me nothing to remember him by, save for my scar and the stolen artifact I kept hidden beneath my tunic.

I had no doubts now. Brynlee, Calina, and I all longed for the same man, though in different ways. Only I knew with certainty he would never come back, could never come back.

"Take it back," I said, thrusting the book upon Calina since she was the closest. "Like I said, I don't know magic, and from the looks of that list, your father didn't either."

I needed to be more careful about losing myself in the past, about falling away. If I kept letting this happen, either Rurik or Calina would figure out that something was wrong—and then it would only be a matter of time until they figured out exactly what that something was.

They knew one of my secrets now, yes, but I could never ever let them learn the one that mattered most. Neither Calina nor Brynlee would ever forgive me if they knew what I'd taken from them, first in life... and then in death.

Our special training arrangement had just become much more important—I owed both of my closest friends a debt—but things were much more dangerous now. This time, the enemy wasn't a master thief or an angry necromancer—it was *me.* I was helping Calina prepare for an adventure she had no way of completing, sending her off in search of a prize that could never be acquired.

I wished I had the strength to spare her the journey, but instead I'd need to settle for preparing her for whatever she faced along the way. And by the time she realized that long road led nowhere, I would hopefully be a different person, a better one, one who could face the full repercussions of what I'd done.

7

And so, I'd agreed to turn a couple of no-good, trouble-making kids into no-good, trouble-making adventurers. I intended to share my wisdom and experience freely, for the most part, while keeping my secret shame buried so deep that even dwarven excavators wouldn't find it.

A part of me relished going through the motions again. I especially enjoyed watching the kids light up as a new lesson stuck. Their lives have only just begun. They could do anything. *Be* anything.

I liked that for them, even though it glutted me with envy. What would I do if I were free to make new choices? Who would I let myself become?

I caught myself asking those same questions on a loop as I spent time in their company. The answers were always the same. I'd just want to be back on the open road with Gaaron at my side and the promise of a new bounty ahead. I'd even listen to him play that blasted gabblewonky again, if it meant having him alive, happy, present, mine.

Every time that I longed for Gaaron, a fresh seed of guilt planted itself in my throbbing heart. I'd had him because they'd lost him. As a thief I was good at stealing things—money, artifacts, even the odd bit of undue praise. But I was having a hard time accepting I'd stolen a person. Especially one that still mattered so very much to both Brynlee and Calina. So many years had passed, and yet they both yearned for him, the same as I did.

Oh, how I wished Gaaron were alive to answer for all he'd done. He'd had the perfect family, and he'd just walked away. Why? Try as I may, I couldn't make sense of his choices. Here I'd thought I knew both his heart and mind completely...

Turned out he'd had secrets too—secrets that, thanks to his untimely death, would never be truly uncovered. A part of me tried to hate him for what he'd done, for who he'd hurt. But more than anything, I still just missed my partner and friend.

He'd abandoned her young, but still Calina was his daughter. I was certain of that now. And I would keep her safe for both of her parents—for the two greatest friends I'd known in all my days. It was no wonder they'd found and loved each other as well.

Rogues weren't supposed to get taken by surprise, yet here I was with my jaw hanging open once again. Every day, the shock of my discovery knocked me off balance. It was really becoming quite tiring.

Especially given that only four days had passed since that early morning in the snag forest where I'd learned the truth of Calina's parentage. We'd had precious little time to train on the mornings that followed, but I had big plans for the resting moons. We'd still meet at dawn, but on those two school-free days, we'd be able to stick together well into the late afternoon. Just so long as I made it to my shift at the Mystic Mug in time, we had the rest of the day to really dig deep into our training.

I'd given both the kids homework to keep them busy at night while I worked—and hopefully also out of trouble, as they'd promised me. Rurik was to give up on the healing spell and shift his focus to a second-level pyromancy cantrip. He'd already mastered his small flame, and I wanted to see how he'd be able to handle something bigger.

I gave Calina the spare dagger I kept beneath my pillow and instructed her to find someplace secluded and to practice throwing it both with her main hand—the left—and her off-hand. Just because she'd crafted herself a bow didn't mean that was automatically the correct choice of weapon for her. Her father hadn't liked getting himself bloodied in battle, but he could throw with astonishing accuracy and force.

I had a feeling Calina might be the same. They were bound by blood after all.

The days that followed the town centennial had been quiet compared to the loosely organized chaos of the festivities. Locals were venturing back out, returning to the bucolic slog of Briarhaven. This, of course, included the regulars of the Mug, sign adequately slapped, they'd come in and take a quiet seat in the tavern, slowly nursing their drinks of choice while Durgan pranced around and told a much-exaggerated tale of his victory over the unruly group of centaurs that had taken up shop right outside our front door. He always made sure to mention—and loudly—how much he liked and respected *our* centaurs. It was just that these out-of-towners didn't have the same dignity and grace, he'd say while his eyes roamed every which way to ensure that no one could be mistaken that he was very much a fan of our village's ruling class.

My favorite infernal, Insy, came by one night and

chose to sit with me at the bar after waving off Durgan's attentions. "I love the little guy, but sometimes he's..."

Insy's words fell away, and I happily finished the sentiment for him. "A bit too much."

He nodded and lifted his sweet blend of fruit and spirits in toast. "Yes. Sometimes big things come in small packages."

I couldn't tell whether he was talking about Durgan or about me, but given the slight upward tilt of his lips and approving nod as he set his partially drained glass onto the bar, I suspected that maybe it was both. Or maybe he just had a profound appreciation for my Demon's Delight cocktail.

Whatever the case, I couldn't say that I disagreed.

I'd always been much bigger on the inside than I was on the outside. Few people ever saw that, but Calina had. Rurik too.

I was both grateful and very, very afraid.

If they could see me for who I really was, did that mean someone else might too? If so, then even our casual training would somehow be enough to attract the wrong kind of attention. That's why I made sure we always returned to that ghastly forest. No one else dared to venture there. The place was too depressing and had nothing to offer but a small bit of privacy.

So far it had been enough, but could I really expect our luck to last forever?

On the first of our two school-free mornings, I brought my trainees to a large farm on the far north side of the village. The place was owned by a family of forest gnomes who claimed a special knack for tending to all matter of flora and fauna. They also owned an artisan shop in town, renowned for its fine honey and cheeses.

The proprietor of both farm and shop had come into the Mug last week, complaining of an infestation that had made itself at home in his vegetable garden. Normally, the talented nature-whisperer only needed to ask that a pest make itself scarce, but the current colony of giant locusts was proving to be particularly stubborn. As I served him up his second drink, I promised that I would help with his bug problem, should it still plague him in a few moons.

I'd stopped by the artisan shop to check yesterday afternoon, and sure enough, the stubborn locusts remained. And they would make excellent target practice for my little ranger and wizard in training.

"What are we doing again?" Calina asked as we

picked our way through a field of overgrown wheat in need of harvesting. The air felt damp on my skin, causing my tunic to stick to my chest. Either a neighborly cloud had unloaded itself, or it was gearing up to do so shortly. At this time of year, it was more than likely that both were true.

"We're embarking on our first official quest," Rurik tutted proudly, standing straighter than usual. He still tripped over his own feet every so often, but I had to hand it to him—the half-orc teen was doing a much better job keeping pace with us now.

"Not really a quest, so much as an errand," I corrected as the farmer came into view across the horizon.

Leicester Dewglen was of slight stature, only a short bit taller than me. His skin was darker than mine, both from his heritage and all the time spent out in the sun tending to his crops and cattle. Spotting our ragtag group, he waved and shouted to us. "Over here. Over here. Come quick!"

Calina and Rurik easily shot ahead of me with their longer strides, but Leicester dutifully waited for me to catch up before launching into a long-winded account of all the damage that had been caused by the giant locusts over the past few days.

Calina wrinkled her nose. Whether in disgust or

with curiosity, I couldn't quite say for sure. "We're here to kill some stupid bugs?" Her voice cracked mid-sentence, much like mine did when I got myself worked up.

"Please. Oh, please. I beg of you. I'll pay you quite handsomely for the trouble." The gnome folded his hands together and shook them at our group. "Only please be sure they go and never come back. The blasted things are already beginning to irritate the oxen, and it won't be long until they find their way to the sheep. Oh, it really is quite the hullabaloo!"

Calina snorted at his dramatic word choice, but at least had the good grace to cover her mouth and look properly apologetic for the outburst.

I shook my head at her, then placed a hand on the agitated farmer's shoulder and waited until his eyes met mine. "Relax. We'll get it handled. The only payment we need is your silence."

Rurik raised his index finger. "Actually, I'd also like to accept the coin."

I made a sharp shushing noise while Calina jabbed him in the ribs. "We only need your discretion in exchange for our services rendered."

"You are too kind. Truly. You'll find the nasty things if you keep to the left. They've set up their nest amidst my prize-winning cabbages," Leicester said, keeping his palms joined as he backed away slowly. It was almost as if he were afraid to turn his backs on us —well, if not us, then Rurik at least. Teenager or not, dude cut a formidable figure.

The three of us watched until Leicester disappeared into a nearby field of corn. Like magic, the vibrant stalks appeared to swallow him whole. That was our cue.

"So bugs," Calina said with a bored expression, crossing her arms over her chest and tilting her weight to one side.

"Yes, bugs! Look alive!" I balled my hands into fists and bounced back and forth, ready for the fight even though I knew I would not personally be taking part. "It may not be an official quest, but this is your first chance to kill something."

"You know, there would have been no harm in accepting the money," Rurik grumped.

Okay, now I was getting annoyed. I stopped bouncing to stare him down, which was hard to do given the fact he was more than two times my height. I was convinced that a bold personality could overcome any physical shortcomings, and this moment was proof enough of that. "Who pays you to read your book? Who gave you coin while you bumbled your way through learning to produce a flame? While you're learning, you're not earning. Now, do you want the experience or not?"

"Fine, we'll go kill the bugs." Calina drew her bow and charged in the direction the farmer had indicated.

"Not so fast. You've had lots of practice with that bow. I want to see you throw the dagger."

She pouted her lower lip as if about to throw a tantrum. "But I'll miss."

"That's the point. The only way to get better is to practice."

"So let me practice with my bow."

"Calina," I huffed. "Just throw the blessed dagger. Rurik, see if you can use your flame to do some damage. You two ready to skewer and barbecue some bugs? Because that sounds like a right good party to me."

Neither said anything, which I took to mean they'd given in. To think I'd expected enthusiasm! I could hardly get compliance.

Well, now I didn't feel so bad about privately arranging for farmer Dewglen's payment to go straight to my own pocket. After all, what did the kids need spare cash for?

8

Calina was the first to locate the swarm amidst farmer Dewglen's cabbages. I watched from several paces back as she hurled the borrowed dagger at a particularly meaty-looking insect that was not-so-innocently crunching merrily away on its ill-gotten snack. The dagger flew end over end in a perfect line—completely off course— and landed on the exposed soil with an unforgiving thud.

The young elf stomped her foot and turned to me with a look of indignation.

"Well, go get it. Try again." I waltzed over and gave her a little shove to get her moving.

Calina didn't even budge. "This would be a whole

lot easier if I could use my bow. You've seen how good I am with it."

"Yes, which is why I need you to practice with something else. What happens if you lose your bow in battle? Or if the opponent closes in on you and your arrows are no longer effective? You need to be comfortable with a backup weapon. The dagger's a good choice."

"Fine." Calina jogged ahead, moving fast as she bent to collect the discarded dagger. Then, raising both arms overhead with the knife firmly clutched in a double-fisted grip, she screamed and drove the sharp point right between the locust's large black eyes.

Blood and guts splashed in every direction, painting Calina an odd mix of colors and textures. She let out a little harumph, pried the dagger loose from the bug's carcass, and turned triumphantly to face me.

Behind her the insect continued to twitch as the last throes of life worked themselves out of its lobotomized body.

"Look, I figured out how to do the stabby thing. Now can I please use my bow?"

"You killed one. Out of hundreds. Keep up the theatrics and you'll quickly find yourself exhausted. Overrun too. But, hey, I'll make you a deal. Kill five using the dagger as a projectile, and then I'll give you back your bow."

Calina's eyes widened as she reached over her shoulder and found the quiver missing. She hadn't even noticed me take it from her when I'd shoved her along. The kid would make an easy mark, except I wasn't supposed to be showing off my thieving skills... Oh, and we were on the same side.

"That's mine," she said between clenched teeth.

"Not until you keep up your end of the bargain." I grinned. Maybe this teaching thing wasn't so bad after all. Because in this situation, I held all the power. Rurik and I both knew it, and soon Calina would figure that out as well. Until then, I was going to have an awful lot of fun messing with her.

The massive insects chittered and closed in on their fallen comrade... or, maybe it was brother... Really, I had no idea what these things were to each other.

Apparently, they weren't entirely sure either, because a couple appeared to mourn the dead while one of the others decided to make a snack of him. Others became enraged and charged straight at Calina with their antennae whirling and bodies bouncing as they half sprinted, half leaped toward my charge.

They couldn't do much more than knock her over —a feat I hadn't even managed—so I wasn't worried about Calina's safety. I'd chosen the easiest possible practice quest on purpose. We had lots of targets and no real risk of sustaining any damage ourselves... Well, not unless Rurik's clumsiness somehow led to friendly fire. That or he tripped and fell straight into Calina's blade.

Anything was possible, I supposed.

"Aren't locusts supposed to be vegetarians?" Rurik appeared absolutely horrified. As if he hadn't witnessed countless moments of blood lust from his time in the cradle onward.

"Honestly, kid, I don't know. Maybe it's a weird mating ritual. Or maybe they're confused. You can study them later. After we kill them." Just to show the kids I had their backs, I hurled my dagger at the angriest of the insects right as it was about to leap at Calina's throat. My blade's course was true and not only made impact but beheaded the blessed thing too.

"And that's how it's done," I said, as the locust's body landed at Calina's feet and its head went flying across the vegetable patch. The dagger continued to sail straight ahead. Its course stayed true, not even altered by the decapitation—so steady was my throw. *Yup, this old girl's still got it.*

Calina looked as if she wanted to speak but knew

she had no good comeback this time. At last, my authority had started to sink in. Good.

"You," I called to Rurik, who still stood a good distance off. I could see he'd taken that old spell book from his pocket and was feverishly flipping through its pages. "Put the book away. You want to learn? Learn by doing. Torch those bugs with your magical flame. Show me what you've got."

Meanwhile, Calina kicked and punched at the locusts that had surrounded her. Her weapon lay a few feet to the left and mine had landed a good twenty paces out, but she didn't seem to notice either. That girl had a lot of work to do if she wanted to make it as a ranger.

Rurik tucked the old tome back into his massive pocket. "Shouldn't we be helping Callie?" he asked, tilting his head like an inquisitive little dragonling and not the fierce orcish creature he actually was.

I had to work hard not to sigh. "Well, then help her. Start killing."

Rurik closed his eyes and summoned his flame. I watched the small magical wisp of fire float above his palm in the open air, waiting to see what he'd do next—while also ready to pat Calina down should he misfire and set his BFF ablaze.

"I've never used my flame as a weapon before," he

mumbled, focusing intently on Calina and her chittering group of opponents rather than minding the glowing orb that now hovered just past his fingertips.

"Get closer," I urged. "Instead of hurling the flame, light it up right under the thing's butt. Killing them will be much easier at close range."

Rurik nodded and paced forward. He moved as if he were walking into a boardroom—not a battlefield.

"Look alive!" I called after him, which only seemed to confuse him even more. At least he kept going though. I knew the lowly bugs couldn't hurt Calina, but I wasn't certain Rurik had that part figured out just yet. Smart as he was, his attachment to Calina seemed to both strengthen his resolve and hobble his intellect at the exact same time.

Finally, after a few very agonizing moments in which I did everything in my power to keep from mocking the guy, Rurik made it to the fight. I watched in an unwelcome combo of horror and humiliation as he guided his flame to the nearest bug with a soft gesture that looked more like he was caressing a lover than smacking down a foe.

The locust he'd targeted simply stepped to the side and out of range.

I shaped my hands into a funnel and shouted

through them to make sure I was heard. "You've got to be quicker than that. Try again."

If Rurik heard my instructions, then he willfully ignored them, continuing to bat at the air like a playful kitten rather than tearing through it as a powerful warrior. The locusts easily evaded him. In fact, they seemed to dismiss him as a threat all together and kept their soft-footed attacks focused solely on Calina, who by now looked like she was in the middle of an especially epic tavern brawl. She kicked and punched wildly, sending bugs flying every which way. She still hadn't located either of the daggers but had picked up the headless corpse of a fallen opponent and was using it as a makeshift weapon against the others.

So much blood, gore, and ichor coated her clothes that I could scarcely tell what color they'd been to begin with. "Can I get a little help here?" she shouted between gasps for air. "There are hundreds of these things. I can't possibly kill them all by myself."

"I'm trying," Rurik moaned and shifted his flame yet again.

"Try turning it off and then back on again," I directed from the sidelines, doing my best not to laugh at the ridiculous scene.

Rurik slammed his fingers against his palm to close the magical flame and then straightened and summoned a fresh ball of fire. This one was smaller than the first. He was losing stamina, and quickly.

Rurik moved a bit faster now, but not quite fast enough. Not even close. The locusts had already figured out his patterns and had no trouble stepping away before he could so much as choose which of them to target next.

"Rurik!" Calina shrieked as she continued to fight with jerky, inexperienced motions. "I can't do everything. We're supposed to be a team!"

If this continued for much longer, I'd need to step in. At the very least, I could retrieve the daggers for Calina or hand her the bow, but first I wanted to see what her partner would do. I was starting to suspect that, while naturally adept in the arcane arts, Rurik didn't work well under pressure.

He stretched his arms wide and summoned a second flame over his opposite palm. Dude looked like a candelabra now, and he just stood there, glowing uselessly in the daylight as the buggy battle raged before him.

Okay, I needed to help them out. I crept closer, planning to grab both knives, deliver them to Calina, and then creep back out just as quickly.

"GRRRAAAAAAAHHH!" Rurik's enraged cry stopped me dead on my feet.

I turned just in time to watch as he snapped off his flames and pushed his fist straight through one of the giant locust's face. Yes, *through*. He hit the thing with so much force that his fist passed through the bug's head and wound up somewhere deep inside its abdomen.

He bellowed again as he shook one chitinous corpse off and pounded into another. Calina heaved a massive sigh—of relief, exhaustion, and who knows what else—and stepped to the side while Rurik continued in full-fledged barbarian mode.

Five minutes later, all the locusts had been slain. Yeah, somehow this clumsy, methodical kid had taken out an entire swarm with breath-taking speed. Calina had used this opportunity to retrieve both daggers. She now stood at my side as we both watched Rurik take in the scene around him with a disapproving shake of his head.

"Are you sure you're not..." I began, but did I even really have to ask?

"I'm not a barbarian." His chest heaved, not with exhaustion but anger. "I'm going to be a wizard if it's the last thing I do."

After seeing his battle magic in action, I could confirm it may very well be the last thing he ever did. Rurik was smart and determined. He could be a talented wizard one day, but he was already a fearsome barbarian. Why was he so dead set against harnessing his natural born talents?

I said nothing. Instead I just waited, knowing full well that one of the kids would rush to fill the silence.

The longer I waited, the more it looked as if Rurik might cry... and then he did cry huge, wracking sobs of anguish. Calina moved to comfort him. I froze, utterly stupefied. What could I possibly say here?

The locusts had been an easy challenge, but what would happen if the two of them faced an opponent that could inflict real damage? Calina had some skills, but Rurik would be a massive liability... unless he fought with his fists instead of his flame.

"I don't think..." My words fell away as a massive figure moved in the sky overhead, turning the entire garden dark for a few tense moments before blinking away right before my very eyes.

Calina gasped and leaned in close to her friend. "What was that?"

"A dragon." I searched the sky for any tell-tale signs of invisibility, but it seemed as if the creature had tele-ported away entirely. That couldn't be right...

"Why would there be a dragon out here?" one of the kids asked, but I was so fixated on the environment, I couldn't even say which one it had been.

That would be just my luck to get attacked by a bloody dragon while out in the middle of nowhere with only two untrained miscreants to lend a hand. We'd be toast before the thing even finished making its landing.

"Where did it go?" Calina asked. This time I could tell it had been her, because her voice came out in a high, tinny soprano that reminded me so much of her mother I could cry.

"I don't know," I murmured as my eyes continued to scrutinize every inch of land and sky. "I don't know."

9

I kept my eyes on the sky, searching, searching, but coming up short. "We need to get out of here."

For once, Calina didn't argue. We'd seen a freaking dragon for divinity's sake. Of course, they were afraid. Though I would never admit it, I was afraid too. Such a reaction was instinctual. Intelligent even.

The kids didn't know what I suspected though. That this hadn't been just any old fearsome dragon, but rather one very specific dragon who'd been hunting me ever since my last quest ended in disaster. Ten years ago, I made myself disappear into the small-town bustle of Briarhaven, but she had never given up the hunt.

Cindara.

If she'd found me, then my days—minutes—were numbered. I had to get out of here. Away from the farm, away from Briarhaven, away from anyone whose life I wasn't willing to forfeit as payment for my sins of the past.

The magical burn on my arm ignited with a fresh tidal wave of pain. I tried to run but found my feet stuck fast to the dirt. What the... Was this the work of a powerful spellcaster or my own corrosive anxiety?

I didn't know. Couldn't know.

And then he appeared as if from the air itself. That same hooded figure who had assaulted me at the Mystic Mug the week prior. He floated toward the three of us.

I couldn't see them, but I felt Calina and Rurik's panic rising from where they stood, trapped beside me. Their breaths came out strained, as if they had to fight for each one.

The world fell silent, still, as the shrouded figure in the billowing cloak continued to cut slowly through the air as he made his path toward our trio.

My heart rammed into my throat and felt as if it got stuck there. I was going to either vomit, suffocate, or both.

"What do you want?" I called—or at least tried to. The words wouldn't come. Couldn't.

The mysterious assailant closed the remaining distance between us and grabbed my injured arm. The intense pain threatened to bring me to my knees, only I still couldn't move, still couldn't talk. I had no recourse, no relief.

I raised my eyes the best I could to peer beneath the hood, but all was dark and undiscerning. The creature clenched at my arm with long, bony fingers that circled my wrist two times over, then it pushed my sleeve up above my elbow, exposing my wound.

"Yessssss." The voice was creepy and undeniably male. He spoke the way I imagined a serpent might. I had no desire to talk to a snake, and even less of a desire to converse with this strange being.

"My servant has not marked you in vain." His servant, so he was not the one who'd assaulted me at the tavern. This was also not just some lowly hench-man. The creature before me had some degree of power and control, although I knew he wasn't the big boss.

Maltherius had that honor. He commanded Cindara, the dragon we'd spied just moments earlier, and he also commanded an unending undead horde, which I suspected this fellow belonged to. I knew Maltherius would never come for me himself, not when he had so many others who could do his dirty work for him.

The creature before me dragged a clawed finger of bone across my skin, and amidst the bumpy red terrain of my burn, something new arose. A glowing outline of some mystic sigil that I couldn't recognize. I'd never seen it before, especially not on my own body. How long had it been there? And why?

The creature threw back his hood and stared at me from hollow eye sockets. I had no doubt he could see me quite clearly despite the obvious lack of eyeballs. He appeared to be half skeleton and half ghoul. Chunks of rancid, decayed flesh clung to his exposed bone, threatening to fall at any moment and making him a sight to behold.

Calina sucked in a sharp breath beside me.

Rurik remained perfectly silent.

"Why was I marked?" I tried to ask, but still couldn't access my words. It didn't matter anyway. Not when I already knew the answer. The figure loomed over me but let my arm go; it fell lifelessly to my side—still not under my control. He raised both hands toward my chest and tore at my tunic, exposing my undergarments in one deft slash of his clawed fingers.

If there was pain, I didn't feel it. Such was my terror.

The artifact I'd worked so hard to protect now lay exposed upon my breast. The elongated diamond shape of the pendant glinted, though there was no sun for it to reflect.

"The Genesis Crest," the creature hissed then hooted in excitement. "At last. Maltherius will be most pleased to see its safe return."

Nooooo! I wanted to scream, wanted to tear myself away or tear the necrotic creature's arm clean off him. But I still couldn't do a single blessed thing.

The undead sorcerer reached for the crest with trembling fingers. With the slightest caress of the pendant's surface, it surged with a power I hadn't known it possessed—a power that blew him back several paces. Hunks of blackened flesh fell from his bony frame, and he hissed in outrage.

I don't know why the pendant had come to life on my behalf, but its defensive attack was enough to break the creature's spell over us.

Calina discovered this first and bent down to grab the nearest weapon she could find—the same bow I'd secretly filched from her earlier. Within seconds, she had an arrow nocked and aimed at the skeletal ghoul as it struggled back to its feet. "What do you want?" she demanded.

Rurik drew a flame in each palm and placed

himself between the two of us and the necrotic soldier. "Stay back!"

My daggers. I needed my daggers.

I kept my gaze locked straight ahead but searched the ground as best I could with my peripheral vision. My best bet now was to stand my ground, to allow the pendant to protect me, should the creature lunge forward again. If I ran, I'd make a much easier target. I wouldn't survive, and neither would the kids.

The silver glint of my favored dagger caught my eye, lodged several paces away. Could I reach it in time to make a difference?

The zombie hung his head and laughed bitterly. "The crest has bonded to you. It shall not part with you unless you command it to do so. And you will do so, or you will die. Give it to me. Now."

"No. No way." I did a good job hiding the quiver in my voice, but my body betrayed me, shaking violently as the creature floated toward me once more. A hunk of rancid, bruised flesh hung from his brow, and looked as if it might tear away at any second. I waited for it to drop, hoping it would present the distraction I needed to retrieve my fallen weapon.

"Silly halfling! You have no idea what power that artifact holds. It is not yours to command. Give it here so that I may return it to my master."

"I owe you nothing. Leave this place and tell your master you failed on your quest." I found myself speaking the way Gaaron would have when confronted with situations such as this one—lyrical and confident, just a few marks short of a well-practiced and hard-won hubris.

"You have been marked. Maltherius will not stop coming for you. Not until he has his prize." Yup, that's exactly what I'd feared all this time. Even if I survived this confrontation, I'd never be able to rest. I'd always be in danger, always need to watch my back and be ready to run.

The kids though, they still had a chance.

If we could overpower this undead soldier, none of the others back in the village would ever need to know that Calina and Rurik had borne witness to this calamity. I could leave town, draw the enemy's focus elsewhere, and give the two of them the chance to grow up and live out the rest of their days unharmed.

"Give it to me now, and I'll let you keep your lives."

Lives, plural.

He was threatening us all, but I knew better than anyone that he planned to kill us no matter what we did next. Our only chance at survival would come from taking him out first. Killing the undead was difficult, but not impossible. Gaaron had mastered a number of melodies to improve our damage against necrotic-powered foes, but my old friend wasn't here now.

Meaning: it all fell to me.

The glob of flesh on the creature's forehead continued to peel from his bone, promising to fall at any moment. He hovered just inches above the ground, pulling closer and closer to the three of us. I couldn't wait for the distraction any longer. I needed to get to my weapon. It was the only chance any of us had.

I darted to the side and tucked my tiny body into a roll as I raced for the dagger. At the same time, Calina let loose one arrow, then another, driving each into our foe's hollowed-out eye sockets.

He snarled in pain and crumpled to the ground. The desecrated hunk of flesh detached at last, falling to the ground along with him.

After that everything happened so fast, it was hard to keep track of it all.

Rurik lunged forward, both flames alight and bigger than I'd ever seen them before. He shoved both of his palms onto the sorcerer's chest, igniting the old, tattered cloak in a mighty blaze.

Calina unloaded her remaining arrows into the

zombie, then dodged to the side and retrieved the other dagger.

I raced forward with my dagger, coming in straight for the throat. The undead were hard to kill, but there was one thing that always worked.

Earlier, I'd easily separated that locust's head from its body. It would be a bit more of a challenge, but I could sever this freak at the neck too.

I let out a throaty roar, channeling my inner warrior who'd lain dormant for so, so long, and hurled myself toward our aggressor.

As soon as I made contact, my tunic caught fire, forcing me to stop, drop, and roll.

Learning from my bad example, Calina fell back. She threw her dagger... and missed. Rurik had already made full use of the only spell he knew, and even if he were willing to go into a full-blown barbarian rage again, the flames that engulfed our opponent had grown too powerful, were climbing too high.

The zombie soldier laughed hysterically, almost as if he were enjoying this whole thing. "You think you can defeat me?" he asked as his flesh sparked, and burned, then quickly turned to ash.

"I am but one of thousands. My master commands death itself." He was nothing more than bone now; his cloak and hunks of flesh had all turned to dust and been gobbled up by the raging flames. "Maltherius will see the value of the work I have done here and reward me with a swift resurrection. Then once granted, I will tear you each apart limb by limb until you're begging for death to take you. This is not the end. It is only the—"

The last of him vanished. All evidence of his corporeal form disappeared as if it had never been.

"The beginning," Rurik said, crouching down to investigate the spot where the creature had once stood. "He was going to say it's only the beginning."

"Yeah, thanks, big guy. Now help me put out this fire before it claims farmer Dewglen's land."

The three of us rushed forward and stomped out the remaining wisps of flame. Much of the fire had disappeared with the last of the creature's ashes. It seemed as if the magic inherent in the creature had made Rurik's blaze all the more powerful, and now that our opponent was no more, the fire had lost its main source of fuel.

He'd been powerful, this servant of Maltherius. Yet somehow we'd won the battle against him. And far too easily at that. I had a feeling that many more members of his undead army would soon be coming our way.

The kids had helped to secure victory today, but I sensed the confrontation had been rigged from the jump. This had been a fact-finding mission, and a test of my grit.

The necromancer must have known I would not surrender easily. Not when I'd already been evading him for nearly a decade. When his soldier didn't return, he'd have proof of our confrontation—and my location.

And he would come back with a larger army and a better plan. Maybe even Maltherius himself would descend upon us now. Whatever the case, I had to make sure that I wasn't here when any of them arrived. Briarhaven had been my home for ten long years, but it couldn't keep me safe any longer.

It was time to leave so that I could protect the others.

I was coming out of retirement. This time it was official.

I needed to face my foe head-on. And on my own terms.

10

I left the farm in a hurry, not even stopping to tell farmer Dewglen the job was done nor to collect the coin purse he'd secretly promised me for our trouble. The kids and I had obliterated the undead sorcerer, but we didn't exactly know what had happened to the massive dragon. She could still be nearby, waiting to finish us off. Maltherius and his legions might also be on their way to Briarhaven. Either way, he'd be sure to finish what his scouts had started. His next move would come swiftly.

And I had to make sure I was his only target.

"What was that all about? I thought you were retired!" Calina practically exploded at my side as she matched me pace for pace in my flee.

Rurik stumbled along just behind. "It's the amulet. I'm guessing it doesn't belong to her."

"Uh, ya think!" Calina balled both her hands into fists and kept them clenched close to her sides, giving her an odd and jerky gait.

I shook my head and tried not to cry. Years of the easy life had destroyed my fortitude. I now felt like a big gooey mess as I grappled with the implications of what I'd need to do next. "It doesn't matter. Your part in it is over."

"Doesn't matter?" Calina jogged ahead and then turned to face me, walking backward so that I was forced to converse with her as I fled toward town. "How can you say it doesn't matter? It almost got us killed!"

"This was a mistake. I shouldn't have given in to your stupid blackmail scheme." I tried to dodge past her, but even walking backward Calina moved too fast for me to outmaneuver. I was stuck.

"I thought you wanted to help me find my dad," she demanded, her face turning a bright rose to match her long, flowing hair. Its tendrils whipped around her face, reminding me of the billowing cloak on our assailant. Did she not realize how close we'd all come to the end just now?

"Your dad is dead!" I shouted, allowing my frustration to overtake me. But just for a moment. I wasn't mad at the kid. I was mad that I'd been found out, that I would have to leave it all behind... Again.

"I mean, he's *probably* dead," I corrected, placing undue emphasis on the probably. After all, I wasn't supposed to know anything beyond what she'd shared with me. At least it would be easier to keep this new secret once I was back on my own. I'd have no one to tell, no one to care.

"I'm sorry, Calina. But it's time to face the facts here. Your father could very well be dead by now. And even if he's not, you have almost nothing to go on. You're never going to find him, and you're never going to be an adventurer. You could barely handle a harmless swarm of locusts, and if that showdown with the sorcerer guy hadn't been rigged from the start, we'd all be feeding the vultures right about now. Agreeing to train you was a mistake—involving you in this, coming to Briarhaven—all of it. But they're mistakes I won't make again."

"You're leaving." Rurik didn't appear angry or even hurt by my decree, only deeply contemplative as he took in all the information and considered it plainly.

"Of course, I'm leaving. Didn't you hear what that undead freak said? He's got thousands upon thousands of friends, and they're all coming for me. I need to get out of here, or Briarhaven's going to get blown straight off the map."

"But where will you go? This is your home. You have people who love you." Calina's rage slowly morphed into sorrow. She'd grown to care about me, just in time for me to leave her behind. Just like her father once had.

I stopped walking and shook my head. "Yes, and I will never forgive myself if my error in judgment gets them *or you* killed. I don't know where I'll go next. Only that I have to go."

"We're coming with you," Rurik said, surprising us both.

"The heck you are! You're both going home and forgetting this whole thing ever happened. You're just a couple of wannabe heroes. You can't handle a real quest like this one." The way Calina's face crumpled and Rurik's surprisingly smooth strides broke into a sudden awkward stumble told me everything I needed to know. This hurt them, but did it hurt them enough to encourage them to give up? To let me go?

"You can't handle this thing alone," Calina argued, but she'd lost much of her fire.

"You're right," I said, striding forward once again. "You're right. I'll need help. But not from you."

"We're a part of this now," Calina insisted as she

once again fell into step beside me. "We were here when it all started. This is our quest just as much as it is yours."

"Little girl, this started more than ten years ago. It has *nothing* to do with you." I knew that was wrong, knew that the necromancer who was now threatening to kill me had also been the one to murder the father she so desperately sought to reconnect with. But if I let Calina discover this connection, she'd never let me go on my own. It was vital that I go on my own. That only I answer for the mistakes I'd been attempting to outrun for the past decade.

I had to work hard to keep my burning tears at bay. I didn't want to let the kids know how much this hurt me. "Now like I said, go home and forget any of this ever happened. And while you're at it, forget about your misguided dream of becoming an adventurer. That life can only ever end in pain. It's not for you."

"Excuse me, Muh-Muh-Miss Quickthatch," Rurik piped up from just behind us. With any luck, he would fill the rest of the distance with his inane rambles, giving me a break from Calina's demands and my attempts to evade them. I was not ready for what he said next.

"How dare you tell Calina what is and isn't for her?" Rurik's voice boomed, and I swear I felt it rise up from the ground and reverberate through my body. "I thought you were on our side, but you're no better than my parents who say I have to make all the same choices they did, or the kids at school who say I'm a loser and a freak and that everyone hates me. You think you get to decide what other people can do, what they can be, but you have absolutely no right." He paused for a moment to suck in a giant breath of air. "You are correct about one thing though. This was a mistake. Calina and I are going to be heroes, but we're going to do it without your help. You're nothing more than a mean, old coward. You've been hiding for more than half our lives, and at the first sign of trouble you're running away. We thought we wanted to be like you, but no. We're *not* going to be like you. We're going to be better than you."

Calina slowed and laced her long, slender fingers between Rurik's stumpy digits. "He's right. We're both going to be somebody special some day, and a big part of that is because we have each other. A true hero knows that attachments aren't a weakness. They're a strength. When you told us about the partner you lost, I saw how you smiled and got that far-off look in your eye... And it told me that you once knew the power of love. You could know it again too if you'd just give us a chance. We don't have anything to prove to you, Tilda. All we wanted was the chance to prove what we can become *to ourselves*. It's all we've ever wanted."

I was done with their philosophical soliloquies. "You're teenagers! You have no idea what you want. When I was your age, I was—"

"We're our own people, Tilda, and we get to make our own decisions."

"Actually, you're still very much both children, which means your parents get to make your decisions. At least for another couple years, and by then, I'll have moved on. By the divine's unending grace, I'll probably be dead. Are you really so eager to join me in that plight?"

"You have no faith. No love. No wonder you're so sad," Rurik said. The stutter had completely vanished now, and he spoke with an uncharacteristic fluidity to his words. "No wonder you only see doom when instead you could see hope. This is your chance to change the world, and rather than accept the hero's mantle, you're planning to run and hide."

"You don't even know what the artifact is or who's chasing it. You have no idea what's at stake here."

"Then tell us." Calina reached around and grabbed my shoulder so that I spun to face her. I hated being so small that it was often easy for others to physically manipulate me. They could command my body, but they'd never break my mind... or my heart.

"No. I know you think you're both some big hotshots because you're halfway decent at wielding a bow while your partner can produce a dinky little magic flame, but you two are nothing. Don't you get it? You're young. You can still make different choices. So do it. *Choose life* instead of certain death."

Rurik let out a long sigh and offered me a piteous glance. His tusks quivered as he regarded me, and his voice grew flat and cold. "If you're so sure you're going to die, then you've already sealed your fate. You *will* die."

"Great, then we're all agreed. I'll die, and you two will grow up and live out your lives as... I don't know, dairy farmers or blacksmiths or any blessed thing you want, because *you* won't be dead. Now by the divine, go away. Leave me to my misery. It's mine and mine alone to bear."

I hated how I left things with the kids, but I needed to scare them off somehow. If I could make them hate me, then they wouldn't try to follow me out of town. It was for the best. Really.

After an afternoon spent preparing my travel gear, I slowly began to make my way toward the tavern. As I wandered, I took in all the sights, sounds, smells, knowing it would all be for the last time. In the midday breeze, curtains from open windows danced, waving to me as I wandered. The dull but animated murmur of townsfolk talking to one another about the weather from their porches. Even the mud, dirt, and dung smell of our simple roads hit me like a hammer on an anvil. This place had become my home. The only true home I'd ever known, and I would miss it with every fiber of my tiny little being.

I didn't worry about being late to work that evening. Truth be told, nothing much mattered. Not anymore. I'd leave at the dawn's first light, hoping my hardest that it wasn't too late to save the others.

"You're late," Brynlee said when I walked into the tavern ten minutes later. I'd forgotten to slap the sign on my way in, and by the way she looked at me now, it seemed she had noticed. "And sad. Why sad?"

"I'm leaving, and I'll miss you," I answered truthfully. She didn't need to know anything more than that.

"Leaving? Where are you going? Are you finally taking that vacation Durgan has been harassing you about all these years?" She started to giggle, but stopped abruptly when she realized my sullen expression had not changed.

"I'll miss you so, so much," I said again. A wretched, little tear fell and rolled down my plump cheek, landing on the fresh tunic I'd changed into after the battles that morning. It was the nicest thing I owned—embroidered with small flowers that were pink and red on a bright orange background. Brynlee had once told me it brought out the rose in my cheeks, and whenever I wore it now, I thought of her.

She shook her head slightly and abandoned the bar mid-wipe down. "Tilda, what's wrong? What's going on?"

My throat felt dry, thirsting not just for water but for the words to truly communicate my despair without giving away any of the details I needed to keep concealed. "I need to speak to Durgan." I turned away to hide the rapidly building tears. My vision blurred as I searched the tavern for the bald-headed, orange-bearded boss who had become like a brother to me over the years.

I spotted him in the back, near the fireplace with Insy, and headed over to offer a verbal resignation from my post. "We need to speak in private," I informed him, tugging on my left ear to reveal that all was not well.

Durgan jumped right to his feet, without even bothering to crack a joke. I wore my doom as clear as the little flowers that adorned my tunic. And when the two of us were standing alone in the stock room, I could no longer hold back the raging torrent of tears that I'd tried so hard to fight all afternoon.

I'd never been a crier before, but I'd softened in my retirement. I'd changed, and not for the better. All the little changes that had helped me to build a good life in Briarhaven would become enormous burdens upon leaving it. I was no match for Maltherius, nor even a lesser necromancer. But I still had to face him.

"I'm leaving," I said, not knowing how else to embellish the statement. This was the one fact that mattered most. None of my reasons changed the outcome, and I didn't want to worry Durgan with them.

"Your past finally caught up to you, eh?" he said with a small tilt of his chin. And impossibly, he smiled. He must have been very drunk already, although it was hard to see any of the usual signs that marked his flag-ging sobriety.

"Something like that. I need to go and finish something I've left undone for far too long. If you want to join me, your maul may come in handy." He was the only person I could think to ask for help, the only one in town who shared my adventuring past.

"My sweet, little halfling friend, would that I could. But I have the Mug and Pat to look after." Both Durgan and I knew that it was actually Brynlee who looked after the tavern, and Pat who looked after his partner, but neither of us bothered to point that out. The moment was too tender, too fragile.

"A life of adventure, it changes a man," Durgan said as he wistfully stroked his beard, fingering one particular bauble as if trying to polish it to a shine. "One day I realized that it was never really a life at all. That I was never my own man. Not until Briarhaven. Not until Pat... Why do you think I drown all my memories with mead? Every night, I drink to forget those days, but every morning they find me again. The past has a hard time of letting go."

I nodded my agreement.

"But you can choose a different path, Tilda." He placed a meaty palm upon my shoulder and searched my eyes as if trying to find something in them.

I tore my gaze away, unable to withstand his scrutiny or his compassion. "The path has already chosen for me. If I stay, people will die. People we both care deeply about."

He let out a deep breath from his belly and waited

a few moments before speaking again. Perhaps hoping I would fill the silence. I did not.

"Then it seems you really haven't got a choice. I'm sorry, Tilda. The past can be a cruel mistress. I'm so sorry she got her claws into you again."

"You'll take care of Brynlee? And Calina?"

"Aye, I will. And I'll save a spot for you behind the bar for when you return to us, triumphant from the glow of your victory."

That wasn't going to happen. Even if I somehow managed to defeat Maltherius, there would be others who wanted the artifact—the Genesis Crest, as my undead assailant had called it. Others who would hunt me down, follow me to this place, and wreak untold havoc.

A big city might have the defenses necessary to hold its own, but Briarhaven was far too small, far too vulnerable. I could never return.

"I appreciate all that you have given me. And I will never forget you." I wrapped the old dwarf in a fat hug. My hands couldn't reach all the way around his barrel chest, so I dug my fingers into his back and held on tight. For a few precious moments, we clung to each other. Our tears flowed freely as a twin cyclone of memories best left forgotten tormented us both.

The ghoulish creature who'd attacked us that day

had said this was only the beginning, but it sure felt like the end.

11

I agreed to work that one last evening behind the tavern bar, both to ease the sting of my sudden departure and so that I could enjoy my happy, little life one last time before the whole thing came crashing to an end.

As I greeted customers, poured drinks, and tidied up the tavern, I took special efforts to catalog every action, every memory for when I needed to call upon their comfort later. This small-town existence had started as a cover, but over time, it had become the real me.

Brynlee had attempted to linger at the Mug in hopes of extracting some kind of explanation from me, but Durgan shooed her off. He understood all too well how much the very act of leaving was breaking me. I couldn't handle seeing that it just might break Brynlee too. She would recover though. I'd never been anything more than a friend and colleague to her. It was Gaaron she wanted. Eventually her longing for him would eclipse any she had for me. This sad truth made me feel a bit better about leaving her.

After all, I was leaving *for* her—to protect her and the others. She didn't need to understand. She only needed to be safe.

Leaving my past life behind ten years ago had been hard, but this time it was brutal. It would have been impossible, had I not loved it so much. No matter what monsters I faced or what fate ultimately befell me, I could accept it all, knowing that Briarhaven and its inhabitants remained just as I had experienced them. Just as I would always remember them. Life would carry on here, one way or another.

Farmer Dewglen came in to thank me for slaying the swarm that had plagued him and offer me the coin purse he'd promised. I accepted it, knowing I might need it. But blessed be, that battle with the giant locusts felt like it had happened ages ago rather than that very morning.

I hoped to connect with Insy one last time before I had to go, but the sweet infernal remained scarce that evening. Like me, he was so much more than he seemed upon just a first glance. I'd known a few others of his kind over the years, but none could hold a flame to Insy. He would be missed.

They would all be missed.

Durgan kept a watchful eye on me as I worked. He seemed to be saving memories for later as well. I wondered if he might one day add a new bauble to his beard in my honor, whether he'd tell my story to the patrons, and what he'd say if he said anything at all.

"This one's for Tilda," he would regale the future faceless customers of my imagination while pointing to a small clay bead, smooth and unassuming with a nasty fracture threatening to split it in two. "She was more than she seemed. Small in stature, yes, but still too big for our peaceful village in the end."

I would not cry. Not over some stupid made-up talisman. Not over all the wonderful things I was about to throw away either. I'd done this to myself. The fact I'd been able to enjoy a decade of peaceful living was more than I'd ever deserved, more than I'd ever even dared to hope for as a young urchin struggling to survive a cruel city's streets.

Well, I was taking to the road again. I'd now decided that my destination would be Mirathane. Going back to that same city that had been such a dysfunctional home for me in my youth made the most sense. I still remembered its alleyways intimately. I could hide for a long time by dodging in and out of them.

If I kept Maltherius searching, he'd be too busy to cause trouble for anyone else.

At least, that was my hope.

I knew I couldn't outmatch Verandel's most powerful necromancer, but I just might be able to evade him long enough to make a difference in the fate of the world. I didn't know what all the artifact could do. With a name like the Genesis Crest, it seemed like some kind of a creation thing. The exact type of object that would be best kept out of the hands of one who'd already mastered death.

When Gaaron and I had accepted the bounty to retrieve it for our anonymous quest master, we hadn't asked many questions. And the questions we had asked went largely unanswered. For ten years I'd kept the mysterious macguffin tucked beneath my tunic, close to my heart, not knowing what kind of power it wielded or even who, besides Maltherius, wanted it for their own.

I could sense its importance, which is why I'd kept it hidden on my person for the past decade. It had never, not once, showed any sign of sentience. Not until it had blasted the undead sorcerer away from me.

Was I somehow chosen? And if so, why me?

I didn't know, couldn't know, but perhaps I would soon be on my way to finding out.

As closing time approached, the crowds slowly began to disperse into the night. This was it then. My last few moments of small-town bliss.

I moved to take inventory of our spirits, knowing it was the last time. We'd gone through a healthy amount of gin lately, due to a recent increase in human patrons. That meant we'd need more of the magic tonic water as well, and the fizzing water was not always easy to secure. I had to make sure Durgan knew, so he wouldn't find himself in need.

A loud smack startled me from my task, causing me to lose track of the list I had been populating in my head for later. I glanced over at the door and spotted my old friend, Insy.

So I would be able to say goodbye after all. Oh sweet divinity, thank you for your small blessings.

I moved to make his preferred cocktail, but he stopped me with a firm shake of his head. "Something told me I needed to be here tonight. To see you," he revealed. "Is everything all right?"

"Everything is perfect," I answered without hesitation.

The infernal studied me for several moments

without speaking, then sucked in a deep breath through his oversized nostrils. "I know you would not lie unless you had a good reason. Be well, Tilda Quick-thatch. Until we meet again."

He turned to leave, and I let him. The infernal worked hard to remain placid and defy his violent nature; I didn't need to worry him with my troubles even if he sensed them already.

I thought Insy would be the last, but as soon as he departed, another tavern-goer slid up to the bar. Bramble Thistledown, the halfling baker who had a not-so-secret crush on me. Alas, I would even miss him and his failed flirtations. It was nice to be wanted by someone for benevolent reasons.

I greeted him with a sincere smile. "Bramble, what can I pour for you today?"

He pulled himself up onto one of the barrel seats to get a better view of me over the bar. "Nothing for me tonight. I'm afraid I don't have any coin to spare."

"On the house," I offered, wanting to keep him there for long enough to have one last meaningful exchange.

Bramble shook his head and deep worry lines creased his usually smooth face. "I'm not here to talk. I'm here to warn you." He reached into his pocket and pulled out a piece of aged parchment that had been folded in half twice so that it resembled a square.

"What's this?" I asked as he pushed it across the counter, rapidly shifting my gaze from Bramble's face to the parchment and back again.

He tensed on his stool and shrunk away from the bar. "The fellow who gave it to me... Something wasn't right about him. I don't know what you've gotten yourself into Tilda, but you need to be careful."

I yanked the letter from the wooden bar top and clutched it to my chest. "Who gave this to you? What did they say?"

"The funny thing is he didn't say much at all. Just that I needed to deliver this here note to you. And quick. Now, I'll confess, I read it first. I had to make sure you were okay, Tilda. I know you'll understand. And I was right to read it. Whatever you've gotten yourself mixed up in, it's bad. Real bad."

I hung my head and took a deep breath. "I know."

"I may be just a humble baker, but I can protect you. However you need me to help, I'll do it. Just say the word." He puffed up and fiddled with his shirt collar, offering a hesitant smile.

"Oh, Bramble. I know that too. But what this is—" I raised the folded piece of parchment into the air and shook it at him twice. "I need to do it on my own."

"That's part of why I like you so much. You're stronger than the common stock, Tilda, but being strong doesn't mean you have to be alone." He paused for a moment and lowered his eyes before hopping off the stool. "Anyway... If you change your mind, you know where to find me."

"Thank you," I called after him, then swept my eyes around the Mug to make sure that no one else needed me just then. Seeing that I had at least a few moments to myself, I tucked myself into the small kitchen and unfolded the parchment.

A dark, shining script filled the page. The impeccable penmanship made the contents of the letter all the more unnerving, made it feel more official, like an invitation of sorts. Dread roiled in my gut as I realized exactly who'd written these words to me and what they meant concerning the next steps of my impending journey.

The bard lives. Bring me the crest, and we will make a trade. This more than generous offer expires when the sun sets on the solstice. You do not want to find out what will happen should you fail to meet these terms. —M

I read the first three words over and over again, for they were the ones that mattered most. *The bard lives.* The bard. Gaaron. My long-lost partner and friend. I'd buried him in my mind, but all these years he'd lived on as Maltherius's prisoner. All these years he'd been waiting for a rescue that hadn't been coming. I simply hadn't known.

I also didn't know whether I could trust Maltherius's words, but I couldn't risk ignoring them. I couldn't continue to let Gaaron down. For ten long years, he'd suffered, because I hadn't known he needed me to save him.

What difference would it make if I died next week rather than after who-know-how-many years spent on the run?

Yes, if it meant saving Gaaron. Calina could have her father, and Brynlee the love her heart so badly ached for. My life would be a small sacrifice to secure so much happiness.

I had to meet with Maltherius.

His deadline didn't give me much time. We were already well into Beltane.

It would be a long journey back to the cliffs that housed his lair, but I could make it. All that arduous travel by foot would give me time to think, to plan for anything he might throw my way.

Was I expecting him to keep his word? Absolutely not.

Would I still go? Yes. Yes, I would.

There was one major advantage I had in this scenario. I knew how powerful my opponent was, but Maltherius had no idea what to expect from me. This old girl still had a trick or two up her sleeve, and it was time to play every last card I'd been dealt.

I'd leave at dawn's first light.

A new hope swelled within me. I would still be leaving the only place I'd ever belonged, but I was no longer running away. I was now running *toward*.

And that small change of perspective made all the difference.

12

I shoved Maltherius's note deep within my pocket, highly aware of its presence as I worked to close down the tavern for the night. While I cleaned up, Durgan shepherded the few remaining patrons toward the exit. The merry boom of his voice stretched to fill the entire establishment, making the air feel thick with his easy charm.

But it wasn't so easy, was it?

He'd confided something in me tonight, and I felt ashamed for not having noticed it before. Durgan's joyful demeanor didn't come naturally to him like I'd always suspected. He had to choose it each and every day. *Fake it even* so that others would never have to bear the weight of his phantom pains. The metaphorical dagger had been pulled clean, but his old wounds still bled. They were wounds of the heart, the kind that never healed.

"Hello, Tilda. Is my quarry ready?" Pat had entered without me noticing, which showed how distracted my inner thoughts had made me that night. The half-giant could hardly squeeze through the doorframe without dipping his head to his chest, and yet he'd managed to make it all the way to the bar without my even realizing he'd arrived. I couldn't afford to make mistakes like this once I set off. Getting distracted often meant getting dead, especially for someone like me who relied so heavily on her stealth abilities.

"He was just here, saying goodbye to the last of our customers."

"Well, he's not here now. Did he leave on his own? You know how I worry." Unlike his partner, Pat had a full head of hair. Thick and curly, it hung just past his ears. He tugged at his golden locks with both hands in frustration and contorted his features so that I couldn't tell whether he would scream or cry.

"Don't worry. He can't be far." I searched the tavern but couldn't spot its missing mascot. Strange. I wouldn't be able to lock up the Mystic Mug without a second key, and I also wouldn't be able to leave without first securing the property. Durgan knows both these facts very well, so then why had he secreted away?

"I'll just go check the kitchen and the storage room." I scooted toward the back of house, somewhat frightened by what Pat might do if he grew too worried. Giants were infamous for their bad tempers, and while Pat was only half, he loved his dwarfish husband more than life itself. He'd pound anyone who threatened the little guy straight into the cobblestones. In fact, I'd seen him take out his frustration with the blacksmith's hammer more than one time. His intense strength made for sleek and smooth blades. I should have liked to own one but had never gotten up the nerve to ask. Shame.

My search for Durgan came up short, and I returned to the front of the establishment dreading making the reveal of this failure to Pat. How would I close shop? A wing scout wouldn't be available at this late hour, which meant that I either had to find Durgan, find Brynlee... or risk leaving the Mug unlocked overnight.

Briarhaven was a quiet village, but that didn't mean someone wouldn't take advantage. I was already leaving Durgan short-handed, I couldn't also leave him short-changed.

"He's not here. Maybe he went home ahead of you. Do you want to go check, and I'll wait here?"

Pat snorted, and I could almost swear I saw small puffs of steam billow from his nostrils. "He knows to wait for me."

"Um, maybe you can wait here for him to come back, and I'll go ask Brynlee if I can borrow her key to close up for the night?"

"He should be here," Pat insisted rather unhelpfully. If I left, could I count on him to wait for my return? If he left, could I count on him to come back? This predicament was actively stealing sleep that I would very much need for tomorrow's journey.

I couldn't believe my old friend would leave me in such a bind. I thought he understood...

"Need my help?" a soft, lilting voice asked before its speaker swept into the tavern.

"Brynlee! What are you doing here? You should be at home sleeping." I could have cried when I spotted her. I never thought I'd see her again, my sweet girl. And now she'd come to rescue me when I needed it.

"I woke her up," Durgan announced, scrambling in just behind her.

"And I told her everything," Calina added, hanging back near the tavern door rather than entering fully with the others.

Rurik's bulky body hovered just outside of the entrance, but he didn't announce himself. Nor did he step inside.

"What's going on?" I placed a hand on each hip, bracing myself against my friends. They had something planned, and whatever that something was, I knew I wouldn't much care for it.

Pat only had eyes for his partner; he opened his arms and waited for Durgan to fold himself into them. "You shouldn't have left. You could have tripped and fallen into the river or got run over by a run-away wagon, or... Truly, there are nigh a hundred ways you could have met your end tonight, my honeybug."

"I took it easy on the ale tonight. This was important, but it was also only a one-time thing, I promise. Now take me home, you big lug." Durgan sighed happily as he leaned into Pat's much larger form, but quickly unfurled himself from the embrace and began to tug the other man toward the door.

"Brynlee, be a dear and help Tilda lock up tonight," he called over his shoulder as our group was cut from six to four.

"Let's close up. I have an early morning ahead of me," I said, refusing to make eye contact with any of the others.

"Oh, I know you do," Brynlee snapped. Her words

crashed into me instead of offering their usual caress. "You were going to leave without saying goodbye."

"I already told you goodbye when we saw each other this afternoon." I jammed both hands into my pockets and tugged at the fabric inside to distract myself, to keep from saying or doing something I would regret. I'd already have enough unwelcome memories to haunt me on the road. I couldn't leave things with Brynlee in a bad way. I just couldn't.

She raised one eyebrow, then the other. "You didn't tell me anything. I had to wrest it out of Calina. Are you really leaving town to fight some scary necromancer?"

"Yes, but it's fine. I can handle myself, Brynlee. Really." I pull-pull-pulled on that fabric until I felt it rip away.

"Calina told me that too. You used to be an adventurer, and you never said a word about it."

"I didn't want you to look at me differently," I admitted, my voice cracking partway through the sentiment. "And I didn't want my past to endanger your future. Or your kid's."

She stepped closer, looming above me in a way I didn't like. "But you thought you could train Calina and Rurik in secret?"

I stepped back several paces until I bumped into a

table. "Hey, they forced my hand on that one. You know how she is."

"Yes, I do, which is why I want you to take her with you."

"Come again now?" Surely, I'd misheard her.

Brynlee moved toward me again, but her steps and words both came softer now. "Take Calina with you. Rurik too, if his parents will allow it. It's better than charging off alone."

"Have you lost your mind? It's dangerous, and they're untrained. Besides, don't they have school?"

"School finishes in a handful of moons. We wouldn't miss much," Rurik piped up from outside. A smack rang out as he accidentally beaned himself with the sign that hung there. He muttered something under his breath and then at last stepped into the Mug to join the rest of us.

"You can train us along the way," Calina added as her friend came to stand at her side. She wore a smirk that made me inexplicably proud. Her father's smirk, I realized, the weight of Maltherius's letter growing in my pocket. But this journey was about doing what needed to be done. Feelings didn't matter, especially not feelings of love, pride, or camaraderie.

"No, I go alone." I pulled out my dagger and rotated it in my main hand, needing something to help keep my mind focused on the present without letting it become flooded with anxiety.

"Oh, Tilda. You've kept us all out for years, but enough's enough. I'm not letting you fight this monster on your own. And we both know that my child will go out adventuring just the moment she gets the chance. I'd feel much better about it if I knew she was with a trusted friend." Brynlee drew near and placed both hands on my shoulders, rubbing small, smoothing circles with her fingers. Her signature scent of sun-kissed berries and fresh morning dew swirled in my nostrils, and I felt myself relax into her touch.

"Why didn't you ever share this part of yourself with me?" she asked softly, dropping one hand to relieve me of my weapon.

I sucked in a sharp breath and whispered, "I wasn't the only one who buried and tended gardens full of secrets."

"What does that mean? I always let you in, Tilda. Always. And I'd thought you did the same. Aren't... Weren't we friends?" Her eyes bore into mine, searching though I couldn't tell for what.

I grabbed one of her hands from my shoulder and ran a fingertip over her palm, eliciting a shiver—whether from her or from myself, I couldn't tell. "The best of friends. That's why I can't endanger your child.

She's all you have left, especially now that I'm going away too."

We fell silent for a few heartbeats. Not even that mouthy kid of hers dared to interrupt as we stood and breathed together.

"I was going to run away," I confessed. "I was going to run, so that my enemy wouldn't come looking for me here. But everything changed tonight when I received a note hand-delivered by Bramble Thistledown."

Brynlee crinkled her nose in confusion while both children remained blessedly quiet.

"He has something of mine, something that I thought I'd lost forever, and he's willing to make a trade."

"You can't give up the artifact!" Rurik shouted, causing both Brynlee and I to jump from the sudden intensity of his outburst.

"I have to, because that something is a *someone*. Someone I should have rescued long ago, but I didn't know... Now that I do, I'm going." I considered telling Brynlee my suspicions that the bards we'd each loved separately in the past were really one and the same. I wanted to so badly, but I couldn't hurt her in that way. What if my suspicions were wrong? What if Maltherius had lied about Gaaron's safety? And what if I failed to make the rescue? No, I couldn't do that to Brynlee. She had enough to worry about as it was—too much.

Calina tugged on my shoulder, ripping me away from her mother. "We're coming with you. We can help make a plan, so that you can save your friend and keep the artifact. We might not even have to face the bad guy. We can sneak in and sneak back out before he ever even notices we've arrived." Calina didn't know it, but she was suggesting the exact plan that her father had concocted all those years ago, the plan that got him captured, maybe even killed. I still knew so little about what awaited me on this journey, but I had to go. I had to believe that everything could be set right, that the world could be made better.

"Your chances at winning the game are much higher when you have three players on your side," Rurik mumbled thoughtfully, leaning against the doorframe in a relaxed posture that was atypical for him.

I moved away from Calina and turned back to her mother. "Please understand. This guy I'll be going up against, he's powerful. *Supremely* powerful. There's a good chance I won't escape our encounter with my life. You can't possibly want me to take your child along."

Calina kicked at the ground and shouted, "Stop calling me a child!"

"Her father was an adventurer," Brynlee confided with a far-off look. She didn't know that this detail had already been revealed to me. "He left when she was still very small. He said we'd be safer if he were somewhere far away. I always thought he'd come back to us one day, but he never did. Still, it's a choice he made, because adventuring was too big a part of him to ignore. It's a part of who Calina is too. It's in her blood, and that's something that will not change, no matter how much I wish she'd stay put. Please, Tilda. Guide her. Keep her safe while she learns to follow her dreams."

I shook my head as hard as I could without making myself dizzy. Why wouldn't she understand? "I would never forgive myself if something happened to her."

"I know, and that's exactly why I trust you so much. I also know that your chances of survival are better if you have help on your journey. So go, all of you. And then come back to me, all three."

My heart froze on the word "three." Did she know? It took a moment for me to realize she meant Rurik and not Calina's father. I searched Brynlee's eyes for even the slightest hint of hesitation, but I found none. She understood what was at stake, but she was willing to accept the risks, if it meant her child's happiness. I couldn't remember my own mother, so I didn't know if she would have done the same for me. I'd planned to run away to protect those I loved, but I never gave them a choice in the matter. Here, Brynlee was actively telling me that I had a choice, yes—but that others did too. I'd worked hard and valued these relationships. I didn't have to abandon every part of my life here, and I didn't have to forget everything I'd come to love during my decade in Briarhaven. I could be my past self and this new version at the same time. I could accept aid and offer the kids the training they craved.

I could rescue Gaaron and bring him home.

I could defeat Maltherius and stop his reign of corruption over the blighted territories.

I didn't have to die, didn't have to accept defeat before I'd even took the first step of my journey.

What Brynlee was asking of me felt scary, monumental... but also cathartic. I had changed, and that improved my chances of success—it did not diminish them. I'd faced Maltherius before as my old self, and I'd lost.

But the time? This time maybe I didn't have to. I could actually win. I could win and return to Briarhaven—not as a place to hide, but as my home, hard-won and true.

I let out a deep breath and stretched as tall as I could. "All right. They can come, and I'll offer them my guidance and protection, Brynlee. By the divine's everlasting grace, I will make sure your daughter comes home to you, safe and unharmed." Once more, I contemplated telling her the identity of the friend we'd be setting out to rescue but decided it would be better as a nice surprise. Telling her now would only heighten her anxiety for the season of our absence, and I'd never want that for someone I loved so dearly.

Brynlee wrapped me in her tightest hug yet. I felt like I might faint but in the best possible way. "Thank you so much, Tilda. I wouldn't ask this of you if I didn't know for certain you could do it."

I reluctantly freed myself from her embrace. "I'll be back, and you'll owe me big time. So get ready for that." I imagined the smile that would bloom upon my friend's lips when I delivered not only her child but also her long-lost love. She'd be thrilled to see them returned to her, but she'd also be overcome with joy at having her friend back.

I was part of the family, part of her bliss, and that gave me the strength of a thousand sorcerers, undead or otherwise.

13

I slept little that night despite knowing how much I needed it. Alas, my mind was too busy to allow my body any respite.

It was silly, really. I knew better than anyone how important it was to take life as it came. All my worries in those wee hours wouldn't change—or even help to better prepare me for—what awaited me on the road ahead. I needed to be sharper than ever, considering I'd have two giant walking liabilities with me.

But Brynlee, she had surprised me in the best possible way. I'd always considered her soft and in need of protection; last night she'd proven just how strong she was when she'd insisted I take Calina with me.

She had wants and needs but put her child's dreams and desires ahead of her own. I wondered briefly if that had been what happened when Gaaron left—if he'd left at her prompting.

I always liked Brynlee but considered the two of us to be opposites. Her willingness to sacrifice for those she cared about showed me just how well we matched in the ways that mattered most.

And I would miss her terribly.

I enjoyed a hearty, meat-filled breakfast, situated my overstuffed pack on my back, and locked up behind me for what I hoped wouldn't be the last time. Despite being relatively strong for a halfling, my traveling gear wasn't exactly on the lighter side. It nearly doubled my mass, rising about a pace above my head and hanging down to my knees. Hey, just because I was small didn't mean I wouldn't need a lot of stuff.

As I ventured the cobblestone streets that would lead us north out of Briarhaven, I tried to focus on how the rising sun felt against my cheeks, how the cool morning breeze swept through my curls. These were the small pleasures that would keep my spirits high, and I needed to indulge them every chance I got.

I reached the riverbank first and considered leaving before the others could arrive. Alas, I did not. I'd made a promise, and this time I intended to keep it.

I bided my time by searching out birds in the trees above as I listened to the brightly gurgling waters. A nest of sparsely feathered flitterwips cheeped hungrily as their mother returned carrying a fat, wriggling grub. I watched in wonder as they fed, thanking sweet grace that I'd been born a halfling and not a sky fowl. Ah, the circle of life.

When the birds had finished their morning meal, I returned my gaze to the village. A thick wall of flesh appeared, moving toward me at a daunting clip. I reached for my dagger, ready to face off with the unexpected blob, when at last the wall drew close enough for me to make out the individual shapes. Three people moved in perfect sync as if they were of one flesh—a flesh made of green, peach, and some shade in between.

The in-betweener was Rurik, and the others were presumably his parents.

The peachy-skinned woman was a human warrior with a fierce expression and wild mane of tousled dreads. Tattoos and wounds decorated her in equal measure, making her quite the tapestry to behold. Like Durgan, she seemed to keep mementos tucked into her hair. Her dreads had been festooned with feathers and quills and—sweet divinity, *was that an ear?*

She stood close to her orc partner's side—that would be the green mountain. While Rurik's skin was dull like a vegetable seed, his father's glowed bright and verdant as a leafy plant at the height of maturity.

His arm had been chopped short at the elbow, and the partial limb was capped off with a gnomish helmet that had been crimped down around the stump. The barbarian orc looked me up and down a smile playing at the corners of his tusked mouth. It was either that or the many scars across his face were pulling his flesh in strange ways... even for an orc.

"Good," he growled, the low note of his voice sounding more like a calving glacier. "You fighter. No *fifhthic.*"

I didn't need to speak orc to understand the implication. The way Rurik's face crumpled at his father's assessment told me everything I needed to know. He was pleased to see I was non-magical.

The orc continued, oblivious to his son's aggravation. "Maybe you take Rurik." He gestured with his one hand, his only hand. All three fingers—or rather two beefy fingers and a thumb—pointed toward the would-be mage. "Bring back fighter. Or maybe *chikchakis* Rurik."

With that the barbarian clapped me on the back, nearly sending me to the ground. I redirected his hand with a sweep of my arm just in time to save my footing. That's when I noticed how Rurik's mother moved perfectly in time with his father, constantly and expertly guarding his weak side. She locked eyes with me and nodded almost imperceptibly. She'd wanted me to see. They were a unit, the two of them. Because of the orc's injury, she'd become his protector. I assumed this meant there wasn't always someone to watch out for Rurik.

"My chief jokes," she said through a tight smile as she stepped closer. "We would prefer Rurik remain whole."

I balked at this. "Whole? What did he say? I don't speak orc."

"He said *chikchakis*. It means you don't need to bring back all of Rurik. My chief believes that if Rurik can learn to fight, he'll be a boon to our tribe. And if he lost a couple fingers like his father, then maybe he wouldn't try so hard at the magic."

Rurik's father grumbled the word *fifhthic* again and spat on the ground in obvious contempt.

"Right, okay. So I guess we have your blessing then." I attempted a smile, but barbarians made me nervous. All my cunning agility was useless if I got smashed into the ground with a single punch, and these two could definitely pull off such a move if they wanted to do so. Either of them could probably even use me as a club in their meaty hands.

Rurik's mother offered another curt nod and then grabbed her husband by the arm and guided him back into town without so much as a thank you or a goodbye.

Their son remained, standing silently across from me. He had what looked like an old trunk fitted with leather belts harnessed to his back. I hoped for his sake, he'd packed well. As soon as Calina arrived, we'd be on our way, which meant I didn't have time to send him back for better supplies. Whatever he brought would have to be enough.

Rurik raised his arm and wiggled his fingers. "That's why I started trying to learn magic," he confided.

"For your father?"

He gulped then nodded. "Yeah, we can't afford a healer who's powerful enough to heal an injury like his, so I figured maybe if I could learn it, then he wouldn't have to be... Well, I muh-muh-mean, he could just be himself again. His whole self."

"I like that," I told him, and I did. Meeting his parents, however briefly, told me a lot about the kid. It was insight I appreciated, insight I could use when it came to preparing him for the dangers ahead.

"I started studying for him—for them—but I kept studying for me. I didn't expect to love it so much," he continued, apparently eager to unload his life story now that he had an in.

He stopped when the sound of fast-approaching footsteps thudded in the distance. I squinted my eyes until I spied the slender form of Calina racing toward us. With Brynlee trailing after.

"Sorry I'm late," she called, loud enough to wake the whole village. "But Mom insisted on making me a special breakfast, then she insisted on having a heart-to-heart conversation. And then she insisted on coming to see me off!" Calina made no attempts to hide her irritation, but I knew that both Rurik and I wished we'd been loved like that by our parents. His meant well but didn't understand him, while mine didn't stay alive long enough to leave any kind of mark, be it good or bad.

I waited wordlessly for them to catch up. The moment they did, Brynlee started fussing over her daughter, adjusting the straps on her pack and finger-combing her long rose locks.

"Mooooom, enough!"

"I'm just going to miss you so much!" Brynlee cried and squeezed her daughter tight, rocking back and forth.

"Brynlee, you have to let her go. Remember you're the one who insisted I bring her."

She tutted at this and pressed her forehead to Calina's. "Is it too late to change my mind?"

"Yes," Calina, Rurik, and I all shouted in unison. It was the first action we'd taken as a party, and that realization made me smile to myself. I hadn't chosen this crew, and I didn't really want them either. But they were mine and I'd make the best of it.

Brynlee finally let go. "Fine, fine, but you have to go now. I can't stand the waiting."

"Not a problem," Calina sang, charging across the small footbridge and over the river.

I moved to follow her but was stopped when Brynlee grabbed me from my feet and hugged me to her chest. "Not so fast, ma'am. I need hugs from all my brave adventurers."

Feeling emboldened, I pressed a kiss to Brynlee's cheek. It was a gesture of friendship and love with no expectation of return, though it brought an adorable blush to her cheeks.

She said nothing as she set me back to my feet and moved to embrace Rurik. "You know you're like a son to me, right?"

He avoided her eyes, keeping his gaze fixed to the same tree where I'd spotted the nest of flitterwips earlier. "I know."

"And you're going to listen to everything Tilda says

and make sure my headstrong daughter does the same?"

"I will," he said, at the same time Calina shouted her protest.

"Then you best be off." She gave him a tap on his upper arm since she couldn't quite reach his shoulder, then shifted her attention back to me.

"This is for you," she said, handing me a small object from her pocket. "I don't think it has any magic, but still, it's the most valuable thing I own. I want you to wear it and remember the promise you made to return in one piece."

I shivered as she clasped the beautiful gold and jewel-encrusted bracelet around my wrist. The gems were all berry-toned and polished to a beautiful sheen. The precious metal caught the first rays of sunlight and reflected them back at us. It sure felt like magic to me.

"I adjusted it for you. Looks like I got the size right."

I wrapped my arms around her waist and gave her one last hug. I hated leaving Brynlee behind, but I knew this life wasn't for her. Besides, I'd have two precious pieces of her with me on the way—the gifted piece of jewelry and her very life blood in Calina. It would be enough until I managed to get home again.

Brynlee smiled at us all one last time then turned her back. "Go, go. I can't stand to watch!"

And so, we went.

"My mom is so sentimental. It's embarrassing," Calina groused, but she wore a small, sad smile as she did.

I contemplated telling her just how lucky she was, but I had a feeling she already knew. Instead, I decided to share some key quest details with my companions. "We'll be walking for many moons, but we can't stop to rest more than we absolutely have to. We must reach our destination by solstice. We absolutely cannot be late."

"Where are we going?" Rurik asked.

"To Maltherius's lair," I answered.

"Who's Maltherius?" Calina asked.

Oh, boy. They knew so little. It was time to change that. I couldn't keep secrets any longer, not when they would endanger us all. I was pretty sure I'd already mentioned Maltherius, but we had a long journey ahead of us. If it took a couple tells to get the right information to sink in, then it would take a couple tells. We had the time.

"He's the necromancer with the dragon and the undead servants. He sent a letter, telling me my partner is still alive. We're going to his lair to trade the Genesis Crest for his freedom."

"What's the Genesis Crest?" Calina asked, but this, Rurik remembered.

"You can't give him that artifact," he shouted, startling a few errant songbirds and causing them to launch into the sky with a cacophony of angry chirps and cheeps. "It's too powerful."

"Right, I know that. Got any great plans ready, or should we—"

"Ah-ha! Now I've caught you in the act!" A young female centaur hopped into our path as if from nowhere. I'd never seen her before. Most likely because she was not yet old enough to imbibe spirits and thus hang around the Mystic Mug. Meanwhile I was neither wealthy enough nor horse enough to frequent Briarhaven's preferred centaur establishments.

I didn't know her, but my two companions appeared to.

"Tulip Thunderhoof," Calina muttered under her breath as she balled her fists. "What are you doing here?"

"I know you and Rurik have been sneaking out to the old snag forest lately. Up to no good, no doubt." She sniffed and looked down her nose at the elf girl. As much as centaurs tended to get on my nerves, I had to admit that this one was stunningly beautiful. She wore her thick blonde mane in a braid entwined with glittering tinsel. Her sharp blue eyes were rimmed with impossibly long lashes, and her flank was an ethereal white that seemed to glow golden when it caught the sun.

"Tuh-Tuh-Tuh-Tulip." Rurik stumbled toward the new arrival and stood uncomfortably close to her. While the orc boy was massive, the centaur stood even taller. His face came up to about her shoulder, which made his unacceptably close proximity all the more awkward—something of which everyone except Rurik himself was suddenly keenly aware.

The centaur girl scoffed and shoved him away. "Back up, you mindless troll."

Rurik's heel caught on the dirt beneath him, and he fell to his rump with a resounding thud.

"Hmmpf!" Tulip huffed and let out a tittering laugh.

Calina growled and nocked an arrow on her bow.

"Hey, hey! What are you doing?" I demanded as I leaped at her and pushed down the weapon.

She pushed me aside and took aim at Tulip once more. "Killing the bad guys. Isn't that the whole point of this quest?"

14

We'd be done for if Calina murdered one of the other townsfolk—especially a kid and especially a centaur—but she was determined. She was also stronger than me.

I groaned in frustration when every single one of my efforts to pull her back was brushed off with ease. "Hey, hey! Knock it off!"

"Oh, I have more arrows I can nock if the first one doesn't do the job." Calina's mouth stretched in a hard line as her eyes narrowed to assess her target. Tulip was enormous, which meant there was really no way Calina's shot would miss. And it would do marked damage, particularly at such a close range. I shuddered as I remembered how she'd sunk an arrow into each of the undead sorcerer's eye sockets. Would she go for Tulip's eyes as well?

Oh, this was not good. Not good at all.

The child wouldn't listen to me, and I couldn't physically overpower her. She was the worst kind of liability, the kind that would get us arrested before we even managed to leave town.

What happened next was not what I'd expected. Rurik came to the rescue. In a shocking show of dexterity, he slammed both his palms into the ground and pushed himself to his feet before rushing at his friend and grabbing her from behind. He locked her to his chest, holding tight with massive, muscled arms.

Calina squirmed and kicked. "Rurik, ugh. What are you doing? Let me go!"

"You'll regret it if you hurt her," he explained sagely, unmoved by her shouts and struggles, either physically or emotionally.

"Are you kidding? I've fantasized about this for years. Now let me go, so I can prove dreams really do come true." She flung her head back and hit him in the jaw, but his facial hair padded the blow in part. Even if it hadn't, I don't think the action would have hurt him very much. The half-orc was as tough as eagle talons, just as his parents had raised him to be.

I expected him to relent, the way he always did

when it came to Calina and her whims. Rurik kept quiet and squeezed his arms tighter.

That's when Tulip swept her front hooves through the dirt, first one and then the other, drawing all our eyes down. Using the brief distraction to her benefit, she launched herself at the kids. And in his surprise, the orc released his hold on his elven friend. Calina dropped to the ground and rolled out of the way just in time to avoid the crushing hooves.

She made it, but her bow did not.

Tulip whinnied and made a great show of stamping the bow into smithereens beneath her hooves. It only took two clean stomps to absolutely destroy the homemade weapon.

"Calina, Tulip, could you both please calm down for a second?" Rurik begged while struggling to pull himself back to his feet after having been pummeled by the horse-half of Tulip.

"Oh now, I'm really going to kill you," Calina seethed. I half expected her to fly into a rage like her friend had as they'd fought off the swarm at Dewglen's farm.

Tulip snorted and stomped on the bow a third time. "I'd like to see you try." Her normally confident voice trilled with every word as if a neigh or a whinny was trying to break through, and she had to make a conscious choice to choose the common language instead.

I'd never seen a centaur lose their cool like this. They built the world—or at least the town of Briarhaven—according to their own needs and desires, which meant very little ever bristled them. They'd made themselves a paradise and did their best to ignore that we small folk also lived within it.

At this point, I'd had more than enough. If I never saw another centaur again, it would still be too soon. "We don't have time for this. I'm getting on the road. You two can either come with me or abandon the quest. Honestly, I'd probably prefer the latter."

Tulip crossed her pale arms over her chest and glanced down at me. "What's the quest?"

"We're going to go kill a necromancer who's been hunting Tilda for—"

"Rurik, enough!" I shouted. Just because we were leaving town didn't mean I was okay with him haphazardly revealing the secret I'd worked so long to keep.

Tulip grabbed her long braid and began to twirl the fringe at the end with long fingers. "For what?"

I shot Rurik a hostile glance. "One more word, and I'll burn that magic book of yours and make you watch."

His tusks trembled. Calina was a wild card, but at least the orc I could control. Some of the time, anyway.

When Tulip realized she wasn't going to get her way, she stomped on the bow again and swished her tail wildly. "You have to tell me. It's what I want, and I always get my way."

"Not this time, princess," I said, eyeing Calina in an attempt to determine whether she would also fall in line with my wishes.

Her shoulders sagged but the rest of her body appeared quite tense. Losing her battle implements seemed to take most of the fight out of her. She knew she couldn't win against the much larger, much stronger centaur now.

"I told you it was good to have a backup weapon." I sighed and retrieved the dagger I kept tucked into my boot. "Now, I'll give this to you, if you promise not to use it to gauge out her eyes."

"She would never," Tulip said with another violent flick of her tail.

Calina clenched her jaw and flared her nostrils, ironically making her appear somewhat horse-like herself. "Just watch me."

"Okay, then I guess you don't get a weapon today." I pushed the knife back into my boot then started off down the trail.

Fortunately, Calina and Rurik followed.

Unfortunately, Tulip did too. "Not so fast. You still haven't answered my questions."

"Yeah. We're not going to, either." I didn't stop or look back. We simply didn't have time for this stranger's tantrum. Maltherius had made his deadline clear, and every second we wasted now was one we wouldn't have on the road.

"You can't ignore me!" Tulip huffed.

I ignored her.

"I'll tell my parents you tried to kidnap me, then every law lizard in Briarhaven will be out looking for you so they can put you in the stocks! Or worse, the executioner's block!"

I continued to ignore her.

"We're leaving town," Rurik said.

"They'll send wing scouts to the other cities and towns. There's nowhere you can go where you'll be safe from the swift hooves of the law." The weird horse vibrato was back. It would be funny if I weren't so irritated with her.

"Shove off, Tulip. We didn't even do anything," Calina practically snarled. She now carried the broken pieces of her bow before her. I hadn't even realized she'd gone back to get it, but then again, I was focused on getting out of town as blessedly quick as possible.

"Maybe, but who's everyone going to believe. I mean, really. I could destroy you without even trying all that hard. Or you could just tell me what I want to know."

I'd had just about enough of this. I abruptly turned to face the equine idiot. "We're traveling across the great chasm, facing down a necromancer in his own lair, and rescuing a friend I'd long thought dead. Satisfied?"

"We're also wielding a mysterious magical artifact that said necromancer is desperate to get his hands on," Rurik added matter-of-factly.

I punched him.

Yeesh. Not that hard, okay? I know he's a kid. But honestly even if I'd hit him with all my might, he still wouldn't have felt much of anything. And besides, I'd been waiting a long time to do that, and it felt divine to finally take out a bit of my frustration.

Tulip's huge blue eyes grew even more fantastically large as they locked on me. "A mysterious magical artifact? I want to see."

"No."

"Where is it? Do you have it? Give it to me."

"The last guy who tried to take it from her turned to ash, so, yes, please try and take it," Calina challenged with a grin. "She keeps it on a necklace. Beneath her tunic."

Tulip trotted forward to cut off my path, bent her knees to lower herself, then reached both hands behind my neck in search of the chain. She found it quickly and tugged.

I grabbed both of her wrists and pushed her away, but she didn't budge. Didn't even strain to counterbalance my attempted show of strength.

"Oh, it's beautiful!" She held the chain high, letting the crest dangle in front of her face.

"No fair, why didn't it incinerate her?" Calina demanded. And that was a great question. I also wanted answers.

"You said the necromancer guy wants this. I'll just keep it safe for you." Tulip undid the clasp on the chain and then secured it around her own neck. "It looks better on me anyway."

"What do I have to do to get you to return the artifact and leave us alone?" I asked. There was no talking a centaur out of something they wanted. There was only finding something they wanted more and offering them a trade, which is what I was trying to do now. We'd wasted more than enough time already. Far more than I had to spare on our already tight deadline. We were literally dealing with life and death here, but none of the teens seemed to get that.

Tulip fingered the crest and twisted her mouth to the side in thought. "Hmmm. Well... The three of you are off on some adventure, and it's pretty boring here. I want to come with you."

"No."

"Then you're not getting your artifact back."

"Oh sweet divinity, we do not have time for this. Give me the blessed thing and gallop off already."

"No," Tulip said with a smug smile. She seemed to enjoy tormenting us—or at least, me. I could see why Calina hated her so much and wasn't far from that sentiment myself. "I'm coming whether you like it or not."

"Why?" Rurik asked.

"Because I'm bored. And I'm better than this place. I deserve a bigger life."

"We have absolutely no reason to take you with us."

"Except that I have your trinket. You need it, right?" She took it off her neck and dangled it above her head. Only Rurik might be able to reach it there, but he didn't even try.

Calina jumped after it, but Tulip easily jerked it out of the way.

"We're going to be fighting a freaking necromancer. You understand how dangerous that is, right?"

The centaur reaffixed the pendant and patted it down without making eye contact. "I can handle a necromancer, thank you very much."

"Because you've done it so many times before?" Calina cried, clenching her grip so tight around the broken pieces of the bow that her knuckles turned white.

"Because I'm strong and smart and enormously beautiful."

"Yeah, enormous is right," Calina muttered under her breath, which made me chuckle.

Sobering up, I asked, "But do you know anything about fighting or adventure? You seem to have lived an impossibly pampered life."

"She has literally no skills. She's also the worst person I know," Calina interjected. "Why are we even talking to her? I thought we had to go."

Tulip curled her lip and refused to address Calina. "I contain multitudes," she told me. "I'd be a good asset on your adventure. My mother is the mayor of this town. She's got a lot of power and people know her name in the other settlements too. You can make her a friend by giving me what I want, or you can make her an enemy by upsetting mommy's little pony. Which would you rather do?"

Well, this at least was intriguing. "What can she do to help us?" I wanted to know.

"Tilda, no. You can't be serious. She'll only mess things up for us," Calina argued.

"Now you know how I feel about dragging the two of you along. Tulip, tell me how your mother will help us."

She flashed Calina a triumphant smile. "Diplomacy. Coin. Supplies. All of the above. You decide."

While that all sounded pretty good, the real value in adding Tulip to our party would be as a counterbalance to Calina. If Calina fired all her vitriol at the centaur, she wouldn't fling so much of it at me. She'd also start listening better. She'd want to prove her mettle, to prove she was a better adventurer than her schoolyard enemy.

I was already saddled with two gawky would-be-heroes. Adding a third wouldn't be too much more work, especially since this third would increase my influence over the party—once I actually got them on the road. The longer we spent arguing with Tulip, the more I knew I could control her. When it came right down to it, centaurs were simple creatures. They wanted what they wanted when they wanted it. Transparent motivations were good. I could work with that.

And so I spoke three little words that I could possibly come to regret later, but felt pretty good about in that moment. "Okay. Prove it."

15

Tulip trotted ahead, swinging both sets of hips as she guided our party back into town. The movement was so strange; it looked like she might fall over at any moment or at least veer suddenly off course. I didn't know whether she was trying to appear seductive, throw a dance party, or if she just always moved like a drunken imbecile.

Seemed I'd find out soon enough since she'd now joined our adventuring party. For the millionth time that morning I wondered what I was getting myself into, and if, in fact, I hated myself.

The two kids I'd agreed to bring with me were already problem enough, but now I had a spoiled princess to mind as well. I really needed to stop second-guessing my initial intuition on this, because the more I thought about inviting Tulip to join us, the more deeply I regretted what I'd done.

"Oh, Calina," the horse girl crowed without bothering to glance back. "Do keep up. I wouldn't want you to fall behind just because the maker cursed you with those unfortunate stubby legs."

Calina growled, pumped her arms, and surged ahead. Just before she could pull past Tulip, the centaur switched into a cantor. And she threw her head back and giggled, moving effortlessly as the rest of us raced to keep up.

If these two were going to try to out-pace each other the whole journey, they'd reach Maltherius days before I ever managed to catch up. I could barely match pace with Calina, let alone a blasted half-horse. Tulip had a nasty personality, but her physique was flawless. Very few creatures were stronger, faster, or more stalwart than a centaur, especially one as well-bred as Tulip Thunderhoof.

Rurik, for his part, had no trouble sprinting alongside Tulip. She ran a straight course, which made it easy for him to follow versus Calina's and my tendency to dodge and dart. Like Tulip, the orc kid was strong. His reflexes were slow, which didn't bode well for him as an aspiring mage, but surely I'd be able to point him toward a more physical role in the party when the going actually got tough.

Even if he fell into line, our party would still come off as lopsided. Tulip only wanted to join because she was bored, and I still had no idea what the spoiled small-town royal could actually do to aid our group—and whether she'd be willing to do it.

Yup, our party was pretty much unbalanced in every way possible. The biggest problem was that none of these kids had any clue what they were doing. Okay, if I could somehow manage to secure a new bow for Calina, she might actually prove an asset. She could pick off any bad guys from a distance while I snuck in for the kill. Tulip and Rurik were massive targets and would make good distractions. I just had to make sure they didn't get killed while I was the one responsible for their safety.

That was a tall order, but I'd faced worse and lived to tell the tale.

Tulip stopped outside a sleek three-story building with multiple domes that rose high into the sky. The white stone facade was trimmed in polished gold and the roof was made of shining slabs of obsidian. I'd caught sight of this place before, but always from a great distance. The so-called "Stable" was the height of luxury in

Briarhaven. Only monied, titled nobility were allowed entry, which meant only the most elite centaurian citizens. Halfling tavern wenches such as myself were not even permitted to occupy the streets outside.

Standing so close to the Stable gave me a fluttering feeling that I did not like. I felt as if I needed to run away and fast—or else risk some great ordeal. The newly reawakened rogue in me refused to flee, greedily contemplating what kind of loot I might be able to score from such an opulent mansion.

"We're here," Tulip announced as if it were no big deal at all. "Jonquil holds a table for my family at all times, just in case we decide to stop by. Let's go claim it. Shall we?"

Calina craned her neck as she examined each of the massive bay windows in turn. "Are your parents in there now? Where should we wait?" As rebellious as the young elf tended to be, even she knew we wouldn't be welcomed here. I wondered if she had that same fluttery feeling I did.

"Hmm. I have always wondered what it's like in there," Rurik said, breezing past Tulip and up the short ramp that led inside. He didn't even pause before pulling the door open and crossing the forbidden threshold.

Tulip followed, swishing her tail and shimmying her hips.

Calina and I exchanged a tense glance before tiptoeing after the others.

"Good morning, Jonquil. Is my mother in?" Tulip addressed this to the elder gelding who stood at a small kiosk opposite the grand entrance. He wore a ruffled shirt with a collar that stretched all the way up to his chin and tiny spectacles that looked as if they'd been filched from a much smaller creature. His flank was dappled with gray, complementing the short salt and pepper curls that topped his head. He did not speak, but rather answered Tulip with a series of head bobs, snorts, and subtle facial expressions. Luckily, this all seemed to make perfect sense to our upper-crust guide.

Tulip frowned. "No, not yet? Then please send for her. My guests and I will wait at the Thunderhoof family table."

Jonquil raised a hand, but promptly lowered it when Tulip shook her chin and moved her gaze toward the archway that led into the grand dining hall.

I wordlessly followed Tulip to the back corner of the club. Calina stayed close at my heels, while Rurik veered off to examine the artwork and portraiture that adorned the walls. The same gold accents from outside decorated the inside, weaving into a delicate lattice that framed the upper walls and extended onto the ceiling. Scattered about, stood high tables with gleaming obsidian tops and no cloth coverings. There were also no seats, making it quite clear the type of creature who frequented this establishment.

The food I could spy looked tasty—roasted pheasant, griffin eggs, and sea-flower salad, and all for breakfast no less. The scents swirled together to create a lovely aroma, one that had both my mouth and my eyes watering as hunger took hold.

Oh, to live a life such as this! How could Tulip possibly be bored with it?

"This is our table," she said, taking the head spot for herself.

A server appeared and poured fizzy water from a green bottle into a crystal goblet. Was this the same magical tonic water that the humans were so fond of? I bet it wouldn't taste so bad without the bitter gin mixed in. No one offered me a taste though.

Tulip yawned and waved the server away when she tried to hand her a menu. The server was young like Tulip, but didn't have her beauty or grace. In fact she looked down-right intimidated by her patron. When Tulip refused the menu, she dipped her head and backed away slowly in a weird hunched position without ever turning her back.

"I'd like a menu," Rurik said, hustling after her.

Appearing even more afraid than before, she shook her head and hugged the menus to her chest, then turned tail and ran—actually ran—away.

"Technically, you're not really supposed to be in here." Tulip punctuated her sentence by raising the crystal goblet to her mouth, imbibing a small amount of the liquid, and swishing it around thoughtfully. "But as a Thunderhoof, the rules don't really apply to me."

Calina scoffed at this but remained blessedly quiet.

"What are we doing here, Tulip?" I asked from beneath the table. Even if I lifted my arms straight into the air, I still wouldn't be able to touch the surface. Let alone feast from upon it.

"Mmm, what's that?" I'd never heard anything about centaurs having unusually poor hearing, which meant I didn't know whether this was an actual issue now or just Tulip being difficult for difficulty's sake.

"She wants to know why we're here," Calina hissed. "I do too."

Rurik had wandered off again. I spotted him across the dining hall, running his thick fingers over a gorgeous brocade of damask fabric and mumbling something to himself.

The other diners eyed us warily, and I couldn't

really say I blamed them. One pair even abandoned their meals mostly uneaten and left while snorting noisily and making pointed glances in our direction.

Jonquil glided toward our table, placing one hoof in front of the other in a slow, practiced walk that I found rather disconcerting. He widened his eyes at Tulip, then lowered his lashes and tilted his head slightly to the left.

Tulip let out a hearty huff adding a little soprano to the sound, like her horse and human sides were competing to show which was the most irritated at present. "Fine. I will go to them. Please ensure my guests are attended properly in my absence."

She backed away from the table and charged across the club back toward the foyer. Jonquil narrowed his eyes first at Calina, then at Rurik, and then he left. Had he already forgotten that I was here too?

"This place gives me the creeps," Calina confided in me while Rurik did gods knows what in his continued exploration of the club.

And so we waited.

At one point, Calina picked up Tulip's abandoned chalice and took a tentative sip before smacking her lips contentedly and then downing the rest of the fizzy liquid. She tried to signal to the waitress for more, but was summarily ignored.

"No wonder Tulip is such a brat. She was literally born and bred to be just that," she muttered as I watched Jonquil slow-step toward one of the last occupied tables, do that weird not-speaking thing, and then escort the guests from the club.

I peered out the nearest window trying to ascertain the angle of the sun so that I could figure out how much time we'd been waiting for Tulip to return with her parents. If she hadn't lifted the artifact from me, I'd have already left.

As it was, we were stuck until she returned.

The waitress hadn't shown face again, not since Rurik had scared her off by requesting a menu. The audacity.

I remained under the table, feeling safer in the confined space. The Stable was far too large and open for my comfort. Despite the delicious scents coming from the kitchen, I'd take Mystic Mug's rugged charm over this place any day. It was too clean, too quiet... too off.

And when Jonquil returned to shoo off another table, I loosed my pack and set it on the floor beside me. As I watched them go, I cracked my neck on either side and shook out my arms.

I placed a hand on Calina's ankle to get her attention then slipped a dagger into her boot. "Get ready," I whispered as I palmed my second dagger.

A moment later, the enormous front door slammed open and many steps of quick footsteps pounded into the club.

"Arrest! Arrest!" a shrill and hysterical voice cried out.

"Arrest! Arrest!" several more parroted in perfect unison. Then, moving as one fluid mass, roughly two dozen kobold guards flooded the Stable, screaming wildly and pointing with crude spears as they crossed the dining room.

They may have been shouting for our arrest, but I knew they'd come to kill.

Their target?

The most obvious threat in the room, of course.

Who just so happened to also be the least prepared for their assault.

Rurik.

16

"**R**urik! Look out!" I shouted, somersaulting out from beneath the table and rolling head first into the mindless lizard brigade.

They poked at me with their spears, which thankfully weren't very sharp. Still hurt though.

I unfurled myself from the tiny ball I'd formed and yanked at the first thing I could reach. A loincloth.

"Ahhh, Naked!" the red lizard creature screeched and moved to cover his privates with his spear hand.

I yanked the wooden shaft and swung, sending him crashing into his fellow law enforcers. Finally, I was fighting someone my size. And it felt good. *Real good.*

"Naked?" another kobold echoed. I turned in the direction of the cry and flung the stolen loincloth at it.

"Blind! Blind!" it shrieked and scratched at its head while trying to dislodge the fabric. Oh sweet divinity, this was nice.

With kobolds, you never had to guess if your blow had landed, because they always conveniently shouted the play by play. I liked that about them.

I liked this. Missed it even.

In truth, I hadn't had a good brawl in far too long.

The red sea of scales split, surging past me in pursuit of Rurik who was standing with his back pressed to the far wall. He had both hands out before him and was staring at his palms intently while he muttered to himself.

Kobolds were easy opponents, but could still do some very real damage. Not like the locusts we'd faced in farmer Dewglen's cabbage patch and not like the rigged battle against Maltherius's undead servant. These little lizard-like guys didn't often win fights, but when they did, it came down to a numbers game.

Mother kobolds laid clutches of nearly one-hundred eggs at a go several times per year. To keep their population from overwhelming the continent, the powers that be required kobolds to conscript for five full years upon reaching adulthood. The ones that survived their service were given full rights and a place of honor in society.

But very few ever made it.

Whatever. They'd started this.

Poof! Rurik's left-hand flame blazed to life and promptly caught on the same damask curtains he'd been admiring earlier.

"Ugh, sorry! Sorry!" he shouted and ripped the heavy fabric from the rod, tossing it to the floor and trapping a few of our cold-blooded opponents beneath it.

"Blind! Blind! Ooh, hot! Hot!"

I almost laughed as I watched their tiny figures struggle beneath the blazing tarp, and then I nearly cried as I watched Rurik bend down to help the blessed things escape.

"Kid, you're killing me! What are you doing?" I shouted at him while slicing a couple throats with a thirsty dagger.

He did not answer.

Calina zipped past me and pulled the curtains back onto the writhing mass of scales. "Stand here!" she told her friend, moving him onto one of the corners. She then grabbed the dagger I'd slipped into her boot and hammered it into another corner. I hurled myself to the center of the action and dug my own dagger into the floorboards at the third corner, then Calina and I worked together to topple one of the tables and move it into place.

"Can I muh-muh-move now?" Rurik stuttered as the flames began to lap at his pants.

"Yes, get out of there, you buffoon!" I didn't know whether those words had torn from Calina's mouth, mine, or both. Yeah, probably both.

Another wave of kobold enforcers marched into the club while the first set screamed a litany of adjectives from beneath the burning fabric.

My heart pounded with excitement as the battle raged on. I waited behind the inferno, certain that at least a few of the new arrivals would charge straight into the flames and remove themselves from the fray without any effort on my part. Kobolds were almost too stupid to live sometimes, especially when swarming.

I smirked as the first wandered into the fire and shouted a string of superlatives. "Hot! Hurt! Dying!"

Over his bobbing head, something higher up caught my eye. Too high to be a kobold. Also too solitary. It quickly shifted from view, but not quick enough.

Jonquil. He was really failing at the whole hospitality thing. In fact, if I didn't know any better, I'd say... Yeah, he definitely orchestrated the whole affair. And that reminded me of another important thing I knew about kobold battalions. Take out their commander, and the whole thing falls apart.

"There are too many!" Calina cried as she darted behind Rurik. She was now without a weapon.

So was I, but I had a plan. "Give me a boost, big guy!" I shouted and tugged Rurik toward the Thunderhoof family table.

"Bend down!"

Thankfully, he listened without asking for an explanation, and I climbed up his arm then leaped to the table's surface.

The green bottle of fizzy water was still there just as I'd hoped, so I grabbed the thing, smashed it on the side of the table, then jumped back onto Rurik's shoulders. "Run toward the archway," I shouted in his ear, then readied myself for the jump. "Don't stop until I tell you."

He charged straight through the second troop of kobolds, knocking several over in the process as he raced toward the door.

"Stop!" I cried, knowing he'd need a few seconds to properly react to my command and hoping I'd told him fast enough to avoid him smashing into the wall.

I had not.

He hit it face-first and crashed onto the ground with a mighty thud. *Whoops.*

I, however, had timed my leap just right, effortlessly vaulting from one oversized mount to another. "Call off your goons!" I snarled, holding the broken bottle to Jonquil's throat. "You've already lost your balls. But I think you might miss your head a little more. Shall we see if I'm right?"

He kicked his hindquarters back and forcibly expelled air from his nostrils and mouth at the same time.

"I don't speak horse. Call off your goons in a language I understand. Or die with them."

He reared back and stamped his front hooves, and I almost shanked him right there, but then the lizardfolk began to disperse.

"Retreat! Retreat!" they shouted and laughed, leaving just as quickly as they'd entered. "Peace! Peace!"

Eh, good riddance.

I slid off the centaur's back, landing easily on both feet, then I gave him the stink eye. Even though Jonquil was nearly three times my height, he backed away in fright. He now knew I'd been trained for combat—perhaps even respected me for it.

And by the divine, it felt marvelous.

"If there's any more trouble, my orc friend will make sure the rest of this place matches that curtain," I threatened, grabbing my chin and forehead and then yanking my head to the side with a satisfying crack.

"She means we'll burn it down," Rurik muttered as he struggled to sit upright.

Calina had remained in the dining room and was now helping the waitress and kitchen staff stamp out the fire before it could spread any farther.

When I turned back to Jonquil, I found that he had fled. The coward. A trio of new arrivals entered the foyer. Centaurs, all. One of them was Tulip. I recognized the woman with her as our town mayor and assumed the man was her father. He had not been gelded, I noted with wide eyes. Centaurs really were big *everywhere*. This both fascinated and terrified me in equal measures, but it was also beside the point.

"I know this was your doing. Why did you attack us?" I demanded, still wielding the jagged bottle I'd used to threaten Jonquil.

"That's easy, my dear," the woman spoke with perfect diction despite the heightened emotions of the situation. "We had to give you a chance to prove your worth."

"I have nothing to prove to you."

"No," the man said, shaking his head. "You don't. Mostly, because, well, you already did. Well done, you. That's exactly the kind of can-do-attitude we love to see from our sweet Tulip's tutors."

"Does that mean I can go?" Tulip neighed and fingered the artifact that hung around her neck. *My artifact.*

I crossed both arms over my chest. "Um, excuse me, but I am not okay with this."

"With what part?" the mother asked.

"With any of it. You sent like fifty kobolds to their death. And for what?" I stared the woman down— well, up; she was much taller than me, after all—for a good long moment as I tried to decide whether her aid would be worth the trouble.

She simply smiled. "They are happy to die in service. It is an honor for their kind. And they shall be memorialized in the village annals."

Like her daughter, the mare mayor was flawlessly beautiful. She also seemed to be—as Calina had put it—a bit of a brat. That's where the similarities ended though. Tulip's mane and flank were both white-blonde, but her mother's were a rich auburn.

Even her eyes had a slight reddish tint, which gave her a dangerous and otherworldly sense of authority.

The man looked like half a human had been stuck to half a horse. He was much less beautiful to behold, and I'd already cataloged the most interesting thing about him upon his initial entry.

"Yes, you can go, pony," the mayor said, offering first me and then her daughter a simpering grin.

Tulip squealed in delight and the three centaurs began to chatter animatedly among themselves. Much of their communication was non-verbal. That gave me the creeps.

"Now just you wait a second. Seriously. Slow down!" I had to jump into the air and wave my arms to direct their attention back to me.

Being stared down by three beings who could easily crush me beneath their hooves was not an experience I relished, especially since they'd already tried to kill via the whole kobold affair. And even though I could handle the scaly swarms with one arm tied behind my back... they hadn't known that when they had set them upon our group.

Tulip's mother blinked at me several times, as if trying to make sure I was real. "Yes, what is it?"

"And why are you asking us to slow down? I

thought you were in a hurry," Tulip added with an exaggerated roll of her large blue eyes.

"I was in a hurry. I mean, I am. But I don't exactly take kindly to being attacked. Honestly, I'm pretty miffed at that stunt your parents just pulled, and I don't really feel amenable to doing them any favors."

"This is about money, isn't it? It's always about money with you people." The mayor sighed and reached into the satchel she held clutched beneath an arm.

"You people?!"

She flapped a hand to wave off my concern as she rummaged about her wallet. "Oh, relax. I don't mean little folk. I just mean the poor. Now, how much do you need? Five hundred? Six? I really don't know the going price for this sort of thing." She palmed several paper bills, the likes of which I'd never seen before. I was so used to making all my transactions in coin.

My rage subsided ever so slightly, or at least enough for me to get curious. "The going price for what sort of thing?"

"Oh, you know." She blew a raspberry as she continued to rummage in her satchel. "Adventure guide. Protector. Teacher. I don't know what you're calling yourselves these days. Do I need to sign a liability waiver?"

"Um..." I usually knew exactly what to say, but I was out of my element here.

It was Tulip who came to my rescue. "Honestly, Mom. Just give her the whole wallet. Also I chipped a hoof last week and would prefer not to put any extra weight on it, so we'll need some kind of conveyance. Oh, and I'll need that fabulous gift Great-Aunt Dahlia got me for my birthday last year. You know the pretty shiny stabby thing?"

"Yes, of course, and you shall have it all," Tulip's mother promised as she dropped the purse into my waiting arms. "Tell you what, we'll send Amariel along to chaperone as well."

It was like I wasn't even part of the conversation anymore. "Excuse me, what? Who's Amariel?"

"Why I am," a faint voice croaked from somewhere behind the row of horse backsides. Bells tinkled in my ears, and I whipped around in search of the sound's source.

The centaurs moved to the side to reveal a fourth person I hadn't notice enter with them. She was much closer to my size, although a head or two taller and also quite frail. Her skin was creased with age, and her eyes were so far sunken back, I couldn't tell what color they were. She stared at me with obvious interest as her stark white hair blew in the breeze.

Except there wasn't any breeze in this place. The air was still, and yet that hair danced on nonexistent wind. And she had wings, a giant honking set of white feathered wings. I seriously almost peed myself from the shock of meeting her acquaintance.

"Is that... Are you..." Oh bless, I sounded like Rurik now, fumbling my words.

"Amariel is a celestial," Tulip's father explained with a flat affect. "One of the last of her kind and a great family friend."

I'd thought the celestials died out centuries ago when the fae realm had invaded. In all my years, I had never seen one—not alive anyway. That meant, Amariel had to be ancient. Yes, ancient. She was the very definition of the word.

"How old are you?" I asked, knowing if I didn't it would bother me until at last I happened upon the answer. Better to ask now and save myself the trouble of wondering.

I was answered by a sorrowful womp of brass... and a snore as the old woman crumpled in on herself. Tulip caught the angelic creature before she could crash into the floor.

"Amariel is pretty old, so she's tired a lot," the centaur girl explained. "But she's fine. It'll be fine."

Fine, right.

I'd started this day worrying that I'd be running a daycare of baby adventurers, thinking that my luck couldn't possibly get any worse. And now as I studied the spoiled princess and her decrepit chaperone, I realized how much of a fool I'd been.

Because in truth? Things could always get worse.

And—hey, look at that—they just had for me again.

17

We were treated to a quiet brunch at the Stable while Tulip and her parents went about gathering the bountiful supplies they'd promised for our journey. This time, we didn't have to contend with any slack-jawed stares from other diners—mostly because the ridiculous, short-lived battle with the kobolds had scared all the other diners off.

The food was fantastic and far more than I could fit in my measly stomach, though I definitely tried to shove as many griffin eggs in there as I could. Never had I feasted on such delicacies, and even if I lived to tell the tale of our upcoming adventure, I probably wouldn't ever get such an indulgent chance again.

I'd like to say I took it all in with the appropriate

amount of awe and appreciation, but in truth, I stuffed my face so fast, I barely had time to notice the flavors. Oversized plates made of silver made the entire table look like a glittering city of legend. That was my favorite part. Had I spotted a good opportunity, I'd have made sure to stick a few of them in my pack, but the waitress kept too close an eye on us for me to sate that particular hunger.

So I kept my pockets pitifully light but filled my belly until it announced that it had taken its fill.

Rurik was only too happy to help himself to my leftovers. Blessedly, he didn't speak a word as he worked on cleaning off everyone's plates with single-minded focus. I had a feeling he would have done this exact thing with any rations we'd been offered, no matter how basic.

This worked for me because I didn't feel much like talking. I'd need all my energy for the journey ahead, and a good deal of it would need to be spent on controlling my temper. As a duo, Gaaron and I had frequently found ourselves outmatched by opponents, but we'd always found a way to ensnare victory because of how well we worked together. Well, almost always. A flush swept over my magical burn, reminding me of just how quickly even the best things could fall apart.

This was, in part, why Gaaron and I had preferred to remain a duo rather than joining up with a larger adventuring group. We only had the two egos to account for. Also fewer weaknesses to balance, less chances of it all going wrong. And our approach had worked splendidly... until it didn't.

My new adventuring party, on the other hand, comprised five members who didn't even remotely look well-balanced from the outside. All we did was bicker. The headstrong teenagers were a liability, even though they had no concept toward the fact.

"That was great thinking, lighting the curtains on fire!" Calina practically sang in praise of Rurik. "And then the way I staked it into the ground? Epic. Even Sylric would be proud."

Two quavering notes of reed sounded in my ear. "Sylric owes me five coin," a soft, withered voice then added to the conversation. But who? And from where?

My eyes darted around the disheveled and partially demolished dining hall. Across the way, a lone centaur picked his way through the damages, muttering to himself as he scrawled notes on a small pad.

"I'm right here," the voice came again, this time accompanied by the gentle tinkling of bells. A subtle breeze tickled my cheek, and I whipped my head in the direction of the unbidden assault. Much more accustomed to kicks than kisses, I did not appreciate being touched, and I curled my upper lip to show it.

There, a few short paces away, I finally spotted where Tulip's celestial chaperone stood in a hunched-over position as if she meant to sit down but had simply forgotten how to complete the action. Yes, the ancient one. I thought she'd left with her charge, but apparently she'd been here this whole time. Hmm. What was her name again? Ama-something. Ama-deus? Ama-nana?

Calina rushed over to her and grabbed the old woman by both her withered hands. If she wasn't careful the young half-elf could break the old celestial —or perhaps crush her into glittering dust. "Amariel!" she shouted, and I took a quick moment to commit the name to memory. "You know Sylric?" Calina gushed and let out a little squeal to boot. Oh, brother.

She bounced on her heels as she continued to fawn. "What's he like? Tell me everything!"

The same bells sounded, but faster and fiercer, and punctuated by a resonant burst of the gong. "He is a liar and a cheat. Not at all the type of god a decent young girl should be invoking in times of joy."

Calina dropped the elder's hands and backed away. "Who says I'm the decent sort?"

"Not, Miss Tulip. I can assure you of that." Three

staccato notes of a hollowed-out hand-drum followed that little quip. It seemed we'd acquired a soundtrack for our new adventure. Thanks, I hated it. I wanted Gaaron's intentional and well-practiced melodies back. Whatever Amariel was doing, it didn't seem to be on purpose. It just... happened.

"What about me, Amariel?" Tulip's haughty trill preceded her into the dining hall. Her echoing hoof-steps added a steady beat to the backdrop. This would not be a silent journey... were that it ever to actually begin.

"What is that you've fastened to your back?" Rurik spoke for the first time since the waitress set food down before us. He'd polished off all the plates now, and his eyes were wide as he craned his neck in an attempt to better see Tulip's new *accoutrement*.

Tulip's eyes also grew wide as she reached back to grab the gleaming bit of metal she'd strapped to her left haunch. "A gift from my Great-Aunt Dahlia. Isn't it marvelous?" She hefted the thing forward and held it out proudly with both hands greedily clutching at the hilt.

And I couldn't tell whether it was meant to be an oversized piece of jewelry or an underwhelming weapon. It was shaped like a battle axe. It also looked quite sharp around the edges, but somehow—impossibly—the metal gleamed with a pinkish hue. And things just got more ridiculous from there. The object shone with dozens of inset gems varying in size and color. Sapphires, amethysts, aquamarines adorned the monstrosity in neat rings along the edges with one massive diamond seated at center mast.

It was Calina who finally said what I was thinking. "Is that supposed to be some kind of weapon? Like are you planning on fighting actual bad guys with it?"

"I know, right? It's amazing." Tulip just smiled, clearly talking more to herself than to any of us.

Rurik came out from behind the table to get a better look. "It is amazing. We can throw it and wait for our opponents to go running after. It must be worth—"

"Five hundred and forty thousand coin," Tulip interrupted with an almost unbelievable amount of hubris. "At least upon its last assessment."

"Think of what we could buy if we sold it!" Calina stepped right up to Tulip and attempted to dislodge the axe from her grip, but Tulip, who was faster, stronger, and taller, easily moved it out of her reach.

"You will not sell it. You will not even touch it!"

I missed the slobbering mouth noises of listening to Rurik eat while the rest of us kept quiet. I also wanted to filch that bedazzled battle axe, break it down to parts, and fence each off to the highest bidder, but I knew better than to lock eyes on that particular prize while everyone was watching. Maybe I could come up with a plan to make Tulip think she'd lost it on our return journey. I could drop the kids home and journey to my old stomping grounds in Mirathane. I'd been well connected with the criminal rings once upon a time. Surely I could find a place to discreetly sell my booty... Er, treasure. Rule one of thieving: only plunder things others wanted to buy.

And what a price that beautiful battle axe would fetch. Hrrrrmn. Now I was the one at risk of making slobbering mouth noises.

I tore my eyes away from the treasure and focused my lizard brain on the facts. I could take out kobolds with the best of them, but sometimes their stupid stuck for a while. I needed to get my sharp mind back fast. So facts. First we had to face down the most fearsome necromancer in all of Verandel and rescue my old friend Gaaron, then I could steal the stupid, brilliant, amazing axe.

Yup. Best to get on with it then. I sighed to show my impatience and hopefully also to hide my sudden burst of avarice. "Is that everything? Are we ready to go?"

Tulip snorted and tucked the axe back into the

holster she kept on her rear flank. I hadn't gotten the chance to ask if she knew how to wield that thing or for that matter, whether the ostentations bauble was even functional in a fight, but something told me the spoiled young princess would claim both she and the axe could do anything—especially when asked in front of Calina.

"The rest of the supplies have been loaded onto our conveyance, and the conveyance is waiting outside with the valet," she informed me matter-of-factly.

I had to admit that acquiring a wheeled transport was a stroke of good luck. We'd wasted far too much time this morning already, but at least now we could make it up easily and without expending too much of our energy.

"Then let's go," Calina said before I could. Eventually I'd need to have a talk with that girl about who was really in charge here. But it could wait until we'd at least made it onto the road.

The rest of us followed. Even Tulip trotted after despite her obvious preexisting disdain for Calina. Hmm. Maybe she would be easier to control than I'd first expected. The addition of the transport, the money, and the begging-to-be-stolen treasure had endeared her to me greatly in the span of a very short time.

Back on the cobblestone streets of Briarhaven's monied district, it was easy to spot what didn't belong.

Not the conveyance, not even our battle-bloodied group, but the half-giant. He stood holding a large and weathered sack out before him like some kind of holiday gift giver.

"Pat?" I asked, blinking into the sun. "What are you doing here?"

He set the bag on the ground and ran a hand through his tousled golden curls. "I was called to outfit the Stable for some new fixtures. Apparently there was some kind of wild battle inside this morning. I don't suppose you know anything about that. Do you, Tilda?"

I swallowed and glanced at the ground, unable to speak.

"I'm just yanking your leg," Pat boomed with a hearty chuckle that made my heart ache for Durgan even though I'd just seen him last night. I was leaving, perhaps never to return. No, I couldn't fixate on that, or the quest would be forfeited before it even had the chance to really begin.

Pat laughed again, this time adding a wink for good measure. "As soon as I heard what had happened, I knew you must have been involved. No offense."

I didn't know what to say to that, so I said nothing at all.

"It made me glad, because I thought I'd missed my opportunity. But sometimes fate smiles upon us."

"Missed your opportunity for what?"

Pat hoisted up the sack with one hand and motioned for me to join with the other. "Gifts! I have gifts to aid on your adventure."

Tulip pushed her way between us. "Oh, what have you brought for me, you large and glorious man?"

Pat grimaced as a fresh tinge of rose ruddied his cheek. "Um, nothing, Miss. I didn't know you'd be here." He pointed his chin at the pink axe strapped to her rear. "And it seems you already have yourself a fine and glorious weapon."

Tulip snorted and fell back. "Quite right."

"I do have gifts for the others though." He paused and studied Amariel for a moment. "Well, not you, ma'am. I didn't know you would be here either. Uh, sorry about that."

Amariel laughed, and her bells jingled their merriment alongside her.

Pat shrugged as his skin tone returned to its usual pallor. "Yup, anyway. Big guy, this is for you." He reached into the bag and pulled out a long, triangular shield. The bag appeared practically depleted once its largest item had been removed.

Rurik looked confused but accepted the gift with a polite nod. "Um, th-thank you for... for this."

"It's to provide an extra bit of protection while you work on your casting times. Take it from a fellow half-human, we may look big and strong, but we still have that human softness. Shields help. This one will give you some added protection while you work on casting your magic. There won't always be a burning curtain for you to toss over your opponents, I'd imagine."

Rurik flushed, attempting to hide the reaction behind his new shield.

"See, you're already a natural!" Pat patted Rurik on the shoulder, then turned toward Calina. "Okay, next up."

We all waited as Pat pulled a series of metal-tipped arrows from the sack. There were nearly a dozen in all. He handed them to Calina and smiled. "These are prototypes. I haven't done much work with archery equipment, but these arrows are forged from my finest stock of steel. They'll fly farther and sink deeper into their target. When you return, you will have to let me know how they worked for you."

"Thanks," Calina muttered, looking absolutely forlorn as she kicked at the ground. "But my bow is gone. *She* stomped it into smithereens." Calina looked much more like herself as she cast a furious glance toward Tulip.

"Oh, come off your high cart." Tulip sneered right back. "I'm sorry I broke your stupid bow, but there's a better one waiting for you in the conveyance."

Calina's body stiffened while her gaze softened. "Really?"

"Well, you can't very well defend my life without a weapon. We are in the same party, after all. Don't make me regret it."

"That was nice of you," Rurik said, coming up beside Tulip and nudging her in the side with his shoulder.

She let out a huff and side-stepped away.

"And finally..." Pat let the sack fall to the path as he withdrew the final items: a matching pair of golden-hilted daggers.

My breath hitched, and my heart forgot that it was supposed to beat.

"Tilda, these are for you."

For so long, I'd coveted Pat's finely crafted daggers, but could never ask to have them without revealing my past—or the fact that it could still come calling. Yes, Durgan knew some of who I'd been, what I'd done, but I'd tricked him into believing I was retired like he was. For a while there, I'd even tricked myself into believing... But now that everything was well and truly out there, I'd gained something tremendous. No thievery required.

Taking a dagger into each hand, I tested them in my grip. They fit perfectly within my palms, almost as if they had been made just for me and my halfling-sized grasp. But wait...

I raised my eyes to meet Pat's, and he offered a subtle nod before sinking down onto one knee and opening his arms to me.

I'd never given a hug so fast in all my life. Not even to my dear, sweet, beloved Brynlee.

18

"Why are you taking up so much space?" Calina groaned and readjusted herself in the cramped corner she shared with me and Rurik inside the wheeled transport. And by shifting in her spot, Calina jabbed me in the ribs with her elbow and stomped hard on Rurik's foot.

When Tulip's parents had first presented the so-called "conveyance," I'd mistakenly envisioned a luxurious, comfortable ride to the very gates of Maltherius's fortress. But no, the strange magic-powered carriage was truly all style and no substance. The lacquered dark wooden featuring gilded scrollwork of some centaurian history was nothing more than a fancy box on wheels. Sure, it was the size of a decent halfling house, but even that wasn't enough for our bulky party. Tulip, her chaperone, and their massive amounts of luggage occupied almost the entire inside space. And there were still three more of us who'd needed to squeeze in with them.

At first Tulip had suggested the rest of us navigate the journey by foot, but after a rip-roaring argument, she'd finally agreed—mostly at Amariel's insistence— that those of us who remained could use the heavy trunks as makeshift seats. Poor Rurik practically had to fold himself in half at the waist to fit. For once, I was enormously grateful for my diminutive stature.

"This is *my* conveyance. I'll take up as much space as I need," Tulip spat at Calina from the opposite side of the wheeled platform. It seemed that the armistice they'd reached over Tulip's presentation of Calina's new bow had already reached its premature end.

Amariel lay across a trunk, partially snuggled against her charge's side, snoring softly. With each breath out, a soft and hollow tick sounded, merging with those that came before and after to create a metronome by which I could measure the steady beat of my torment.

"We need to stop arguing and start planning," I said. My head felt light from lack of both fresh air in my chest and common sense in my companions. The mayor had claimed the roof was removable, but that it would have to be left behind once detached as there was no good way to stow it while on the road. Right about now I really wished we'd gotten rid of it while we'd had the chance.

"We already have a plan," Rurik argued, his eyes glued on our centaur companion, even though it seemed as if he were speaking to me. Soft light filtered in from the semi-transparent roof, giving his green skin a ghastly glow. "Journey to Maltherius's lair, rescue your old traveling companion, and protect that artifact at all costs."

Tulip pointedly looked away from the half-orc's intense gaze. Calina and Amariel appeared similarly unmoved by the plan he'd laid out.

I pinched the bridge of my nose to stave off an incoming migraine. These kids would be the death of me, and whether that would be a literal or figurative death remained to be seen. "Those are goals, not a plan. You've said what we want to do. Now we've got to work out how we're going to actually do it. You kids have no idea what to expect. I need you to be ready for whatever Maltherius throws at you. Because whatever it is, I can guarantee it'll be a lot to handle. Especially for the uninitiated."

"Sounds like we need training. Not a plan." Calina

adjusted herself again, smushing me up against the side wall.

"Careful," I cried, pushing back at her to regain my space. Calina was small compared to the others, but she could still injure me if she wasn't careful. Or worse, push me off the luggage and possibly through the wall of the blessed cart.

And this cart thing practically gave me hives just thinking about it. It was driven by an unseen source of magic, that not a one of us knew how to control. That made it unpredictable and dangerous. What if it just drove off a cliff? Or smashed into the mountain face? What then? It had no windows or any other easy way to glimpse outside—at least not for me since I wasn't tall enough to peer through the roof. For all I knew, we'd already left the homely plains of Verandel for the steaming streets of the Infernal world. Who could say? This whole situation certainly felt like hell to me.

"We are safe in the conveyance," Amariel rasped with a woodwind accompaniment before she fell back into that same ticking sleep as before.

I studied the slumbering celestial but couldn't seem to make odds or ends of her. Had she read my mind or simply seen the worry reflected on my face? And were we really truly safe in the conveyance? Like, actually?

I'd heard whispered tales of her kind growing up on the crowded streets of Mirathane. But it was hard to discern what was fact and what had been fiction, especially when examined through the lens of time. Omniscience, flight, even teleportation had all been attributed to the heavenly beings. Mind-reading hadn't been expressly mentioned, but maybe that was part of the whole omniscient schtick.

"You're quite easy to read, dear," Amariel chimed, and this time I looked over fast enough to catch her winking at me before she fell back to her slumber. "I am in control of the conveyance. It will not let us down."

"Do you know magic?" Rurik asked, rubbing his large, green palms over his knees.

Amariel kept her eyes closed, but answered with a confidence that rang clear in the dulcet tones that encapsulated her words. "I am magic."

"Is it your magic that powers the cart? Can you... Can you teach me how to do that too?"

"I did not animate the cart. Even my abilities have their limits. But it is a simple enough thing to keep it going. Why, I can even do that in my sleep."

Yeah, no kidding. I was beginning to think this was the longest I had ever seen the celestial stay awake, which wasn't saying much at all. I was also beginning to wish she'd speak a little less. Her words mattered, but the musical accompaniment was giving me a headache. I would rather listen to one song all the way through than experience all the starts and stops that came with the celestial's speech.

Beside me, Calina spun one of her new metal-tipped arrows like a baton, whirling it faster and faster in her grasp. Until—*whoosh*—she lost control and sent it skittering to the other side of the cart.

Tulip deftly reached down and picked it up. "Mine now," she said in case there were any doubts that she was both the largest and the most in chargest here.

"You can't—" Calina began.

"This is my conveyance. I can do whatever I want."

And just like that, we were back to square one with Calina and Tulip casting each other ugly scowls across the cart while Amariel slept, Rurik pondered something quietly while cavorting around inside his own imagination, and I attempted to steel my nerves about the whole thing.

"Uh, excuse me," Rurik said, while at the exact same moment, he inadvertently shoved Calina and me up against the side wall. He crept forward on his hands and knees, then reached out and tapped on Amariel's shoulder.

Tulip was quick to come to her guardian's rescue. "What are you doing? Go away. She needs her rest."

"It's quite all right. Come, Tulip, make some room for our friend to sit with us." This statement came with an instrument I didn't recognize. Strange since I had traveled with a bard for so many years. Was it something specific to her realm? Something that didn't work quite right in the mortal world? A part of me wanted to ask about it, but a much, much larger part of me didn't actually care.

Amazingly, Tulip did just as she was told, shuffling her position and pulling her forelegs beneath her to open up enough of the floor for Rurik to have a seat beside her and Amariel.

"You're muh-muh-magic," Rurik whispered reverently, though still his voice boomed and filled the interior. "I want to be magic too. Would you help me?"

Amariel's response was undercut by a plucky stringed melody. "I belong to a magical race. You do not."

I watched as Rurik's cheeks grew pink beneath his scraggly beard. Poor kid. He was trying so hard to make something very specific of himself, and other than Calina, it didn't seem that anyone believed he would ever accomplish it.

"Oh, I..." he sputtered now.

"You cannot become magic if you are not born of it," Amariel said, then winked again. I thought I heard a flute weaving notes beneath those words. "But you can be taught to wield it." This ended with the trill of a long high note that lasted several seconds past what I would have deemed necessary.

Rurik bowed his head and dutifully waited for the music to silence before asking, "W-would you teach me?"

"I shall give it my best," Amariel assured him. She smiled at him briefly before returning to her slumber.

Rurik stayed in his new spot, affording Calina and I a great deal more comfort than we'd experienced before. Calina appeared agitated, but I, for one, hoped our large, green companion would remain on the opposite side until we pulled up at Maltherius's front door.

"I like your axe." I heard him tell Tulip at one point.

She expelled a quick burst of air through her nostrils but otherwise remained quiet. She also remained quiet when he said, "My dad used to wield an axe, but after his injury, he needed to switch to a single-handed weapon, and—"

"And I don't care, so stop talking to me. Please." Tulip thumped one foot on the floor to further emphasize her point. Why were all my companions so noisy?

"Hey," Calina shouted right into my ear. "We're supposed to be a team here."

So, so noisy.

Tulip pulled her front legs out from under her, forcing Rurik away, then made a huge show of stretching to take up even more of the meager space. "This is my adventure and my conveyance. You're literally just along for the ride."

My rebel elf girl sprung across the transport before I could even try to stop her. In less than a second, she had fallen upon Tulip and was yanking hard at her thick white-blonde braid.

"Let... Go," Tulip seethed.

How Amariel slept through this, I have zero idea, but that's precisely what she did.

"Do something," Rurik pleaded, but I already knew that the youngsters weren't going to listen to me.

I fixed him with a look that said I was irritated too but also not going to do anything about it. "They clearly have some big issues to sort out, so I say we let them."

"But Calina is hurting her!" Interesting that he'd argue for the creature opposing his best friend, especially given that she was clearly the stronger of the two.

"Let me go, or you will regret it for the rest of your life. Which, by the way, won't be very long," Tulip threatened, then stamped a hoof, sending tremors through the floor of the conveyance.

Calina looked up and caught my eye, then gave me a smug smile, before returning her attention to the centaur in her grasp. "Try me, *pony.*"

"That does it!" Tulip whinnied, or neighed, or made some other such horse sound. I still hadn't learned all the vocabulary associated with the centaur's unique culture and doubted that I ever would. Whatever the case, Tulip was big mad. She was also now on the move. She bent her human half forward and bolted to her feet, slamming Calina into the roof of the conveyance.

And through it.

Calina screamed with rage as she crashed through what had once been a solid wood ceiling and flew out of view. Well, good thing we hadn't stacked all of Tulip's luggage up there. We would've been crushed to death after the first big bump in the road.

Amariel's eyes popped open, and her mouth grew wide. She shouted something that I couldn't hear over the ear-splitting collision of cymbals. It must have been "stop" though, because the next thing I knew the magic wagon had halted so abruptly I had to wonder if we'd hit a literal wall.

Rurik shot to his feet and leaped up and out, only to biggify the newly formed hole in the ceiling.

I remained firmly seated and thoroughly flabbergasted. It wasn't until Amariel took my hand in hers that I finally snapped free of my fog.

"Come," she said like reeds on the water. "This part of the journey has reached its end."

Yeah, that was the understatement of the century, but I dutifully joined her, much to the protestations of Tulip who refused to dismount.

"This is *my* conveyance," she muttered on loop until the rest of us had made it out of earshot and probably even past that.

Rurik, having rushed ahead, had already found Calina's mangled form and now hugged her to his chest as both of them cried, though with different types of pain.

"Is... Is shuh-she going to be o-o-okay?" he asked through big fat tears.

"I'm fine," Calina choked out as my eyes fixated on the gleaming white bone piercing the fabric of her leggings and now boldly jutted out to greet us.

"It's fine. You're fine. It's just a leg. Luckily, you come ready fitted with an extra. I mean, who needs two of those things anyway?" I hoped my joke would lessen the pain, but it seemed to have the opposite effect.

"Rurik, could you please move me closer to Tilda, so I can smack her?" Calina hissed and moaned.

"Put her down," Amariel cooed in a new soothing melody. "I will mend her. You two, pack up the cargo. We'll be taking the rest of this journey by foot, I'm afraid."

"Can I watch?" Rurik asked after carefully depositing Calina on the soil.

"Not this time. You'll need to do most of the lifting I'm afraid."

Amariel confirmed what I already suspected—that our strongest party member would be of no help when it came to solving the problem she herself had caused.

I had no doubts that this would be a pattern on our journey.

Not a single doubt at all.

19

I t took a few heated minutes of arguments and threats before I was finally able to convince Tulip to get off the broken-down transport.

"But my hoof! It's chipped!" she whined in protest, making sure to pout her lips, and sucked in a sharp breath of obviously faked pain when she lifted her hoof demonstratively.

It was actually Rurik who got her horse butt up and moving. "You shouldn't put too much weight on it," he said with a sympathetic frown. "Don't you worry about anything other than yourself. I will carry the rest of our supplies. I'll do it by myself if I have to, and it looks like I do, in fact, have to."

And I had to bite my tongue to keep from

pointing out that Tulip never worried about anyone besides herself, with the possible exception of Amariel.

"Oh, bless you, you sweet, green hero," Tulip answered breathily as Rurik and I pressed ourselves against the inner walls so she could pass, finally taking her exit. She limped heavily as she moved but wasn't exactly consistent as to which side she favored. I kept my thoughts to myself but mentally gave the princess a promotion to queen, *drama queen.*

Once Tulip was out of the way, I grabbed the original pack I had prepared for myself—it already pushed the limits of what I could manage on my small frame, but I knew exactly what I could handle, and I also knew not to tempt fate by trying to take on more. That was probably a lesson Rurik would have to learn the hard way, and sooner rather than later too.

I'd let him figure that out for himself though. At least his willingness to make up the slack meant we could get ourselves moving again.

Yeah, moving was good. I hopped through the oversized door and onto the dirt outside.

But Rurik remained inside for so long, I had to climb back in to check after him. As it turned out, he just sat kneeling in the same place I had left him, having made no move to pack up anything at all.

I hesitated before speaking up. "What's wrong? Do you need help?"

He lifts a hand to his hairy cheek and smiled, tusks out on full display. "She called me sweet... a-a-and a hero. That's one step above adventurer."

Hero, ha. The worst part was that Rurik had no idea he was letting himself be led by the least heroic among us. What was it about love that made even the most intelligent people into bumbling fools? And why on earth would clever, shy Rurik fall for brash and brassy Tulip?

I did my best to hide my disdain as I said, "It's hardly up to Tulip Thunderhoof to decide what you are or aren't. If you want to be a hero, then prove yourself to me by successfully completing our mission."

He dropped the hand from his cheek and sighed. "I feel as if I have already emerged victorious."

Sweet divinity, what was this line? Was he quoting directly from a romantic storybook now?

I rolled my eyes so hard that I rushed to press the heels of my palms into their sockets to keep them from rolling away. "Don't talk like that in front of Calina. She already hates Tulip, and if you go switching allegiances all of a sudden, she's going to become completely unhinged, which will make her impossible to deal with."

He let out a long, wavering sigh, casting his eyes toward the ceiling or the celestial realm or something like that. "Calina is my best friend and always will be, but Tulip—"

"Don't. Just don't. This quest is already hard enough without adding this dynamic. Plus, I'm pretty sure Tulip isn't capable of loving anyone but herself, okay? So just... relax already."

Rurik's face fell, but he quickly recovered, arranging his orcish features back into an odd, dreamy smile. We were so screwed.

"Pack whatever you can carry and leave the rest. Maybe we'll find someone who can get the cart going again when we hit the next town. Amariel said she can steer it once it's already powered up, but that she can't get it started on her own. I think that basically means we're stuck unless we get really lucky really fast." I hopped back outside and zipped my eyes across the horizon. Despite my many years spent adventuring, I still wasn't the best at directions. Our current situation was complicated by the fact I hadn't seen where we were heading while inside the wheeled box. I also had no idea how much ground we'd covered.

I spotted Amariel in the near distance and took a moment to study her while she tended to Calina's injuries. The girl's bone was now back inside her leg, which was huge progress, but I wondered and worried about how much longer would it take for her to be able to walk on it?

Oh, Amariel. The old coot was such a mystery to me. How had a celestial resided in Briarhaven all this time without me catching so much as a whisper of her existence? And why was she working as some kind of glorified servant for the Thunderhoofs?

I had to admit it was good luck that we had a healer amongst our party, but what else could she do? Could she fight? And if so, would she? I so badly wanted to ask her, but doubted she would give me a straight answer. Besides, she needed to focus all her energy on healing our pink-headed girl before sleep overtook her yet again.

Ugh. How long was all this going to take anyway?

Our journey kept throwing us obstacle after obstacle. I didn't want to lose the rest of the day but understood that we couldn't leave Calina in her current state. It wasn't just impractical. There was also the small matter that Brynlee would kill me, absolutely murder me.

Of course, it was entirely ridiculous that this was even a problem, given that our party did, in fact, have a mount, capable of carrying both Calina and Amariel with ease while they continued their healing ministrations. But I knew better than to even ask Tulip to debase herself in such a way, especially on behalf of her avowed enemy.

I glanced over at the self-important centaur and found her frolicking back and forth along the road. She'd let her thick braid down and now had a cascade of gentle whitish-blonde curls blowing behind her in the wind. Tulip had beauty, riches, power; she appeared to have it all. I frowned. Why did the divine give some people so much while others were left with so very little?

I watched Tulip gallop with wild abandon before she abruptly stopped and began to turn in tight, fast circles. Oh sweet divinity, she was chasing her own tail. So maybe she hadn't been blessed with *everything*. Brains clearly seemed to be lacking.

What on earth drew Rurik to admire her? They had absolutely nothing in common. Even with the apparent touch of idiocy, Tulip was so far out of Rurik's league that he couldn't even reach it by a whole day's walking.

At least I knew Brynlee would never love me back, but Rurik? He'd somehow acquired the most dangerous companion of all: hope. And hope in a hopeless situation, no less.

I'd need to keep an eye on him, to make sure he

didn't go spewing any bold declarations to further split our party. And then, as if my thoughts had summoned him, Rurik appeared behind me, looming even larger than usual.

"I've... I think I've... got it... all." Each word was a struggle, given how over-encumbered he'd allowed himself to become. He carried his original trunk on his back and had an additional large leather trunk secured at each hip with thick rope. He also carried a fourth bundle in front of him. How had he even managed to get through the blessed door?

"This is ridiculous. Surely, we don't need to bring everything." I gave myself the luxury of rolling my eyes since I knew there was no way the half-orc could see me from behind his mountainous burden.

"These are... Tulip's... things. She... might need them... on the journey."

"If she needs all this, then she can help carry it. Set it all down. I'll help you sort through it."

Rurik cast a longing glance toward the horizon, where Tulip had apparently caught her tail and was now working it into a braid, but he did eventually do as he was told.

I sorted through the loose sack first. It held mostly food and camping supplies, all things we would most certainly need. When I moved to examine the first of the added trunks, Tulip let out a thunderous cry and came galloping over, barely managing to stop before ramming straight into us.

"That's mine. Don't touch it."

I pointedly resisted making eye contact. If she wanted to be treated with respect, then Tulip would have to act respectably. "Rurik can't carry all this. We need to determine what to take and what we should leave."

"Then leave that stuff," she argued, pointing firmly at the sack of supplies I'd already deemed necessary. "I need my trunks."

"If you need them, then you can carry them."

"It's fine. I can," Rurik attempted to interject but stopped short when two sets of very mismatched eyes glared daggers and battle axes at him.

"I am injured." Tulip raised one hoof, bringing it to my eye level.

I couldn't see a single thing wrong with it. "No, *Calina* is injured, thanks to you. You are fine, and perfectly capable of carrying a load."

She let out a long, exaggerated snort. "Oh, so because I'm a half-horse, I have to be your pack mule? You sound so ignorant right now. Centaurs are regal, intelligent beings."

"Clearly." I felt my breath getting stuck in my chest as anxiety mounted. Each of my companions was entirely unreasonable and each in their own unique way. It would be a long journey, longer still if we had to move at a snail's pace to accommodate all this cargo on foot.

"What do you have in there that's so important we can't leave it behind?"

"My travel wardrobe," Tulip answered blithely.

I'm not proud of what I did next, mainly because the only person it hurt was me. But I kicked the ever-loving crud out of that trunk. My fists and feet worked themselves into a fury, but the trunk remained stoic and unyielding despite my best efforts to punch it into oblivion.

"What are you doing?" Tulip exploded while Rurik watched in a quiet stupor.

"This is what I think of your stupid travel wardrobe," I shouted then spat at the ground very near to the trunks.

Finally, Rurik placed a firm hand on my shoulder, bringing me back to the present moment and to my mostly rational mind.

I heaved big, dramatic breaths as my shoulders bobbed up and down from the effort. It took a solid few minutes for me to find myself again, and the whole time the two large kids watched on in a mix of disgust and confusion.

"If you need this stuff, you will carry it. End of story," I spat out, then spat on the ground once more for good measure.

Tulip crossed her arms and wrinkled her nose. "Whatever. I'll just buy new clothes when we get where we're going."

Yes, because the first thing we would do when we reached the necromancer's lair would be to go on a shopping spree. To my credit, I resisted taking out my rage on that trunk a second time.

Late afternoon came, and we finally left the busted transport behind, Amariel having fully healed Calina. The agile half-elf was still a bit ungainly but made a good effort in not slowing the group down.

Waiting had never been my strong suit. I still marveled at how I'd managed to lay low in Briarhaven for so long despite knowing that Maltherius would still be looking for me. Maybe it was that whole out of sight, out of mind thing. It was easy to lose track of people, things, and especially time when they weren't standing right in front of you and demanding you pay attention.

It was days like this one that I wished I had retreated to some remote mountaintop and taken up a monk's lifestyle rather than choosing Briarhaven as my long-term hiding spot. I'd loved my life in Briarhaven while I was able to live it and had no regrets, especially when it came to any of the time spent talking with, working alongside, or thinking of Brynlee.

Yup, no regrets. *Yet.* But that didn't mean I wasn't currently annoyed out of my skull though.

We were moving slowly toward our destination and thank the divine for that.

Of course, Tulip wouldn't speak with anybody, not even her chaperone. At one point, she threatened to leave us and run back home to Briarhaven. When I called her on her bluff, she grew quiet... and angry. Each fall of her hooves came so loud and heavy, it shook the earth beneath her. The tantrum looked ridiculously silly, but it also produced a very real threat. I'd have to make sure I didn't get caught beneath one of those heavy hoof falls. I doubted that even Amariel would be able to repair a shattered spinal column.

Hopefully, we could all reach some kind of a settlement before Tulip completely wore herself out and demanded we stop for the night. We had way too much ground to cover in order to keep taking breaks like this. And Maltherius's deadline had been firm. A literal *dead*line at that. We had to reach him by solstice, or he would kill us all—or at the very least me... and also Gaaron if he were well and truly alive.

I did wonder why the kids hadn't asked for more details about the man we were attempting to rescue. I'd concocted many a lie to explain our relationship without ever so much as hinting at his connection to Brynlee or Calina. But the youngsters were so fixated on their own issues, they didn't ask for even the most basic of details. No doubt their heads had been filled with tales of heroic deeds and adventurers who managed to save the day, thanks to some unwieldy combination of divine providence, dumb luck, and poor storytelling.

Dumb or not, I hoped this particular stroke of luck would continue for the rest of our journey, but even I had to admit that this small blessing couldn't last forever.

20

The sun was just starting to set over the mountain's top when we finally stumbled upon a tiny settlement at its base. The town appeared long and narrow, wedged within the pass between one mountain and the next. Despite the abundance of rock provided by the landscape, all of the buildings and even the paths themselves were made from wood and dried grass, giving the village a rustic and outdated feel. More than anything though, it appeared damaged. Several of the buildings sported large holes, many of which nobody had bothered to patch up. And while the dried grass didn't look like it was thriving exactly, it had somehow found its way into almost every nook and cranny of the town.

Tulip turned her nose up at the shabby dwellings

that appeared before us, each in varying states of disrepair. She even went so far as to roll her eyes and sigh when she spotted a nearby domicile with its roof collapsed inward. The whole vibe was definitely abandoned chic, and our party's appointed princess was duly unimpressed with the display.

Calina, who seemed to be back to her normal, pre-injury levels of vitality, raced ahead, her footsteps thudding heavily on the wood-planked walkway. This willful lack of both stealth and caution was not a good look for an aspiring ranger. "Hello, hello!" she called at the top of her lungs. "Is anyone here to welcome us?"

Not surprisingly, nobody came to answer.

"We can stop here for the night and start up again at dawn's first light." I picked my way over some strewn debris that had busted up the footpath and stopped on the porch of a mostly intact cottage. The crooked door swung ominously, opening and almost closing in the faint breeze that swept through the town. If this town had once been inhabited, it was long, long ago. Our arrival was probably the most action these broken, old buildings had seen in years.

Placing both fists on my hips, I stood with my legs shoulder-width apart and sucked in a deep breath of the clean mountain air. We were stopping again, yes, but I couldn't wait to take some time to myself. In fact, it seemed like a great stroke of luck that I'd have thick cabin walls to protect me from my companions' irritating chatter and ridiculous problems for the next several hours at least.

"Not having to set up or tear down camp will save us time," I said simply with a shrug.

"It smells. And not in a good way," Tulip complained but followed the path I had cut all the same. It seemed even she was growing tired of the diva act by this point.

"Something's not right about this place," Rurik said, but I did my best to ignore him. First he had problems with too many people, now with too few. Between his social issues, Calina's Tulip issues, and Tulip's... well, Tulip issue, I was just done. Besides, what did this kid who'd never ventured past his home-town know about anything, really?

Amariel remained silent as she floated after the rest of us. I couldn't tell whether her feet actually connected with the ground, thanks to her long, flowing robe, and this bothered me. She was a puzzle I had yet to figure out, which meant she could very well present problems that I was unprepared to handle.

I'd just need to rely on my quick wit and even quicker movement to handle whatever happened our way. And the value of a good night's rest was certainly not to be undersold.

"Tuck in," I called to the others. "When I wake you in the morning, you'll have exactly five minutes to get yourselves sorted and ready for the road. Otherwise you'll be left behind. Got it?" I didn't wait for any kind of a response before disappearing into my chosen dwelling and securing the door tight. I even pulled over a busted-up chair and wedged it under the handle to make sure nobody would enter without my say so. It had been a long time since I'd last traveled the open road, but I could still secure a safe place to sleep—I could do it in my sleep even, should the need ever arise.

Right now though, I needed this break, this time away from the others. It came as no surprise that they were grating on me, but I still found it all extremely exhausting at the end of this very long day. I was also beginning to question whether I could successfully face down Maltherius and rescue Gaaron with such a ragtag group as my companions.

I spun the gem-encrusted bracelet Brynlee had clasped around my wrist, sliding it faster and faster as I attempted to count the revolutions and quiet my mind. Brynlee had trusted me with her child. She believed I could do this, that we could do it. I'd hate to let her down, but at the same time, it would be so much worse were I to let any harm come to Calina.

Perhaps it was better to continue the journey on my own. Calina had already been grievously injured once, and I'd done nothing to prevent it—or to heal her. Maybe I wasn't cut out for this role after all.

I stopped spinning my wristlet and fixed my eyes on one of the shining green jewels, letting my focus soften around the edges as I tuned out the external world and focused entirely on the storm picking up windspeed inside of me.

If I left now, the kids wouldn't be alone. They'd have Amariel to protect and guide them, and even though she'd been asleep more often than not, she still did a better job in that role than I'd ever managed. It would be kindness to them if I spared them from the dangers ahead, if I left.

Yes, they were better off without me. Just as Gaaron would have been, ultimately.

I'd only ever let down those who were foolish enough to care for me.

And these kids, they still had their whole lives in front of them. I'd hate to be the reason they missed the chance to live a little, to make mistakes they could laugh about later. Mistakes that would help them learn and grow and eventually become real, honest-to-divinity adventurers.

More than anything though, I knew I had a better chance without them. Selfish, sure. But Gaaron was counting on me. He'd already been waiting for so long...

I stayed up with my thoughts for what felt an eternity, and then when I was certain the others had been given enough time to find sleep, I found the door, unstuck my makeshift lock, settled my pack onto my shoulders, and crept outside. As a halfling, I could move easily while evading detection. My steps were fast and light, my form small and unassuming. Both of these things aided me well as I slipped through that abandoned town under the cloak of night.

I would find a way to retrieve the artifact from Tulip later. I hadn't planned on actually giving it to Maltherius anyway. No, I would merely let him think I had it with me, use that ruse to lure him out of his lair, and then murder him while saving Gaaron. Finally. He'd been waiting so long, and if Maltherius hadn't sought me out, I'd never have known it. I was the worst friend. The worst person, really.

And it was time I made things right with or without that artifact in my possession.

Besides, what's the worst that the stuck-up centaur

could manage to do with the Genesis Crest when none of us even knew how the blasted thing worked?

It wasn't as if she would suddenly take up necromancy, master it, and then build an undead army of sycophants to help her conquer Verandel. Hmm, actually, that could totally happen. Tulip already thought she owned the whole world. What if the artifact gave her the power to do just that?

No, no, it would be better if I lifted it off her before I went. I'd just have to figure out which cottage she'd chosen for her night's rest, then I could creep in, pluck the necklace from her chest, and creep back out. I still wouldn't give it to Maltherius, but at least this way, I could guarantee that Tulip Thunderhoof wouldn't use it for her own nefarious means before I managed to retrieve the blasted thing again later.

I turned and did a quick survey of the abandoned town, trying my best to determine which cabin would have been most to the centaur's liking...

"What are you doing?" a deep voice slammed into me from behind and then echoed through the mountains on a horrible loop.

I spun to face Rurik, who'd somehow crept up behind me on the path without my noticing. *"What are you doing?"*

"Orcs don't need as much sleep. Once I get my fill,

I spend the rest of the night reading by my flame, seeing what new things I can learn. Only here, my flame doesn't seem to work. I don't know why. I've never had that happen before."

"Oh." Well, at least he had no idea what I was actually up to. Rurik's mind was every bit as restless as my own. He just needed an outlet. He didn't suspect anything.

"You were running away, weren't you?" he asked, blowing that particular theory to smithereens.

"What does it matter?" I grumbled. The only thing worse than being caught out was also being called out. And by Rurik blessed Bane, no less.

"It matters a lot. You keep telling us we're all on the same team, but that's not exactly true. Is it?" Rurik took another step forward and held out his hand, palm up. He then blessedly changed the subject. "Why can't I summon my flame? Any ideas?"

"I told you, I don't know magic. Maybe Amariel could—"

"Amariel needs her sleep more than any of the rest of us. C'mon, we can figure this out together. Tulip brought lots of great magic books, but I can't read any of them without my flame."

"I thought we left all that extra junk behind?"

He reared back like a serpent getting ready to

strike. His glistening tusks and green skin made the metaphor all the more appropriate. Rurik looked at me, not with anger but with pity. "Books are the most precious thing in all of Verandel. They are not junk. Apologize."

"Apologize," I said, then hummed a quick beat before asking for a bit of clarification. "To the books?"

"To me for what you said and for trying to abandon us." He sucked air in through his teeth, which made a weird slurping sound, given the tusks.

"I don't—"

"Apologize, and I won't tell the others," he insisted, crossing his arms over his barrel chest and digging his heels into the ground. Every time I thought I had this orc kid figured out, he went and did something like this. It was a good thing he was so focused on his books most of the time, because I really hated it when he looked at me like he could see every single pump of my heart—not just see it, but also anticipate it. The whole thing was seriously unsettling.

And so I caved. "Fine, I'm sorry. But didn't we leave those *precious* books behind with the busted-up cart?"

"I put them in my own trunk so that I'd always have them handy. That was before your outburst, of course."

"I did not... You know what? Fine. I did have an outburst. You three are impossible and way too big a chore for me to handle." I needed to help Rurik get the stupid flame back so he could go back to reading books —instead of me and what I thought were my *hidden* doubts and anxieties.

"There are four of us. Did you forget Amariel?" He cocked his head to the side and then shook it before continuing. "Anyway, we don't mean to be difficult. We just don't have the experience you do. That's what this trip is all about, right? By the time we reach the end point of our journey, I'm sure we'll all be in fighting shape."

I quirked an eyebrow at that. I couldn't help it. "Yeah, but will you actually fight the bad guys, or will you just keep fighting each other?"

Rurik shrugged. "Help me with my flame. Without my magic, I'm useless, right? So let's fix this one problem now, then take the rest as they come."

Curse this kid and his very reasonable wisdom. It seemed I wouldn't be making my escape just yet. I probably wouldn't be making it ever if Rurik had a habit of wandering around at night. And now he knew to keep an eye on me, which meant I was well and truly stuck with the lot of them.

Sigh. Okay. I'd help him fix his stupid flame, and

then I'd go grab a few hours of shut eye before the sun dawned and forced us all out again. I didn't exactly know the ins and outs of magic, but I'd traveled with Gaaron long enough to pick up a few odds here and a few ends there.

"We're stuck in a pass," I pointed out, motioning to the tall mountains on either side. "Sometimes the thick walls of rock block the flow of magic. It's possible this whole town is a dead zone."

"So we need to step out of town and try again?" Rurik said, then took off at a sprint.

I hung back, exhaustion suddenly seeping deep into my tiny, little bones.

He reached the edge of town. His once hulking form was now a tiny blip just barely visible in the starlight. And then a burst of bright and brilliant flame joined him.

"It worked!" he shouted with joy and maybe also a touch of hard-won pride.

I wanted to shout at him to keep quiet so he wouldn't wake the others but that would have been rather counterintuitive.

Rurik began to jog back my way, flame held out proudly in front of him. But as he drew nearer, the magic zapped away, taking his summon with it. He groaned loudly in frustration, then raced back a few paces and reignited the spark.

A giant rumbling sounded overhead. An avalanche? Really? At this time of year?

Rurik's flame snapped off, and we both searched the area with frantic glances. "What's going on?" he shouted. Without the stutter, I noted. I'd have been proud of his growing confidence, if I'd had a moment to think about it.

Instead the roar of falling rocks sounded again. And this time I saw exactly where the sound was coming from. And it was so not good.

"Rurik, get back!" I screamed, just as an enormous creature slammed into him from the side.

21

I gasped when the first rock monster slammed into Rurik at such an impossibly high speed that I could have missed it if I'd blinked. When the second golem smashed into him from above, I screamed with everything I had in me. This was bad. This was really, really bad.

I ran out of sounds to make as more and more stony creatures flung themselves from the mountains; every single one of them only had eyes—if they even had eyes, that is—for my young charge.

My charge, my responsibility. I'd signed on to this, and it wasn't time for me to sign off yet. Not until we got the job done. Not until I made sure that we all survived this.

And so I shucked off my pack and ran toward the

battle, but it was like I was invisible. Rurik at least had the good sense to fight with his fists, but that seemed to make little difference. One after another, the rock monsters slammed their bodies into Rurik until he passed out from their assault.

"Help!" I screamed into the thick night air, praying it would be enough to roust the others. And then, because I knew better than anyone that you could only really ever count on yourself, I leaped forward and thrust myself upon the back of the nearest golem. I punched and kicked with all my might, but it barely even noticed my presence.

"Leave him alone!" I shouted, hoping to turn their attention away from the out-cold half-orc. I couldn't just leave him to die. Oh, what a wicked turn that would be. No sooner had Rurik convinced me to stay, than he received the ultimate punishment for following me out into the night.

When would I finally learn?

And when would those I cared about stop getting hurt?

Keeping others at a distance hadn't worked. It wasn't enough. Something in me had to change. Right here, right now. It was the only hope either Rurik or I had against this practically invulnerable horde.

"Mmmmgggrffff," Rurik moaned and raised a

hand. A small flame sparked to life, but quickly burnt out again. It was enough to draw even more monsters from the nearby mountains. One after another they all descended upon the poor wizard in training.

And that's when I got it.

Our opponents weren't golems. They were siphons, or magic eaters.

As I'd told the kids many times before, I had no magic. And that simple fact is why these golems didn't give a lick about me. They needed Rurik to keep fighting, to keep casting, so they could consume every last magical mote and then perhaps the kid himself.

Okay, so now I knew what we were up against, but I still hadn't the foggiest idea how to actually defeat it. Rurik would probably know, or at least have the answer in one of the many books he'd dragged along from the busted-up conveyance. Fat load of good that did us in the moment.

I'd just been freed from the heavy guilt of Gaaron's death, and I wasn't ready to watch this oversized kid die due to my ineptitude.

Think, Tilda, think!

Couldn't use my fists. Couldn't use my daggers.

Could I use the rock monsters against one another? I still sat mounted on one of the big guys, who hadn't cared enough about my meager attempt at an attack to even bother flinging me away. Could I somehow steer him into one of the others? Get them to fight each other instead of continuing to wail on Rurik?

It was the best chance we had, at least if I could get my off-the-cuff plan to work.

"Hey, idiot!" I taunted as I pounded on the thing's head. "Your buddy over there wants all that magic to himself. He's going to suck away every last drop and leave you hungry!"

But could the siphons actually understand my words? Did they have any capacity for language at all?

I was just starting to think that this new plan had already failed miserably when a high, lilting voice rang out from behind. "Nobody's eating my friend! Not today! Not ever!"

Calina came charging out of her chosen cottage, bow at the ready. Before I could shout to warn her, she fired one of her new steel-tipped arrows straight at the monster I was riding and very narrowly missed clipping me in the heel.

I yanked my foot out of the way and watched as the arrow snapped upon impact with the ravenous creature's rocky hide. Yeah, there'd be no repairing that. The attack did no damage, but it did get the monster's attention. He spun in a quick half circle, forcing me to hang on for dear life as he picked up speed and charged full force at Calina... who as a half-elf was magical, whether or not she chose to practice wielding the element in battle. Denying her innate gifts wasn't enough to curtail the siphon's appetite for them.

"Get out of the way! Get out of the way!" I screamed uselessly.

Calina braced herself—and her bow. I didn't know how Rurik had survived the assault against him so far, but I knew for a fact that there was absolutely no way Calina would stand up against similar treatment. She was so lithe and frail compared to her should-have-been-a-barbarian friend. One hit from this rocky monstrosity would take her out of the battle for good.

"No, what are you doing?" I screamed so hard that something in my throat seemed to snap. "Your arrows won't work on it. Get out of here. Go hide!"

Unsurprisingly but seriously disappointingly, Calina ignored my warnings. Her headstrong nature was going to get her killed for divinity's sake!

I yanked on my living rock throne's shoulders and tried to reroute its path, but it was hopeless. Maybe I could jump down in just enough time to push Calina out of its way. But if she was frail, I was something far worse than that. And I had no doubts that I'd be dead on impact. I'd just have to hope my sacrifice would be enough to buy her some time and finally make her see sense.

"I'm sorry, Gaaron," I whispered. I wouldn't be able to save him now, but I could help his daughter. If he knew, he would be pleased. For just a flash of a moment, I pictured that debonair smile of his that made so many ladies weak at the knees. It made me smile too.

And then I jumped.

Trumpets blared just before I crashed into Calina, knocking us both down onto the worn, wooden path.

"Ouch," she groaned. "What did you do that for?"

"To save your stupid life. Now get out of here!" My throat burned, proof that I was still alive, even if I wasn't exactly sure how.

Of course, Calina still didn't heed my many warnings. I honestly didn't know why I even bothered issuing commands at this point. Calina stayed rooted to the spot but raised one shaky finger and pointed.

I followed the path with my gaze until it landed upon our ancient friend, who had just joined the battle. Seriously, how had I missed the brassy fanfare?

Oh, that's right. I was in the process of risking my whole stinking life to save one stupid, ungrateful teen. How could I have forgotten so quickly?

My former mount charged furiously toward the little old lady. As it did, every single siphon on that battlefield abruptly stopped what it was doing and raced toward Amariel as if pulled by some kind of unseen force.

Magic, I realized. Rurik's and Calina's sources were slight, but Amariel was a veritable feast of the arcane. They'd probably never come across such a powerful being in all the however many years of their wretched existence.

Amariel was definitely old and probably wise, but did she actually know how to defeat them?

Well, at the very least, she seemed to know how to avoid taking damage from them. In fact, she floated right past them, completely unfazed by their violent overtures. If their powerful blows landed at all, they were clearly of the glancing variety. I watched in pure stupefaction as she breezed past the rushing beasts and made her way over to Rurik's fallen form. Her fingertips glowed with a pale-yellow light as she reached for him.

The siphons swarmed several paces away, but none dared to move closer.

"Is he dead?" I shouted, despite the persistent pain in my throat, and was promptly jabbed in the ribs by Calina's elbow.

"Of course, he's not dead," she hissed. "Don't say things like that!"

"It's a reasonable question," I mumbled as I pawed at the throbbing new pain in my side. So many hurts for not even truly being involved in the battle. "Given the circumstances."

"He's still breathing," Amariel trumpeted back. Apparently she only spoke in brass while on the battlefield. "I can heal him."

Calina let out a long, shaky breath. For all her bluster, she had obviously been worried about her friend. I'd been worried too, but as I watched Rurik awaken and roll over to his side while our cleric tended to his injuries and the siphons paced the invisible barrier she had erected, I knew that everything was going to be okay.

This battle hadn't been won, but it hadn't been lost either.

Yes, everything was going to be all ri—

"What's going on out here?" Tulip whined from the doorway of one of the many abandoned cottages in town. Well, at least now we knew why the townsfolk had left in such a rush. "Why is everyone making so much noise? Don't you know I need—"

The end of that sentence was buried beneath a resounding roar of thunder as every single siphon in the vicinity locked onto the glowing artifact that hung around her neck.

Yup, it sure served me right for allowing myself to get all optimistic.

Battles weren't won or lost until they had ended, and it was time for my pity of a party to learn that lesson the hard way.

22

T he Genesis Crest.

Many years ago, an unidentified quest giver had hired Gaaron and I to steal it. We'd managed to secure the prize, trading the artifact's safety for my partner's.

And for the last decade it had lain dormant, cozily nestled between my bosoms.

I'd never witnessed even the slightest hint as to what the crest could do until it decided it would rather stick with me than go with Maltherius's undead servant when the vile creature had attacked us over at Leicester Dewglen's farm. Strangely though, the mysterious crest hadn't put up a fight when Tulip had snatched it from me on the road leading out of Briarhaven.

And since then, the potent magical object had been more than content to act as simple jewelry, sitting high on the centaur's chest just beneath the dip in her collarbones. Honestly, Tulip probably hadn't even remembered she was wearing it...

And that was very unfortunate for us all.

Because as soon as she turned up in the doorway, the artifact shone with a wave of magic so powerful, that every single siphon whipped itself into a frenzy of bloodlust. Those that had been entranced by Amariel's celestial shield suddenly snapped out of their stupor, and many dozens more that hadn't bothered to join the fight before now hurled themselves from the mountains, crashing onto the wooden path, the ground, and even straight through the roofs of the abandoned village's dilapidated dwellings.

If it hadn't been clear before, the truth of our situation was now as transparent as glass. No one had been here to greet us, because the magic eaters had chased them all from their homes. This meant there was no one here to save us. If we were to survive this encounter, we had to figure it out for ourselves. It was all up to us.

My mind and body seemed to separate then.

Each muscle moved of its own accord. It knew how to run, how to fight. My brain, however, didn't know how to defeat these things. And so it was stuck, spinning wheels at a furious pace but ultimately getting nowhere.

Amariel. She was our best chance.

"What do we do? How do we defeat them?" I yelled, but my voice was lost amidst the thundering footfalls of the rock monsters.

"Amariel, help us fight!" I called again. My throat ached and burned from the force of my words, and this time, I knew the celestial had heard me because she glanced up from Rurik's prone form and locked eyes with me before turning away with a small but unapologetic shake of her head.

By the divine! She was here to protect Tulip. Did she not see how close the centaur was to a very swift but very painful death?

"Amariel, we need to..." I didn't even bother finishing my plea. If the celestial wanted to help, she would. The danger was very obvious here, but the solution, unfortunately, was not.

I couldn't stand around waiting for help that might never come. Of course, while all this was going on in my mind, my body had already brought me all the way over to the place where Tulip had initially appeared. Maybe I could grab the artifact and take it behind the invisible barrier Amariel had erected. The old bat could still be of help whether or not she was actively willing to assist.

Yes, I'd steal it back and retreat to safety. That's what I would do.

Only I couldn't snatch the artifact, because I couldn't find it... or the giant centaur who'd been standing in this same spot only moments before.

The siphons scoured the area, restless and upset about having been misdirected. Apparently, they didn't much enjoy playing with their food. At least not when the game was hide and seek.

Okay, but where in the ever-loving Infernus had Tulip gone? I couldn't make heads or tails of her sudden disappearance, which I guessed made me just as stupid as the mindless monsters.

I didn't much care for that association.

Calina showed up at my side, her chest heaving as she sucked in sharp, rapid breaths. "What's happening? Where did she go?"

I held out a hand to silence her as I studied the rock monsters. They weren't coming after Calina, and they weren't going back to Amariel or Rurik. Instead, they were pacing a tight perimeter around the area where Tulip had stood. A few of them even tilted their craggy faces to the sky and sniffed at the air.

She was still here. *Somewhere.*

I desperately wanted to solve this puzzle. I hated being flummoxed like this, but I also knew that the sudden vanishment was the only reason Tulip hadn't already been violently ripped to shreds by our foes.

The Genesis Crest had acted of its own accord once more. That was the only thing that made any sense at all. Did she even know she'd disappeared? Was she still nearby? Or had the crest taken her to another realm? Judging from the monsters' behavior, she had to be near at hand.

I thought about calling out to her with a warning to remain very still and very quiet, but I didn't trust her to heed my advice. She always had to have the last word, that one. Even if that word could get her killed.

So I decided to stay quiet and wait. The artifact seemed to have a plan even if I didn't. It had protected us before, and it could protect us again.

"Tulip, where are you?" Calina's shrill voice set fire to my nerves, but it was too late to silence her.

"Don't say anything!" I sputtered and shot Calina a mean glance.

But at the same time, Tulip shouted, "I'm right here, duh. How can you not see me?"

I groaned and smacked my forehead, both to channel some of my frustration and because I was again trying really, really hard not to hit the kids.

The monsters roared and rushed toward the sound of the disembodied voice. Even though I'd heard her call out, I still had no idea where Tulip had actually gone or how she'd gotten there. And it seemed like she didn't have any answers either.

Calina paced the area with her weapon drawn, the same weapon that we both knew was absolutely useless against our invulnerable opponents. I forced myself to stay still and wait, and I hated every moment of it.

The siphons continued to swarm like sea monsters waiting for the undertow to ensnare another ship and deliver its freshly killed crew to their bellies.

Amariel disregarded us all. Rurik still hadn't regained consciousness.

We were at a standstill. At least we were, until a horrified neigh echoed through the canyon. "Oh my me, where's my body? What's happening? I don't like this, Tilda. I don't like it at all. Bring me back this instant."

Forget slapping her, I was going to straight-up murder Tulip Thunderhoof. That's if the siphons didn't manage to do it for me first.

They surged forward, collectively as if of one mind, drawn to the greatest source of magical power in the area, even though none of us could see it.

"Why is this thing glowing? Ahh, it's getting hot!"

Tulip complained, cried, and then suddenly popped back into view as my precious artifact went sailing across the deserted town.

As soon as I caught sight of the projectile, I ran for it, performing quick calculations in my head as to its speed, the arc of the throw, and the strength of the one who had thrown it. I needed to figure out where it would land before the monsters did.

I was at least smarter than this ruckus of rocks-for-brains, wasn't I?

"Someone better explain what's happening right this instant!" Tulip called after me. I hated her. I absolutely and unequivocally hated her, which meant I didn't have to answer. I had to save our butts... Tulip's last, and not just because it was the biggest.

"You are impossible!" Calina screamed and shoved the horse girl. Even though I'd just been tempted to smack her myself, I knew exactly where this was going and I was most definitely not happy about it.

"And you are incorrigible!" Tulip shouted back before stomping on the half-elf's foot—the one that was on the same side where she'd sustained her leg injury earlier that day.

Now my adventuring party had one member too wounded to battle, one who refused to do anything to help fight the monsters until the other was fully healed, two who were now fighting each other instead of the army of very scary, nearly invincible monsters, and one who had to do everything for herself.

Yup, that last one was me.

No one was coming to save us. No one would—

A piercing cry sounded overhead. It seemed every time I thought in absolutes lately I summoned a change in luck. Usually for the worse.

My latest bout of bellyaching had somehow managed to call forth Cindara, Maltherius's massive necrotic dragon. The beast herself was practically the size of a whole mountain—a small mountain, true, but that still made for one very large dragon.

But why was she here?

To help the siphons destroy us? Because if she'd have just waited about five minutes, she could have saved herself the trip. We were as good as dead. Doubly so, now that the dragon had arrived.

Honestly, if Maltherius was going to keep such close tabs on us, couldn't he have just given us a ride to his lair and spared us all this whole disaster of a hero's journey?

Great. I was about to die and here rather than thinking of anything pleasant, I was going to go out while angry at everyone and everything in the world. Well, except Brynlee, never, Brynlee.

If I couldn't think productive thoughts, maybe I could at least summon a happy memory or two.

And so I closed my eyes and thought of Brynlee wiping down the already gleaming bar at the Mystic Mug, of Gaaron as I'd last seen him within the dungeons of Maltherius's lair, even of the stupid kids I'd just wanted to kill. They were my family—my life even—and now that life was ending. *Whomp, whomp.*

I kept my eyes closed tight as I waited for the pain to override my senses.

Was there truly a paradise waiting for me in the afterlife? Would I be reunited with the parents I could scarcely remember? Would they want me now even though they hadn't before?

So many questions. And soon I'd have answers to them all. If not answers, then stillness, peace. Yes, either was good. Anything would be welcome at this point...

"Uh, what are you doing?" Calina asked from behind my right shoulder.

"Accepting death with a smile," I muttered. She had to be a hallucination, or maybe she was a spirit. That would make sense if the monsters or dragon took her out first. It meant my time had come. And I was ready as I'd ever be.

"That's really weird," Tulip snorted.

So she was dead too. That snazzy battle axe of hers was of no use against monsters with impenetrable skin. She probably hadn't even thought to wield it anyway, making her an easy target to subdue despite her great size.

Something pushed into my shoulder. It was gentler than I'd expected dragon fangs or rock fists to be, but it still sent me stumbling back.

"Snap out of it already!" Calina growled, and that's what finally convinced me to open my eyes.

Calina and Tulip stood before me, both a little worse for the wear, but also both undeniably solid and more than likely *not* dead. In the distance, Amariel continued to treat Rurik's wounds, humming a soft song as she worked. When combined with her tinkling bells, it made quite the beautiful little melody.

"Where are the monsters? Where's the dragon?"

Calina narrowed her eyes at me. "What dragon?"

"The blessed dragon! How could you have missed it? The thing was as big as the sky itself!" Some ranger this kid was turning out to be. How could she stalk smaller, more stealthy prey, if she hadn't even noticed the enormous predator overhead?

"Oh, that must have been why all the rock guys ran away," Tulip informed me with a disinterested flick of her tail.

Calina pointed in the direction from which we'd initially arrived in town. "They all went off running that way. Do you think maybe we should leave before they come back?"

"Yes, we should leave." I gave both girls a pointed look. "And next time there's a battle, we need to fight our opponents instead of each other. Understood?"

"Yeah, okay. Whatever," Calina said with a shrug.

I probably should have launched into a lecture right then and there, but honestly what was even the point?

23

"We need to get out of here before the siphons realize they'll never catch that dragon and then come back here to make an easy snack of us," I told the girls. Meanwhile I wondered whether Maltherius had meant to help us by sending Cindara as a distraction. Had our salvation come about because of dumb luck, or was the big bad making sure no one else killed us before he got the chance to finish the job himself?

Whatever the case, I was grateful. Begrudgingly so, but still, happy to be alive and ready to fight another day. I just needed... "Where's my artifact?"

I'd lost sight of its trajectory when I'd spotted Cindara, assuming that it no longer mattered, seeing as

I expected to be dead before the pendant could hit the ground. But that pendant had saved our butts, first by turning Tulip invisible and then by drawing Cindara to us.

At least I assumed that's what happened. I still wasn't quite sure.

The more I tried to understand the Genesis Crest, its power, and its attachment to our party, the less it made any sense at all. Especially considering the thing was some kind of necromancy artifact.

Whatever, I could figure it out later.

"Over here," Tulip called, standing where the wooden walkway ended and pointing with one hand and one hoof decisively at the dirt.

I spotted the gleaming crest and raced forward to retrieve it. I even gave it a quick kiss before looping it around my neck and tucking it back beneath my tunic.

"Gross," Tulip said, but this time she didn't look upon me with a sneer, which I considered real progress in our relationship.

"Go get your things," I told her, hoping Calina would also follow suit.

I needed the girls out of the way so that I could go check up on our magic-powered duo since neither of them had said boo since the battle began.

They weren't hard to find, given they hadn't moved so much as a toe's length away from their initial spot. Amariel continued her soft rhythmic chanting as she held Rurik's head in her lap.

"We need to go," I told her gently.

And she ignored me.

So I tried again. "They'll be back. Angrier than before. Hungry. We need to go."

The celestial lifted one hand and used it to motion me away.

Okay, that did it. I reached out and grabbed her limp wrist before she could move it away. "Look, I get that healing is your whole schtick, and it's useful... most of the time. Honestly, I'm still a bit miffed that you couldn't take a quick break to help defeat the monsters before they killed the rest of us but—"

"You're still alive." Each word was punctuated by the mighty boom of a drum.

"No thanks to you!" I boomed right back, no musical accompaniment required.

"He needed me more than you did. Now if you'll please let go of me, so that I can continue my healing work." These words reminded me of a snake slithering through tall grass, which I guessed meant Amariel had summoned the oboe. Did she pick the instruments that played along with her words, or did they pick themselves? I would probably never understand this strange, old woman, but that wouldn't stop me from wondering about her.

I tried to calm myself down. I really, really tried. But it was hard to be a leader when your followers refused to follow. Like ever. They never listened, let alone did what I wanted them to do, and I was more than a little fed up. "Excuse me, *ma'am*, but—"

"It's f-fine," Rurik interjected as he lifted his head and stared up at me with half-lidded eyes. This was the first and would probably be the last time the orcish kid had to look up at me so I relished the moment while I could. "I can walk. I'm strong enough, I th-think."

"I need to finish all at once, or you'll sustain long-term injuries," Amariel said glibly, powered by the reed yet again.

"We don't have the time." I clapped loudly to make sure Amariel was paying attention, and to mock her a bit while I was at it. "Don't you understand?" *Clap.* "Those siphons will be back." *Clap, clap.* So unless you're planning to single-handedly dispose of them, we need to make tracks." *Rousing applause.*

"All life is sacred, and as such, I will not be disposing of anyone." Amariel spoke and musical chaos ensued. I was done trying to figure it out, because every flippant note was making me more and more furious.

I released my hold on her wrist and blinked hard as I attempted to take in her words. "Are you telling me you won't kill the monsters who were, until just minutes ago, very actively trying to kill us?"

"I do not want their blood on my soul."

"But they're rock monsters. They haven't got any blood. So no blood, no problem, right?" Even as I said the words, I knew we, in fact, had a very big problem. If Amariel wouldn't fight, our party was even weaker than I'd feared.

She looked at me and then through me, sending a shiver to my stomach. "I sustain life. I do not destroy it."

Rurik sat up the rest of the way, letting out a pitiful groan as he did. "Thank you for healing me. I will be all right now."

Amariel shook her head and went back to chanting her healing prayer.

But Rurik gently shoved her aside, then staggered onto his feet. "Tilda's right. We have to get out of here before those creatures come back. I'll be fine. Let's go."

Amariel stood too. Well, really she hovered a few inches above the ground, not unlike the undead sorcerer we'd dispatched near farmer Dewglen's cabbage patch. I tucked that interesting fact away for later.

Then I watched in tense silence as Rurik staggered back toward the cottages and Amariel followed after him with glowing, outstretched hands. She clearly planned to finish mending his injuries whether he wanted her to or not.

Well, at least everyone was up and moving again.

I cupped both hands over my mouth and shouted, "Five minutes to grab your things!" After that, I'd be leaving with or without them.

Oh, right. I had things to gather as well. I'd thrown my pack to the ground to race toward Rurik when the siphons had first attacked. I'd thought for sure he was a goner, and so I'd panicked. If I'd been thinking more clearly, I may have taken a few seconds to toss my bag toward the nearest cabin for safe keeping.

But I hadn't thought. I'd merely reacted. And as such, my carefully prepared pack had been trampled to dust—or at least turned into a useless pile of debris beneath the feet of the rock monsters.

My luck was forever changing like the direction of the wind, and I was one bad karmic coin toss away from absolute ruin. But just as I'd earlier determined—

although admittedly with some difficulty—I wasn't dead yet.

Which meant I had to keep going.

I glanced up at the stars twinkling overhead. Pretty, but fairly useless when it came to judging the time. Had five minutes passed yet? Like the stars, I myself was rather useless in keeping track of time. Eh, I'd waited for the others long enough. It was time to go, go, go before we couldn't, couldn't, couldn't.

"We're going north through the pass, and we're going now!" I called in the direction the others had disappeared. The great crane's constellation shone overhead. As if to encourage me, its long neck stretched forward to guide the way. Yes, I needed that. Thanks, stars.

I charged a few paces ahead, trusting the others to eventually fall in line.

"I... I..." Rurik came shuffling after me, half-dragging one side of his large, green body in a horrible, unnatural gait. Amariel tutted and hummed, still attached by her healing spell.

I paused and waited for them to catch up.

"I can't carry it all," the orc informed me after he'd caught his breath.

"Leave the books. They're too heavy."

"I would rather die than leave the books," he said

rather dramatically, but the glint in his eye told me Rurik was dead serious.

"Fine, fine. I'll help with what I can. My pack is wrecked anyway."

He pursed his lips as if he wanted to ask a question but decided against it. Good, we didn't need any more questions until we found some answers. Well, we didn't need any more questions *except one.*

"Where are Calina and Tulip?" I asked with an exasperated sigh.

Rurik shrugged and offered me a baleful glance before turning back to the abandoned town.

Amariel turned with him.

"So you basically don't exist until you finish your healing spell, I take it?" I snarked as I hopped over a caved-in portion of the path.

"Spells are for witches. I am a celestial," she answered with a frown, but otherwise kept right on with her busy work as we headed back into town to grab our cargo.

We passed Calina on our way back to the cottages. She turned to follow us, but I shoved her back.

"Keep going. We'll catch up when we can."

Amazingly, she didn't argue. My heart floated in my chest. Was this what it felt like to be taken seriously as a leader? Because if so, I really, really liked it. Maybe our dysfunctional group dynamic was finally changing for the better.

I held onto that exhausted optimism as I followed Rurik into his former sleeping quarters. "What can I carry?"

"That." He pointed at the large leather sack that held all the camping supplies. It was almost as big as me.

I hesitated, then asked. "Got anything smaller?"

"Just the books. And I'd rather carry those myself."

"Fine." I gritted my teeth, spit on both my palms, and then grabbed hold, dragging the sack after me. I made some progress, but then got stuck in the doorway when the flooring level changed slightly creating an obstacle I couldn't quite conquer.

I let go and looked at my poor hands, reddened from clinging so hard to the heavy burden. "This is ridiculous. Where's Tulip?"

"I haven't seen her," Rurik admitted as he shoved the bag through the entrance for me. That simple act appeared to kick the wind right out of him. No wonder he'd needed my help.

I turned to Amariel. "You're supposed to be here to protect Tulip. Don't you even care that she's missing?"

"I'm not missing," Tulip's voice came from somewhere outside. Her words lacked their usual bluster, immediately telling me something was wrong in a way I probably shouldn't ignore.

So I left the bag behind to search for her. Seriously though, how did we keep losing the largest member of our party?

After a couple minutes of searching, I finally found her sitting behind the cabin on her horse's rump. She cut an odd silhouette, which meant it took me longer than it should have to realize that she was crying.

"We almost died back there," she whispered before choking back a sob. "I didn't know we could die."

I worked super hard not to roll my eyes on that. The kid was in emotional pain, and she needed me to put on my nicest act. "It wouldn't be an adventure if there wasn't anything at stake."

"But my life? Yours? That's not really worth it, I don't think."

"Hey, you're the one who begged and bribed your way into this party. What did you think you'd signed up for?"

"I don't know," she admitted, then let out a big huff through her nostrils. "In the books, the characters battle monsters but you always know they're going to win, that they'll live happily ever after."

"Yeah, well, this isn't exactly a book. It's real life, and in real life, the stakes are always death."

She widened her big, blue eyes in horror, then pouted and whispered, "I don't like that."

"It's not my favorite thing either, but we can't exactly change it."

I lowered myself onto the ground beside her and attempted to pat her side consolingly.

She didn't flinch or say anything mean. Again, our relationship was making real progress here.

"I want to go home," she whimpered.

"Well, you can't. The adventure has already started, and it's one you committed to. Besides, the siphons took off toward Briarhaven. If you go back that way, you'll be walking straight into a death trap."

She sighed but made no attempt to argue or insult me.

"You know what you could do though? To better our chances?"

She turned toward me with a wary expression. "You're going to tell me to be nice to Calina, aren't you?"

"The thought had crossed my mind. I can tell you're strong, Tulip, and now that I also know that you know how to read, I'm guessing you might even be a little smart."

She huffed at this but let me go on.

"You could be a powerful ally if you actually showed up to battle."

Tulip sighed again. If I was supposed to understand all her breathy horse noises, I didn't. But I could sense the frustration, the despair, and the self-loathing. They were all things I felt myself, and I felt them every single day.

She twisted to retrieve her battle axe from its strap on her haunch. "I have no idea how to use this thing," she admitted.

I forced my eyes away from the shining jewels and fixed them on the sad girl before me instead. "I do. I can teach you."

"Really?"

"Really. Just on one condition."

She quirked an eyebrow and motioned for me to proceed.

"You have got to start pulling your weight."

"In battle?"

"Yeah, and also literally. Rurik can't carry everything. He's injured. We need you, Tulip."

"You... need me? Like I'm important?"

"Yeah, exactly like that."

"Like I'm the hero?"

"Uh, sure. You're a hero."

"Not a hero. *The hero.* Like if this were a book, then I'd be the main character?"

"I guess?"

"Say no more. I'll do it."

I was almost afraid to ask, but I did anyway. "Do what?"

"You'll see," was all she said before she pushed her powerful hooves into the ground and sprung back onto her feet as if nothing had ever been the matter.

24

If there was one thing I could count on more than Tulip hating the rest of us, it was how much she absolutely adored herself. The realization that she could actually die on our adventure coupled with our brief and confusing heart-to-heart outside the cabins seemed to be just what was needed to make her a useful companion.

And this included carrying our camp supplies. Rurik still had the heavier burden, but he was also improving with each step as Amariel worked her healing magic.

Tulip was also taking her new self-given role of "the main character" quite seriously. If I'd forgotten that she'd landed the starring role in the kids' stage adaptation of "Legends of Yore," it all came screaming back to me now.

"What's my motivation in this scene?" the centaur asked me while clutching the sparkly axe to her chest.

I kept my eyes on the road ahead, hardly paying her any mind as I answered, "To cover as much ground as possible before we need to set up camp for the night."

Unfortunately, as soon as the words were out of my mouth, Tulip took off at a full gallop quickly becoming nothing more than a tiny dot on the horizon. It took the rest of us close to an hour to catch up to her. This taught me that I'd have to pay closer attention to my words when it came to her. She went from listening to nothing I said to taking it all far too seriously.

Still, progress was progress. No matter how annoying.

"I need my supporting cast. Otherwise there's no show," she explained before falling into step beside me once more. It was quite awkward, the enormous four-legged horse girl attempting to match my small-legged stride. I'd have laughed if I had the energy, but this crew was wearing me out quickly.

"There's got to be a show," Tulip said emphatically as she swung her battle axe out to the side in a big swooping motion. Luckily, it missed my head by several feet due to our great differences in height. "Life is much more interesting that way."

I wasn't sure whether this was supposed to be a novel, a stage play, or something else entirely. Adventures were plenty exciting without the added theatrics; it was literally right in the name: *adventure.* I was more than a little irritated with Tulip's sudden interest in me, but at least we were finally headed in the right direction here.

Another hour passed before Rurik was returned to his full health. Amariel now struggled to keep upright as she floated alongside us. She'd really worn herself out. I'd feel bad for her, if I didn't also partially blame her for all our problems.

"Oh, if only someone could aid this poor damsel in distress," I crooned, hating that I had to debase myself in this way to get results. *Me, a thespian. Bah!*

"Say no more. Everyone's favorite heroine is here." Tulip pulled the drowsy celestial onto her back, arranging her carefully beside the sack of camp supplies, and flashed a glamorous smile to all who were willing to look upon it. Which basically meant to Rurik *and only Rurik.*

Watching the big, burly orc swoon made me even more sick to my stomach, but I couldn't afford to lose whatever meager nutrition remained in my system.

There would be no barfing today, no matter what strange, new ways these kids and their token elder found to nauseate me.

"That was suh-so graceful," Rurik mumbled in Tulip's general direction.

Tulip, as per the usual, ignored him. She so desperately wanted an adoring audience, but failed to notice her biggest admirer was standing right there, staring at her with a slack jaw and heart-shaped eyes.

Still, Rurik was undeterred. It seemed her obliviousness to his affection gave him all the more courage to express it. I really hoped that I wasn't this heart-sickeningly obvious when it came to my feelings for Brynlee. Even so, this was something Rurik and I had in common, the way we longed for women who would never ever return our romantic intentions.

I fingered the bracelet that Brynlee had secured around my wrist and smiled. I didn't need her to love me back—at least not in that way. What we had already was perfect, and it would be made more perfect still when I returned with both a hale-and-happy Calina and an alive-and-well Gaaron at my side.

As we continued our walk, I allowed myself to get lost in the fantasy of our party's triumphant return, living happily in my dream world while Rurik begged Amariel to teach him new spells, Calina practiced nocking her new arrows on her new bow, and Tulip pranced big, histrionic circles around the group.

All in all, it wasn't a bad day...

But night was fast approaching.

"I'm tired," Calina complained however many minutes or hours later. Honestly, by this point, it seemed as though time was overlapping itself, weaving and tangling as it meandered off in some future direction.

"I'm obviously perfectly fine, but I do need my beauty sleep," Tulip agreed with a shake of her golden mane. The fact that Calina didn't dig in with an insult was proof of just how exhausted she had become.

Amariel punctuated Tulip's point with a long snore, bells and all.

I glanced toward Rurik, the only one who hadn't voiced a complaint—if Amariel's snores could be considered that, which I believed they very well could.

During our last nature break, he'd unpacked one of the heavy books from his trunk and now had it out in front of his nose, sucking up all the words like they were the freshest of air and he himself were a greedy, little flame.

It would be getting dark soon, and I could just imagine the chaos that would ensue if our resident spellcaster attempted to read while walking *and* holding a flame cantrip. There would be no consoling him if he accidentally set the grimoire ablaze. Never mind there were a dozen more just like it in the old chest turned backpack.

"All righty then. This is as good a place as any to set up camp," I acquiesced. "Come on, crew. Let's get started."

Rurik helped Tulip settle the sleeping celestial on a soft bed of little blue flowers, then the three kids followed my instructions to set up our first official campsite. They listened to me. They worked together. They were basically perfect until...

"Where am I supposed to sleep?" Tulip wanted to know, and it was a good question.

"The conveyance," Amariel answered in such a way that I couldn't be sure whether she'd actually woken up to say it.

"You mean the wheely thing we left behind ages ago?" I shot back but received not even a grunt in response. In truth, it had only been a day and a half since we'd had to abandon our wheeled transport, but it felt much longer than that. I eyed the setting sun and tried to work out how much time we had left until the solstice.

Would we reach Maltherius in time?

Moreover, what would happen if we didn't? Would he come to us? Would he murder Gaaron and then reanimate his corpse and send him to kill the lot of us?

No, it wasn't good to think like this, even though it was very easy to do. We'd make it in time. *We would.* Mostly because we didn't have any other options. At least not any that I liked.

"You can sh-share my tent, Tulip," Rurik offered, and of course, that suggestion did not go over well.

Tulip stamped a hoof. "I do not share."

His counteroffer came quick and without hesitation. "Then you can have it to yourself. I don't mind sleeping under the stars."

"Fine." Tulip flipped her mane and then moved toward the tent. Entering the small cloth fort required her to get down on her belly and pull herself awkwardly in with her front legs while wiggling her bum. "Don't look," she pleaded, so of course, we all stared without shame.

Rurik, in particular, watched with especially wide eyes.

And Calina, of course, watched him watching with a scowl.

Amariel snored.

I hung my head and sighed.

Tulip may have been the only one who thought we were in some kind of stage play, but each and every one of us was very skilled at playing our assigned part.

"This will do for now," Tulip called, putting an end to my metaphorical musings. Her voice was muffled since she was facing away from us, but she didn't have enough space to turn around in the borrowed tent. "Thank you!"

"You're welcome!" Rurik shouted eagerly and far too loud.

Calina and I both stuck fingers in our ears and spun them around to clear our hearing.

I could sense tension brewing between the friends. I wasn't sure whether Rurik was aware, but Calina most definitely appeared hurt by her bestie's obvious interest in her avowed enemy. They'd have to work the conflict out eventually, but right then wasn't the time. It was late, and I was bone tired.

"Go to bed, both of you," I ordered, voice stern and unwilling to tolerate any arguments.

Once the kids had settled themselves, I rummaged through our remaining camp supplies and found a nice metal mug. The little blue flowers I'd spotted earlier would make a fine brew, and I intended to enjoy it along with the silence of the night before I took my rest.

I made quick work of starting the campfire and settled myself cross-legged on the ground as I waited for the water from my canteen to roll to a boil. My eyes gazed into the lapping flames, watching them dance, remembering the many nights that had come before. Gaaron and I had made the same fires, drank the same wildflower tea, set about the same kinds of quests.

So many years had passed, but it all felt so familiar and so very much the same. Like I'd never left at all. Like maybe the interceding decade had been nothing more than a slight snag in the thread of time. The quiet life had never been meant for me. I could have half-convinced myself that Briarhaven itself had been nothing more than a pleasant dream if not for the rest of my party sleeping scattered about the campsite.

I reached around my neck and unclasped the chain that held the Genesis Crest. Bringing it before me, I let it dangle, swing, and reflect the dancing flames. It didn't appear to be any great treasure, at least not from the outside.

And yet, it had saved us all today. That made two times now.

But I found myself angry with it still. This artifact is the reason I lost my friend. It was the reason everything had changed.

This simple diamond-shaped pendant held great power, most of it unknown to me. Why did Maltherius want it so badly? Why had he continued to seek me out all these years rather than simply letting it go?

If all went to plan, we'd free Gaaron, kill the necromancer, and escape without the crest ever changing hands. That meant I would never know why this silly thing was so important. And that would plague me all my days, the not knowing—but life didn't always provide all the answers in a prettily packed gift. No, it was much crueler than that. Or at least far less predictable.

My fingers shook as I reached out to thumb the pendant. My hands had shaken back then too, which was why it had all gone wrong...

"Over here! To the left!" Gaaron had shouted, running ahead of me with his strong human legs as he strummed at his mandola, casting the notes for a protective wall that was slowly rising between us and the fast-approaching foes.

He'd spotted a hidden door that would provide a swift exit from the dungeon beneath Maltherius's lair, a much-preferred alternative to fighting our way through his entire horde who had now learned of our presence—if not also our theft—and were descending upon us in wave after wave.

"I've got it. Just keep playing." *I darted ahead, fast on my feet as ever.*

It had all happened so fast. It seemed that the most important moments in life zipped by within a blink. Maybe that's why I had such a precarious relationship with time. I didn't trust it.

My gaze softened once more, and I was back in the dungeon, *running, running, running. As I moved, I pulled my favored lock-picking kit from my sack and readied the cool metal in my hand.*

Each time Gaaron plucked another string of his instrument, a giant burst of energy shot across the room in a tight, crashing wave. Some of the horde fell back, but not enough.

I reached the door, tested the handle to make sure it was indeed locked, and then jabbed my pick into the mechanism.

"Be quick, Tilda dear!" Gaaron shouted over the honeyed notes of his performance.

I stabbed and twisted and turned, but the lock did not give. I kept trying, quickly, quickly, but the more I maneuvered my tool, the harder it became for me to control it. My fingers shook from the effort, not because the door was enchanted nor that it was particularly heavy, but because something inside me knew that I had already failed.

That I couldn't do it.

And that something had been correct. That something also kept me from believing I could set things right with my return. But by the divine, I had to try! I had to!

Gaaron's song ended, and he sprang straight into another one, but the spell had been broken. He started to shout my name, but only managed one syllable before his voice was silenced forever...

No, not forever. He could still be alive. I had to keep believing that. Otherwise this entire journey was pointless.

I had failed him then, but this time I wouldn't let him down.

I wouldn't let any of them down.

This time I would quiet the voices that said I was too weak, too small, too foolish. And if I couldn't get them to shut up, then I'd shout over them and drown out their cutting remarks.

I could not fail. Not again.

25

Despite having stayed up well past the others, I was the first to get moving the next morning. Sleep and I had never had the best understanding of one another. My mind and body were both too active to succumb to its embrace for long. What if an enemy snuck into our camp and offed me in my sleep? It would be an easy enough thing for them to do.

When I died, I wanted to make sure I went out fighting, maybe even take a few others with me on the way.

For now though, I took a few precious moments to watch the sunrise before tromping away from camp to retrieve another batch of those delicious wildflowers for my brew. And when I returned, I found Calina hunched before the waning campfire, trying to stoke it back to life.

Well, there went my peace. It would be tea for two then. Except...

I frowned when I realized I didn't have enough of the flowers for two mugs of tea. Come to think of it, we might not even have a second mug itself. Despite the generosity of Tulip's parents in providing our initial bulk of supplies, we had quickly lost much of what we'd started with. First with the conveyance, then the siphons. A few of our supplies also disappeared somewhere along the trail when the bag burst open, and its contents scattered. Tulip had been galloping so far ahead of the rest of us, that none of us noticed the fiasco until it was too late to retrieve all the dropped or damaged rations.

Something told me, this kind of thing would continue to be a problem with our party. That same thing also told me that I had to take my peace—and my tea—while I could still find it.

So I decided not to share. If Calina wanted something, I had no doubts she would find a way to get it. I needed my morning brew, especially now that I wouldn't be getting my quiet.

"What are you doing up?" I asked, my voice rough around the edges. Somehow I had gotten both too little and too much sleep. How did this always end up happening to me? And why after decades of life had I still not figured out a workable solution to this problem?

Calina fell back onto her rear and flung her arms over her knees, letting her hands dangle at the wrists. Apparently, she had decided it was my job to tend the fire. I was the best suited to it, after all.

I set my mug and supplies out of her reach before poking and prodding and transforming the dying embers into hungry young flames.

Calina sighed—perhaps with pleasure, perhaps with exhaustion. It was hard to say which. It also didn't really matter. "You're good at that," she said.

"I'm good at a lot of things." I flashed her a self-assured smile, deciding to shuck off the vulnerability I had wallowed in last night. The others needed me to be strong. Calina most of all. I recognized myself in her, and I'm pretty sure she looked upon me in a similar way. Was I a vision of what was to come? For her sake, I hoped not.

What she said next took me by surprise. "What was he like? Your partner?" The question felt pointed, personal, as if Calina had seen all the memories that haunted me at this very fire last night.

I needed to be careful here. I was not at my best in

the mornings. In fact, if I had a best, I wasn't sure it corresponded to anything as regular or predictable as a certain time of day. Whatever the case, Calina couldn't know who he was. Not yet. Not until we had found him, and maybe not even then.

But Gaaron would see it instantly. The girl looked so much like her mother, the woman he had loved then and that I wished to love now.

Okay, so it was a conversation we would definitely need to have at some point, but not now. It would only create chaos, anxiety, distrust. And our party was hardly hanging together without this added complication.

Calina rolled her shoulders, then twisted at the waist, watching me with those piercing, violet eyes of hers. "It's okay if you don't want to talk about it. I mean, it must be hard, losing a friend like that."

I nodded and dropped onto the ground beside her. "Well, I thought I'd lost him, but it seems I was wrong."

"Can you really trust that Maltherius guy though? What if he's just lying to get you to bring him the thingy?" She tipped her chin toward the artifact, which I then realized I was wearing on the outside of my tunic, rather than hidden beneath as I'd always done before.

I fingered the pendant thoughtfully. "Yeah, I've thought of that too. In fact, I'd say there's a really strong chance he is lying."

"But you can't risk not going," Calina answered for me. "Just in case there's even the teeniest tiniest chance, right?"

"Exactly. And also..." I paused and patted my chest to soothe myself. "Also, something in me knows that he's not. Knows that G... That my partner is still out there. And that he needs me."

She cocked her head and pursed her lips for a few terse moments before speaking. "You know, because you love him. You can feel him out there."

"I do love him, but not like that. It was always different between us." Shame overwhelmed me at Calina's words. I did love Gaaron, and I should have felt him, should have known. Had I been selfish? Too focused on keeping myself safe that I had failed to rescue him?

"You loved him the way I love Rurik, right? Different than a lover, but not any less important." Calina rearranged her delicate features into an angry scowl. She was angry a lot, this one, and I'd never really stopped to wonder why.

Calina was waiting for an answer, and so I gave her the best one I could offer without giving too much away. "I did. I do. I really believe he's still out there."

She smiled and scooted closer to me. "Then I believe it too."

Calina looked so, so much like her mother. It was almost as if Brynlee was here with me now. And if she were, what would I tell her? Would I confide the truth in her?

No, I realized. Probably not.

And yet I so desperately wanted to make everything right, to bring this family back together, but I needed more time to do it and a better plan for how. Not just because we still had to finish our journey, but because, selfishly, I liked being the most important person in Brynlee's life outside of her daughter.

I liked being the third leg of their little stool.

When Brynlee had Gaaron back, she wouldn't need me anymore... or at least not quite as much. She would still be my whole world, but I would be relegated to only a small piece of hers. And what could any of us do with a single stool leg? It became useless when it was on its own.

I fingered the Genesis Crest and sighed.

For so long my past adventures had defined me, the hiding, the secrets, but now it was all coming to an end. I wouldn't be either of my past selves, and I felt too old to reinvent myself a third time.

Maybe I should have tried harder to get some more sleep last night.

"What are you thinking about?" Calina asked.

I stretched my arms overhead then rose to my feet and set some water to heat atop the fire before sitting back down beside my young companion.

"Well? Tell me what you're thinking about," she prompted, making it clear that I could not just dodge the questions I chose not to answer.

"I'm thinking about Rurik," I said, because it was easier than the truth and because Calina seemed to be in a relatively calm and introspective place for whatever reason. It would take a lot more to quell my inner demons, but maybe I could help the kid with hers. "And about Tulip."

She immediately tensed and pushed her heels into the ground. Her gaze swept the camp, searching, but Rurik was nowhere to be seen despite having slept outside. I hadn't spotted him when I first arose either. He was probably off on the top of some mountain, reading one of those spell books under the best possible morning light. Whatever the case, he wasn't here now, which made him safe for the two of us to discuss.

Calina turned back to me, her shoulders sagging under the weight of unseen problems. "He's my best friend, and he knows how awful she's always been to me. To us. How could he—how could he like her?"

"She's pretty," I said with a shrug. "You're pretty too," I then added, in case that was the problem. Calina claimed she and Rurik were just friends, but maybe that was starting to change now that his attention was focused elsewhere. Although to be very, very honest, Rurik would never win Tulip's heart, body, or any other part of her, no matter how many nights he let her sleep in his tent.

"I don't like that word, *pretty*. It's so dismissive and belittling, like if I'm pretty it's the only thing I can be. Looks don't matter to me, and Rurik isn't shallow like that either. There's something he likes about Tulip for her personality, if it can even be called that. I thought I knew him better than anyone, but this, I'll never understand. I'm trying, but it makes no sense, and usually Rurik is the most logical person I know. And before you go suggesting otherwise, I am *not* jealous. I don't want to be with Rurik or anyone else. I want to go on adventures and live my own life, not get all tied up in someone else's."

"I understand that probably better than anyone else in the whole world," I said.

Her eyes narrowed in confusion. "But you... don't you *like* like my mom?"

"It doesn't matter. I'm happy being her friend. Besides she's still very much in love with your dad."

Calina sighed. "Yeah. That's why I've decided love isn't in the cards for me. I want to play a different game, a better one."

"You don't have to commit to one game your entire life, you know. You're young yet. There are so many great adventures ahead of you. Maybe love is one of them. Maybe it isn't, but I've always found it best to go with the flow. You never know what games you'll be good at until you're actually invited to play them, right?"

"I guess." Calina let out a long breath, slowly deflating like a popped balloon. "It's frustrating though when you know you're the best and you should be the one who wins, but—"

"But some people have better luck. They start the game with better cards or more tokens."

Calina scrunched her pretty, little features into a grotesque mask. "You're talking about Tulip."

I just shrugged. "Just stuff I've learned along the way. The game is easier if you read the instruction manual first, understand the rules."

"I hate rules."

Yeah, well, that made two of us, but I was supposed to be the role model here, so I just smiled and nodded. "Yeah but knowing the rules inside and out makes them a lot easier to break."

Calina smiled too. "What game are we playing by the way?"

"Who knows?" My tea began to boil, and I hopped up to grab it from the fire, using the sleeve of my tunic to protect my hands. I blew across the hot liquid, eagerly anticipating the first sip. But it wasn't the right time to take it, not yet. Instead I focused on the fragrant scent, the comforting tickle of the steam, the beauty of the morning.

And then I turned to Calina and felt all of the love Brynlee had for her, her fierce desire not just to provide for her but also to nurture her into the person she was meant to be. It was an honor to be even a small part of that.

Then I said the thing she so desperately needed to hear. I said, "I don't know what game we're playing, but you know what? We're going to win it anyway."

She bumped me in the shoulder, then reached one long arm around me and pulled me into a side hug. "Yeah, we really are."

Oh, how I wished I would have believed the things I told her that morning, that I could make them true for myself as well as for her. I liked that our talk had helped, that Calina seemed less troubled now. But I had been living with my pain, shame, and regret for so long now that I didn't know who I would be without it. And that made it impossible to let go.

The part I'd failed to tell Calina was just how very hard it was to continue playing the game when you were certain that you'd already lost.

26

I drank my tea and got a much-needed pick-me-up. Calina stayed at my side but left me to my own thoughts. Much appreciated.

Rurik eventually staggered back from wherever he'd been but failed to tell us exactly where he'd gotten off to.

Even Amariel floated out to greet the morning, bringing a happy, little piccolo with her as she said her hellos.

In order to get back on the road, the four of us had to work together to drag Tulip from her tent, kicking and screaming. In the ensuing chaos, Rurik took a hoof to the chest, but his bludgeoning damage was quickly healed by our resident cleric.

And then we were back on the road!

Spirits were generally high, but Tulip had notably lost much of her zeal from the day before. Apparently it wasn't all that fun to play make-believe on your own—or at least not for a second day running.

Amariel had far more energy following a good night's rest and lesser demand for her magical talents—whether to heal injuries or navigate conveyances. She walked alongside us rather than hovering nearby or hitching a ride on Tulip's back.

Rurik, of course, took this opportunity to ask her an endless litany of questions: *How does your magic work? What spells do you know? Which do you think I should learn next? Are you able to heal an amputation? Can you teach me?*

Poor guy was still thinking of his parents back home. He longed to impress them, to gain their approval in his own way, even though they had different plans for his life. But would helping his father regrow an arm be enough to convince his folks that magic was a viable path?

Somehow I doubted it, but of course I kept that to myself.

Calina didn't speak much, just kept her focus on her bow as she fired arrows at any tree that dared to cross our path.

"You're getting better," I said after she'd nailed a birch burl right through its heart.

"Well, you aren't training us, so I'm improvising," was all she said before firing off another steel-tipped missile.

So much for our bonding experience that morning. I may have been quick on my feet, but that was nothing next to the rapidly shifting attitudes of these teenagers.

In my defense, I wasn't training them because we needed to spend every waking moment making tracks. My goal was to reach Nexara by early evening. This city was posh, the wealthiest in all of Verandel, meaning I'd never much cared for it. Yes, in theory there were lots of good items to steal. In practice, it was an entirely different matter altogether. It was hard to filch anything when others quickly spotted you as a ruffian vagabond adrift and out of her element. I hated that.

Twice, Finnian Sly had sent me to Nexara with a group of other young thieves under his stifling care. And twice, it had all gone horribly wrong. Each time at record-breaking speed, sending me running away with my tail tucked between my too-short legs. All that had happened before I'd fallen in with Gaaron, of course.

Things had gone far better with Gaaron at my side, although they'd ended terribly.

Now I was nearly back in Nexara, and I wasn't quite sure how to feel about it. Lately it felt like my life's timeline had folded in on itself, that I was repeating earlier events, trying to get a different outcome the second time around.

My return to this place would be brief. We just had to pass through the city that marked the halfway point of our journey and pray that Rurik didn't get sidelined by the prestigious University Nexus Arcana within its boundaries. It was the magic academy that gave Nexara all the things its citizens most celebrated. All of Verandel's top thinkers—and top earners—had walked through its halls, studied in its libraries, and done whatever else smart, rich people did when transitioning from adolescence to adulthood.

Rurik would go nuts for it. He would love all the people here as much as they detested the very idea of him. This kid wanted to be one of them, but he had the wrong parents, the wrong upbringing, and even the wrong biology. Luckily, he probably wouldn't notice their disdain, given how oblivious he was to Tulip's.

I'd have bypassed Nexara altogether if possible, but that would have added too much time to our trip. I was already more than a little concerned about making it to Maltherius by his deadline. I needed shortcuts, not long asides.

And so I did my best to focus on each step, each feel of my toes shifting within my boots as they struck the uneven ground. I really needed to stop worrying about what came next, or I would never get there—to our destination, to the future, to peace, to any of it.

We would either rise to meet the challenge, or we wouldn't. Worrying wouldn't change the outcome. I just had to keep showing up for these kids in whatever way I could.

And that gave me an idea.

"Hey, Tulip. That axe of yours is really amazing," I called to her.

Her blue eyes twinkled as she turned back to look at me. "Isn't it though?"

"It looks sharp."

"It's very sharp. Shiny too."

I spotted a thick stick with a notched head laying several paces ahead and raced forward to grab it. Once I had it, I worked the shaft into my grip and held it aloft in front of me with the hooked part jutting high to my left. "Can you hold it kind of like this?"

Tulip studied me for a moment with her jaw tense, then blessedly began to rearrange her favorite plaything in her hands. "Like this?" she asked in a poor approximation of my example.

"Almost." It wasn't close at all, but I knew telling her that would make Tulip quit in a fit of rage. And I needed to help her build skills whilst being mindful of her pride. What I really needed was to be able to manually manipulate her grip on the weapon myself, but there were several problems with that idea. First, the axe would be very heavy for me given its great size. Also I couldn't reach it. I didn't even come up to Tulip's flank, let alone her shoulder. And lastly, we needed to keep moving even while attempting to train. If we stopped for any length of time, we wouldn't reach Maltherius's lair in time for the solstice. And this all would have been for nothing.

I bit back a smile as a brilliant plan flashed across my mind.

"Rurik," I shouted so that he would hear me over the sound of his own booming voice, which hadn't paused for a single moment in its interrogation of Amariel and its owner's demand for new magical knowledge.

He stopped speaking abruptly and paused his step so that I could catch up with him.

"Do you know how to wield a great axe?"

He looked at me, then at Tulip, and a glowing blush lit his cheeks. "It's not my preferred weapon, but my parents made sure I knew how to use it. And a war hammer. And a spear. And—"

"I'm really only talking about the battle axe right now. Can you show Tulip how to hold it for maximum power when striking?" I mimed a strike with my sticky stand-in.

Calina re-equipped her bow and fell in a few paces behind us to watch. I couldn't see her expression, but I could feel the intensity of her curiosity. What would Rurik do? Who would he pick? Did he even have any idea what was going on apart from the impromptu battle lessons?

Tulip, bless her, had no idea any such power dynamics were being fought behind the scenes. She just held her axe out toward Rurik with both hands and bowed her head ever so slightly. "Be careful with it."

Rurik grinned as he accepted her offering. "Well," he said. "The main thing to remember when wielding an axe is to—"

"Whoa, look out!" Calina shouted before dropping back and flinging her arms out before her body in a protective stance.

A spear struck the spot where she'd been standing, burrowing its way into the ground like it was headed home. It had barely missed striking her. Which meant I had almost gotten Brynlee's daughter killed a third time. Had it even been that many days since we left?

Snap out of it, Tilda. It's not time to beat yourself up; it's time to fight.

I craned my neck to the sky just in time to see a regiment of wing scouts crash land in a broken moon shape as they closed in on our group.

Wing scouts outside Nexara. I should have anticipated it. The most ruthless of their kind tended to hang out around all the big population centers, and this was the biggest of them all.

The mercenaries before us weren't the ordinary civil servants we often called upon to deliver messages in Briarhaven. For one thing, our small-town variety worked solo while this group consisted of at least twelve assorted men and women. They also came bearing weapons, one in each hand, and incredibly menacing expressions.

Their group closed in on ours, pushing us together.

Calina snarled and rushed toward the nearest scout. "Leave us alone. We haven't done anything wrong!"

I admired her bravado, though I knew it was foolish. These weren't the simple scouts she knew. They were proven killing machines, who traded their battle skills for coin. And we had no idea who had hired them, which made them that much more menacing.

"What do you want with us?" I shouted in my most fearsome voice.

One among their rank stepped forward to size me up. She was not the tallest, nor was she the strongest or most beautiful, but she did appear to be the one in charge. "We're here to escort you to Mirathane. Will you come without a fight?"

"We're not going to Mirathane," Rurik said from somewhere behind me. "We're going to Malt—"

"Will you just hush, kid?" I hissed, cutting him off at the quick. The last thing I needed was for him to give our plans away. If the scouts were here to bring us to my old stomping grounds in Mirathane, then I had a pretty good idea who had hired them to escort us.

I really did seem to be an expert at pissing off powerful people who could hold intense grudges. I spat on the ground and crossed my arms over my chest to show that I wasn't afraid. We didn't have time for this. We were barely going to make it to Maltherius on time as it was; Mirathane was even farther from his lair than our starting point in Briarhaven had been.

No, no, no. This was not acceptable. We had one quest, and zero time for asides.

As the fear and irritation crashed into one another, I was left quite literally shaking in my boots. "What does Finnian want?"

"Our job is to collect you. Not to fill you in on all the details," the scout answered, appearing almost bored with the whole affair.

"Who's Finnian?" Tulip demanded of me, as if I had caused this delay on purpose.

"Isn't that the master thief who took you in when you were an orphan?" Rurik recalled. I assumed he looked thoughtful as he said it, but I refused to take my eyes off the looming threat that surrounded us.

I ignored my companions and dug in my heels, both literally and figuratively. It was good to be consistent like that. "I have no business with Finnian. Haven't in years."

"See, that's where you're wrong," the scout said with a smile as she drew a sword from each hip. "Deathly wrong, I'm afraid."

And then because my life was never ever easy, she gave a quick nod to the others.

They descended on all sides, outnumbering our group three to one in manpower and a million to one in battle prowess.

It would have been nice to go a single day without a life-or-death encounter... Yup, it certainly would have been nice.

But it was probably also never going to happen.

27

The wing scout with the swords spun her weapons in her hands as she approached slowly, a challenging glint in her eye—yeah, just one of her eyes. It was weird and made me wonder if one had maybe been lost in battle and replaced with a fake.

Partially blinded or not, she was still rather formidable. Not just because she loomed over me, but also because I knew what it took to earn her rank. Hundreds of young, misguided adventurers died each year trying to achieve the honor, which meant the few that actually managed it were the toughest of the tough.

A scout got its wings by slaying a griffin and

claiming its hide as a mantle to wear atop their armor. Once inducted into the ranks, the cloistered heads of the organization then enchanted the felled wings granting the new wearer the gift of flight. This secret ritual enchantment also imbued the initiate scout with the strength of the lion and the keen sight of the eagle.

Which is part of the reason I found it so curious that this one appeared to have a handicap to what was usually among a wing scout's greatest strengths.

She was still about to kill me though, so I needed to snap out of my woolgathering and focus on the immediate and very real threat looming before me.

The only thing I had going for me was my quick-thinking... and possibly my party if they could pull themselves together in time to be useful. But the battle with the siphons taught me they were just as likely to attack each other as they were our opponents. I'd been so eager to see Gaaron again that I hadn't been focused enough on teaching them the ropes. My fault, yes, but it still meant I couldn't exactly count on the party. So far, we were a "party" in name only. I'd need to work hard to change that, should we survive our current kerfuffle.

For now, I'd have to rely on myself; this would all come down to wits then.

I knew we couldn't win against the wing scouts, which made me long for our previous battle with the kobolds. How easy they'd been to dispatch, what great memories.

If we couldn't win the battle, then I had to do my part to make sure it never even happened. I had to talk our way out of this one—and fast.

"Hey, scruffy!" I shouted even though the scout was now standing little more than a sword's reach away from me. "Finnian's not going to like it very much if you bring him my corpse. Pretty sure if he sent you all this way to retrieve me, that he'd rather have me alive."

The swords stopped spinning. The wing scout blinked, but only one eyelid fully closed. Ah-ha, I'd been right about that one thing, at least. Hopefully my other bid would pay out as well.

"How much is he paying you?" I pressed, moving forward as if unafraid. Honestly, I was terrified, but part of making a good negotiation is always keeping the upper hand—even if that hand was shaking like crazy. "I bet we could pay you more. Not in coin, but in treasure. How much will it cost to make you forget you ever saw us?"

"Tilda!" Tulip neighed and stomped. "You can't just give away my things."

Ugh, of course my party would prove a liability. I didn't have time to reason with the spoiled kid, but I knew she wouldn't let me ignore her either. "Who says I'm giving away your things?" I mumbled, keeping my gaze keenly fixed on the enemy.

"I'm the only one who has anything of value. Of course you're giving away my things, and I don't much appreciate it." Tulip snorted, and it sounded like she may have reached for her axe. But I didn't turn to look.

The next thing I knew, the wing scout flapped her massive wings and in an instant she fell upon the centaur's back, holding both swords beneath her throat. My eyes followed her, quick to confirm that—yes—the idiot princess had pulled out her massive weapon during what I was hoping to keep a peaceful showdown.

The scout snarled, ignoring Tulip's whimpers of protest. "Our order is to deliver you, Tilda Quick-thatch. Alive, yes. But our orders have nothing to do with your companions. And my swords are so, so thirsty." She pressed one of the blades into Tulip's porcelain skin and drew out a fat, scarlet droplet of blood.

This was not going well for us. I was just about to yield, demanding they take me and let the kids head home, when—*whoosh!*—Rurik sent a fireball crashing into the scouts' one-eyed leader and knocking her off our centaur friend.

Okay, not a fireball. That same weak flame cantrip he always used, mostly because it was the only spell he could muster. Regardless, it was enough to light the feathered mantle ablaze.

As soon as she hit the ground, the scout jumped back to a standing position, lifted her arms overhead, and hopped. She'd clearly meant to take flight, but she couldn't. Rurik's measly magic had broken the enchantment.

This luck was dumb, yet in my favor yet again. Could these fearsome warriors really be so easily defeated?

The wing scout growled and then began spinning her swords again. Oh, right, she still had her skills and experience even without the added touch of magic. And now she was powered by rage on top of that all.

Her buddies closed in, each drawing a different kind of weapon. One started chanting a spell that caused vines to burst through the soil and ensnare my feet. Once they had my feet, they climbed up my legs and torso and wrapped around my shoulders. I struggled against the vines, but it was clear there would be no breaking free.

I watched as Tulip stomped and smashed the bonds before they could take hold of her.

Rurik used his flame to prevent them from climbing past his knees, but he was also burning himself in the process.

"Stop!" I shouted, having to raise my chin to make sure my voice didn't get muffled by the thick earthy wall that had more or less devoured me by this point. Only my eyes and the tippity top of my head remained free and unblocked. "We'll stop fighting you. Just take us to Finnian, so we can be done with this already."

"We will take you to him, but first you must pay for the damage you did to my mantle," the sword-wielding scout hissed. For one appearing so human, she certainly made a lot of animal noises. I wondered if that had anything to do with her missing eye.

"Hold him," she crowed, then charged with all her might.

Even if I could have broken free, I still had no time to act. Every last scout converged on Rurik, working together with the vines to hold him in place and nullify both his novice-level magic and his great strength.

The lead scout smiled cruelly, and her one eye flashed with sinister glee as she reached forward and tore one of Rurik's tusks from his jaw.

He remained stoic, but both Calina and Tulip

cried out on his behalf. Blood gushed down, saturating his shirt and dripping from the vines. Oh sweet mother of all creation, I really hoped Amariel could heal that for him!

The vile scout just smiled and waved her prize in front of Rurik's face. "This will make a lovely addition to my battle necklace." She remained rooted before the wounded half-orc, greedily fingering her necklace of battle trophies as she turned to call back to her allies. "We've already wasted far too much time on this bounty. Let's take the whole group back to Mirathane, so we can be done with this whole cursed charade."

A winged druid made a large sweeping motion with his hands and sent each of our ensnared bodies crashing into one another, then the other scouts resumed their crescent moon formation and joined hands. The one-eyed devil who'd ripped out Rurik's fang pressed herself up against me and waited.

And then the chanting began. It seemed to be spoken in Infernal, but I didn't know the language well enough to discern the words. Smoke began to swirl around us, completely clouding my vision.

Whether it lasted a moment or a millennia, I honestly couldn't say. But eventually, the chanting stopped, and little by little the smoke cleared away.

My limbs and torso were still held in place by vines.

Nearby I spotted the axe-like stick I had made into an example weapon for Tulip. Patches of dirt and uprooted flowers covered the ground. But they didn't belong here, and neither did we.

The wing scouts had performed a teleportation ritual. They'd brought us indoors. To Mirathane. To Finnian Sly, my old mentor and jailor in one.

The winged druid waved a hand, making the magic vines shrivel and fade from existence. I fell to my knees and gasped, taking in a full chest's worth of dank, musty air.

The scouts dispersed with the vines. I didn't get a chance to see where they were headed. At my sides the kids choked on the stale air. One of them cried. I couldn't find Amariel. Had they let her behind? Taken her somewhere else?

Or had she been the one to offer up our location to the scouts? My stomach churned at the possibility of her betrayal. The ancient celestial had been irritating, yes, but she hadn't seemed bad. Had I gotten it all wrong?

"It's okay," I told the kids, doing my best to keep the fear from my voice. "This is just a minor detour. I'll have us out of here in no time."

I reached into my pocket to retrieve my favorite lock-pick, but only felt fabric beneath my fingers.

Laughter rose from the shadows on the other side of the room. "Tilda, please, don't insult me. I know you, you sneaky, little trickster. After all, I'm the one who made you, aren't I?"

That voice. I thought I'd never hear it again, but now it chilled my veins and threatened to stop my heart. I lunged across the space until a wall of thick, rusted iron bars forced me to halt.

"Welcome home, Tilda. It has been such a long time, my child."

My lock-pick held aloft in his hand caught a faint glint of torchlight, shining back at me, mocking the fact it had moved from my reach. Just like with Gaaron. Just like before. I couldn't escape. I couldn't save my companions.

Next I saw his shining obsidian eyes, the matching thief's mask. Cunning was so innate in his being that Finnian Sly had been born with a burglar's mask stuck permanently upon his face. He was not from this place. He was not from anywhere within Verandel. As a tanuki, Finnian Sly had spawned from a land so distant he could never hope to return to it in this lifetime.

His thick, bushy tail flicked up and down as he regarded me now. And he hummed a merry tune onto himself. I recognized it as one that Gaaron had favored in our early days together.

Finnian had chosen it on purpose to unnerve me, to defeat me before I ever had the chance to mount a defense. He knew what he wanted, and he also knew that he would get it. He knew how to break me. After all, he was the one who had built me in the first place.

28

I became so transfixed on Finnian's shadowy gaze that the rest of the world fell away for a short while. It wasn't until Calina appeared at my side, her knuckles white as she gripped tight to the iron bars, that I jerked into the present moment. I pushed the heels of my boots into the uneven floor and settled back into my body, while Calina yanked and tugged at the cage with all her might. But her efforts had no effect, other than to make our tanuki captor giggle with glee.

"Who are you? Why have you taken us?" she demanded with sharp eyes and an unforgiving set to her jaw.

"He's Finnian Sly," Rurik answered from behind us, although with the gaping wound left in place of his missing tusk, the words came out quite garbled. Poor kid sounded as if he were drowning in his own blood, and maybe he was.

Calina hesitated before turning back toward her friend. I turned too, surprised to find that Tulip was already there to comfort our wounded warrior.

She'd lain her horse belly on the ground and pulled the half-orc into her flank. She now ran her fingers through his dark mohawk and long ponytail as she made soft, breathy noises to soothe him. "Don't talk until Amariel has the chance to heal you," she cooed in a way that sounded so unlike her usual self I had to do a double take.

Nothing seemed real anymore, and yet here we were.

"Nuh-no," Rurik said as he pulled himself away from Tulip's nurturing embrace—this too came as a surprise. "I don't want her to heal me. I want my parents to see that I faced battle and was brave. I want them to be proud."

At least, I thought that's what he said, because again, he was still fighting back a steady flow of the red stuff. It seemed his mouth wasn't the only part of him to be bleeding. He was choosing to live with this disfiguring pain for even the mere hopes that his parents would approve. Would I have been willing to do the same for my parents if they'd lived?

I would never know, and that would have to be okay.

The tanuki snickered at us again. He was always laughing to himself, as if he found everything and everyone he encountered to be some kind of great joke. "Taking after your old pa. Aren't you, Tilda? Collecting children, sending them in to do your bidding. Hmm? But what will you do now that your big muscle has a nasty tear in him?"

"Shut up," I spat, and my shoulders heaved with the sudden, returned weight of the anger I'd let fester for years and years. I'd stolen many a thing in my day, but Finnian, he had stolen my entire childhood from me. My innocence. And any chance I had of making a better future. I'd run from him then—run as far as I could get—but now I realized that I had never quite escaped his grasp. Finnian's lessons had stuck, and his sticky fingers had continued to reach out for me across the distance of both space and time.

And here we were together. Again. Always.

"Where's Amariel?" Now that Rurik had removed himself from her comfort, Tulip clip-clopped across the craggy stone floor as she ambled to a standing position and moved about the narrow cell. "Look here, you nasty fox-man. If you hurt her, I'll bash your skull in!"

Finnian drew back with a sharp intake of breath, then pressed his face close to the bars on his exhale. "Ouch. Both a nasty insult and a threat in the same breath. I like this one, Tilly."

"*Where. Is. She?*" Tulip demanded, pushing a heavy snort through her nostrils between each word and scraping her hooves against the ground to further underscore her demand.

The tanuki clapped his hands together and hooted. "Yes, I like her very much. I shall keep this one, I think. What's your name, my beautifully blood-thirsty darling?"

Tulip screamed as she approached the bars then turned in the tight space and kicked out with both rear legs at full horse-power. But it just wasn't enough to dislodge the heavy iron bars.

"I'll kill you and turn your hide into a scarf that I only wear on the most wretched of occasions," she half-screamed, half-neighed. "Tell me what you did with her, and tell me right now!"

"So touchy." Finnian chuckled again and ran one clawed finger along the bars. "I'm only trying to make friends. Now, it would really be so nice if you'd introduce yourself, dear."

Calina darted to the side and grabbed hold of his little, black finger before he had the chance to pull away. "Her name is Tulip Thunderhoof, okay? Now just tell us what you did with Amariel, then you can tell us why you took us and what you want."

The tanuki yanked his arm back and then held the assaulted hand to his chest and tutted. "The celestial is safe in her own anti-magic containment chamber. Rest assured, you will all be reunited later. Once you understand and have agreed to the plan."

Taken, but safe.

I assumed the same went for our supplies. My lockpick wasn't the only thing that had been foisted from us. All our weapons and camp gear had also been taken away. I assumed Finnian had already raided our stash for valuables, which meant Tulip's bedazzled battle axe and the new daggers Pat had gifted me had already been looted and were unlikely to be returned.

The daggers. I hadn't even gotten the chance to use them.

But I would. I would. I'd outsmarted this master thief before, and I could do it again. The sooner I got him to reveal his intentions, the sooner I could foil them—and free us.

"What plan?" I did my best to sound uninterested, or at least, only vaguely curious. Finnian was great at reading people, especially those he already knew well. I had to keep a mask drawn firmly on my face if I wanted to keep the upper hand.

"All in good time, my child." The tanuki smiled revealing sharp white fangs within his tight black smile. "First let me set the stage, then I shall issue the call to adventure."

"We're already on an adventure," Calina interjected with a snarl that reminded me of the one-eyed wing scout who'd brought us here. "And you're interrupting it."

Finnian hung back a pace, cautious with Calina now. "This is not an interruption. It's an about-face, dear. Time to go on a bigger adventure, to tell a better story. *Mine.*"

I was not surprised that Finnian had taken a quick liking to Tulip; they both had a flair for the dramatic, and they both put themselves first and all others at a far distant second. Tulip's concern first for Amariel—and now also Rurik—showed she had heart where Finnian had only ever possessed a deep-seated greed.

"You were a difficult quarry to track, Tilda Quickthatch. Quite difficult, indeed. I don't know whether I should feel more irritated or proud. But I did always know we would find each other again. I'm a bit hurt I was the only one who was looking, but children don't always appreciate their parents quite like they should."

"My parents are dead."

"Papa's here, Tilly. I've always been right here, awaiting your inevitable return."

I hated him. I hated him so much. He wouldn't even let me keep my parents in name only. Finnian had never been satisfied unless he'd stolen everything, even the things that weren't really worth taking. Perhaps, especially those.

"Let us go." I slammed my palms flat against the bars. He already knew he'd gotten to me, so I had no reason to hide my upset. Letting some of it out made me feel a bit better.

My old master hung his head and laughed sadly. "If only it were that easy. I owned you then, and I own you now, Tilly. The first time you wronged me, I looked the other way. I let you leave with Gaary, Bluth, and Rami. Gave you the space to strike out on your own. Every child eventually goes through its rebellion, but they all come back whether by choice or by force. I let you leave, but you never came back. Why was that, Tilda? Your betrayal hurt your old pa so. But I am nothing if not a magnanimous creature, and so I gave you and ol' Gaary a second chance, didn't I? An opportunity to set everything right again, but then he was captured and you disappeared. And, yes, I must confess I did worry then, but eventually I remembered who you were, reminded myself that you couldn't stay away forever. And would you just look at us now? True, our reunion was late coming, but now that it is here we shall celebrate to the fullest."

Calina let her hands fall from the bars and hang limply at her sides. "What's he talking about, Tilda? Who's he talking about?"

"You may address me with your questions directly, granddaughter. I am only too happy to explain how my Tilly, the brightest and best of all my children, took my songbird and together they failed the most important mission I'd ever given to them. Why, that I'd ever assigned anyone for that matter."

"Your partner?" Calina kept her eyes and words both focused on me, but I could see the tanuki had gotten through to her. Finnian loved a good monologue, and I could tell he was only just getting started with this one. If Calina hadn't made the missing connection yet, she would within minutes. And then what?

I so badly wanted to explain, to tell her what had happened, why I'd chosen to keep the secret. But how could I without revealing our plans to Finnian? He took all he could see, and if he discovered our plans, he would no doubt co-opt them. Corrupt them.

He was the last partner I wanted on the quest to save Gaaron. Yes, even less than my unskilled and unpredictable group of teenagers. Calina, Rurik, and Tulip were immature, but they had the right stuff. The heart of a hero. Finnian would find the soft flesh and devour it with his sharp teeth and even sharper tongue. I couldn't let him hurt them the way he had hurt me. I couldn't let him stand in the way of our rescue mission. Gaaron had already waited so long.

I didn't know what I could say to balance comforting Calina with keeping Finnian in the dark, and so I remained regrettably quiet.

And Finnian delighted in his continued spotlight. He let out a soft, raspy chuckle before continuing. "Do try a little harder to keep up, child. Tilly and Gaary were meant to sneak into Maltherius's lair and rid him of the Genesis Crest. They were my best thieves, and I thought they could handle the job. But no!" Finnian's voice rose to a shout so suddenly, it caused both me and Calina to fall back in fright. It took another moment before his words fully registered.

"Maltherius? The Genesis Crest? The anonymous quest giver, that was you?" Now I was the one with questions, it seemed. We'd broken free of Finnian's house of thieves many years prior to that quest. I'd never thought to connect the two in my mind.

"Come now, dear. We both know you wouldn't have accepted the quest, had you known it came from me. And I needed that artifact. I still need it, in fact. It was a quest you accepted, and it is one I intend for you to complete."

Rurik spoke up then. "We already have—"

"We already have a quest that we're in the middle of," I quickly course-corrected. I still didn't know what all the Genesis Crest could do, but I knew enough to understand that it should never fall into Finnian Sly's grasp. Rurik was too honest and trusting for his own good—or for mine. "You'll have to wait your turn."

I surreptitiously patted at my bosom to check for the artifact. Finnian had rid us of our cargo, but had he also managed to take the Genesis Crest off my person? Yes, I realized, with a heavy heart. The crest hadn't let the undead sorcerer remove it from my body, but it had willingly gone with Finnian.

And yet he had no idea the object he'd so desperately sought for a great many years was already in his possession...

<h1 style="text-align:center">29</h1>

"What does this Genesis Crest do? Why do you want it so badly?" As I spoke, I crinkled my nose, leaning into my hatred and disgust in hopes that I could hide my curiosity and surprise.

"Nuh, uh, uh." Finnian grinned and waved a pointed finger at me. "One must never tell a hired thief the true value of their target. Things just get messy when you do. All you need to know is that the crest is mine, and I expect you to retrieve it for me."

He brought his claws near his face and scowled as if inspecting them for dirt. Then flicked off a speck and sighed. "Or die, your choice."

I must admit, I strongly considered the "or die" part of the bargain. For the moment, the crest was safe from both of the evil forces that wanted to do something big, terrible, and unknown with it. I also knew that if Finnian and Maltherius were both this committed in their quest for the artifact, others would undoubtedly come searching for it as well.

My death would be such a small price to keep the larger continent safe. My tiny life wasn't worth all that much, really. But the kids were another matter entirely. I simply couldn't bring myself to surrender them to my former master in either life or death. Not even if it meant saving the whole of Verandel.

There had to be another way.

I had to fight for them even though I couldn't yet see a way to win. And this turned my mind back to the conversation with Calina at the campfire that morning. Her surety that this was all a game, and it was one we were going to win. Had she believed me when I'd said all that? Could I bring myself to believe it now?

"I'll help you," Calina said. My heart dropped to the floor when I realized it wasn't me she was talking to this time. "I'll gladly go and get the artifact for you, Finnian Sly, but first I need you to answer a few questions."

The tanuki scoffed at her and began examining the claws of his other hand for dirt. He'd always been fastidious when it came to his hygiene, and I easily recognized the tell. We were getting under his skin. His meticulous ministrations comforted him, gave him back some semblance of control in a situation he feared was getting out of hand. Finnian's eyes narrowed coldly at the elf girl as he spoke. "I do not know you. I'm also not quite sure I like you. And thus I cannot tell you of the crest's power. Quite simply put, it is not for you to know."

"I don't care about the stupid crest." Calina raised her hands and limply clung to the bars that separate them. Her next words were spoken without their usual bluster. She appeared weak, pained. "I want to hear more about Tilda's old partner. About Gaary."

Finnian grinned, dropped both hands to his side, and tilted his chin upward as if combing through all the possible responses before selecting the one that would best manipulate Calina into doing his bidding. He was back in power now, and he knew it.

Which meant this was my last chance to intervene. I'd always been quick on my toes and quicker still when it came to my mind, but when I opened my mouth to speak, all that came out was, "Calina, please. I..."

All the apologies and explanations got stuck as if dammed inside. How desperately I wanted to break it down, but I just couldn't. Years of hiding secrets had made it a challenge to freely share them now.

Calina had no such problems however. Thick tears flooded her violet eyes, then whooshed down like a storm, drenching her fair, freckled cheeks. I counted the tears as they fell, leaving angry splotches on the stone floor below. "How could you, Tilda? I trusted you. My mom trusted you!"

The world went still. Once again I was stuck, neither here nor there. Brynlee had trusted me. Gaaron had trusted me. The kids had trusted me. Even I had once trusted me. But I'd let each and every one of them down.

Such was my lot in life, and there was no redirecting fate once she'd made her mind up about you.

Tiny feet scurried across the dungeon floor and a serious of amused squeaks came with them. I glanced down and saw a fat rat with a furry mask and long, naked tail had joined us in the cell.

Poof! Finnian shifted back into his base form and lay a conciliatory hand on Calina's shoulder.

"Oh, you dear child. It is so hard when those we trust, don't trust us. It's not your fault. My Tilly has always been this way. She was always out for herself, and it seems she still is. In fact, in all her many years, she only ever truly allied with Gaary, and look where that got him. Stuck in a dank necromancer's dungeon. Praying for death, I'd wager, but also knowing it will never come. Hmm. Tell me, what is Gaary to you?"

"He's my dad," Calina sobbed and leaned into the master thief's touch. "He's got to be. I just know it."

Rurik cleared his throat and spat. His words came clearer this time, which I took to mean that the wound was finally closing up a bit. "I have a book that belonged to him. With writing in the margins. I can show you if it would help to confirm."

Finnian glanced toward Rurik briefly but then locked eyes with Calina again, laying a second hand on her shoulder and pulling her close so that their faces were practically touching. "Books, who needs books? Your heart knows what's true, doesn't it, child? Your Tilda knew it too, but all this time and she chose not to tell you. Yes, yes. I can't say this comes as a surprise to ol' Finnian."

Calina leaned forward the rest of the way and pressed her forehead against the tanuki's. More tears fell and soaked his fur. "Tell me about him. He left when I was so small. I don't remember much, but I'd give anything to know him."

"Anything?" I couldn't see his face, but I could hear the machinations behind that one word, hear the rusty cogs grind and hiss as they powered to life, working to activate a new plan. A plan I could guarantee that none of us would like.

"Calina, no. Don't trust him!" I shouted meekly, knowing it would not be enough.

"You say that, but he's the first one to be truly honest with me. You, my mom, you both kept him from me." She wouldn't even look at me as she spat her venomous reply. It was then I knew I'd truly lost her, that I'd failed myself and Brynlee.

"You're stupid, but not this stupid, Calina," Tulip huffed. "Stop talking to this literal villain stereotype. Stop it right this instant!"

"Pah, don't listen to them. I would never lie to you, my dear."

I watched in horror as Finnian shifted his shape yet again. This time, he turned himself into a near replica of Gaaron at the same age I'd last seen him. It was a perfect approximation except the unmistakable mask around his eyes where the skin was discolored and slightly darker than the rest. With enough time to prepare, Finnian could easily disguise the tell-tale tanuki mask with face paints. He'd used his magical gifts and natural charm to take the place of many powerful men and women in his day, but I'd never seen him take the shape of someone I knew personally and missed terribly.

Even though I knew the human man standing before me wasn't my long-lost partner, I still had to hold myself back. I had to keep from running to him and wrapping my arms around him.

But that longing quickly dissipated when he spoke. Finnian couldn't change his voice along with his body, and it sickened me to hear the vile thief's words spill forth from my friend's lips.

"Your father was a good man and a bard of great renown. I never understood why he kept such close company with Tilda. He could have done so much better, and from the gorgeous, good looks of you my dear, he did."

He was calling Calina pretty. She hated that. Would it be enough to free her from his spell? The only magic Finnian could wield was that of changing his own shape, but he was a practiced thief, skilled in the art of manipulation, especially when it came to children.

And he'd now glimpsed Calina's most ardent desire—to be reunited with her father. He would exploit that from every single angle until it ruined us all.

She shook her head sadly but stayed close. If his new appearance affected her, Calina didn't show it. I wondered if she remembered Gaaron well enough to even recognize his likeness. "No, I'm not like my mom. I never have been."

"Oh, but you are so very much like young Gaary. I see him in you," Finnian said while wearing his knock-off version of Gaaron's skin.

Calina sighed, then nodded slowly with big, exaggerated movements as if it were all suddenly coming together for her now. Whatever she said next would decide everything. I knew it in my bones. And I feared it, just as I also deserved whatever came next.

"We're on our way to save him," she revealed with a sniff as she wiped at the drying remains of her earlier tears. "I just didn't know it was him we'd be saving until right now. Until *you* were honest with us, Finnian."

Finnian shifted back into his tanuki self and tilted his head thoughtfully. "You were already headed to Maltherius. Why?"

"I already told you." Calina's brows pinched together before her forehead smoothed again. "To save my dad."

Finnian drew both of his hands before him and began to pick at his nails, twisting his hands quickly as he worked. "But why after all this time? Why all of a sudden?"

Calina glanced at me forlornly. Her mouth was sad

and still, but her eyes appeared busy and alive. It was strange to see the two halves of her face in disagreement, and I couldn't quite work out what it meant. But she continued to stare at me without speaking and without giving away whatever was going on inside.

When Finnian turned away to follow Calina's gaze, she tossed me a wink. The gesture came so fast I couldn't be sure I'd witnessed it at all. But it was enough to suggest that maybe she was still on my side after all.

30

"I'll tell you everything I know, but there's a lot I still don't know. I was hoping you could help maybe fill in some of the blanks." Calina shrugged then mirrored Finnian's hands with her own, winding her fingers around each other as she cast her eyes to the ground apologetically. I couldn't tell whether she was doing this on purpose to win him over or whether it had been a mistake.

Becoming conscious of his behavior now, Finnian stopped and tucked his hands deep into his trouser pockets.

Calina continued to twist and wring her hands. "My friend Rurik and I..." She twisted at her waist and turned to point to the aforementioned half-orc, who waved and tried to smile but then winced when it caused him too much pain.

"The two of us," Calina continued, dropping her hands now. "We figured out Tilda's secret. You know about her past as an adventurer. We figured it out, and we blackmailed her into helping us become adventurers too. And when we were training, this giant dragon flew overhead. I guess it belonged to the Maltherius guy we're supposedly all after? Anyway, he found her and demanded she come see him before the solstice. And then Rurik and I demanded that we come too. Because, I mean, what better way to learn than by doing? Tilda fought us on it, but eventually we convinced her to let us come."

Finnian bobbed his head as he took this all in. "And what of the centaur? How does she factor into all this?"

"Hello, I'm right here!" Tulip snorted and stomped but continued to be ignored.

Calina cast her eyes to the ceiling and shook her head. "She just kind of just happened along the way. The celestial came with her as kind of a package deal."

Now Finnian began to pace up and down the narrow cell. One hand came out of his pocket to caress his chin. "But why? Why does Maltherius insist upon a visit?"

I could see Calina struggling against her urge to follow the tanuki as he walked the length of the cell. She was cunning and clever, I'd give her that, but she was also inexperienced and trying way too hard. If she managed to shine a mirror on Finnian's manipulation tactics and blast the spell right back at him, it would be more to his own blindness than her skill. Still, I had to hand it to her, Calina had gotten farther than I would have on my own. She had also had me fooled. I'd believed in her betrayal with every fiber of my being until, at last, she'd revealed her hand. What did that say about me, that I could so easily believe my friends would abandon me?

"That's a good question, and we don't have an answer," Calina said thoughtfully. It took me a second to realize she was answering the question Finnian had spoken aloud and not the one I'd wondered at internally. "I guess like you, Maltherius doesn't like to reveal his full plan. Honestly, we were probably headed straight into a death trap until you saved us."

Back and forth, they parried. It was either one's match.

"Yes, he is a worthy opponent. One I have not yet managed to best despite so many well-spun attempts." Finnian stopped pacing and began to finger the coarse hairs on his bushy tail.

Calina remained still, single-minded with her mind solely on her words now. "He told us he had my dad. Gaaron. He said we could come get him. Well, really the message was just for Tilda, but again we insisted on coming too. And it's a good thing we did, since she's obviously been lying to us this whole time. What if she wasn't even going to save my dad?"

My throat burned with the heat of the defensive retorts I knew better than to speak. I had to trust Calina, no matter how much her words pained me.

She hooked one eyebrow as she leveled with the tanuki. "Tilly says she didn't know he was alive. But you knew, didn't you? Earlier, you said he was captured. Not that he had died."

"Yes, I know a great many things. There's a reason I am the master thief and little Tilly is a thief no more." A smile played at the end of his snout. It was coming to a close now. Soon either Calina or Finnian would emerge victorious over the other. I still didn't know who held the better hand, the upper hand.

"Can you help save my dad?" The elf girl asked pointedly.

Finnian chuckled drolly at this. "Child, please understand. I command an army of thieves, but I do not march among them."

"Can you send your army with us? I just know we can save my dad if you're on our side."

"I could be swayed to help, but what's in it for me?" He moved toward her swift as a shadow; whereas, before they had stood head-to-head, Finnian now loomed above her. I hadn't even noticed him adjust his shape.

To her credit, Calina did not blink, cower, or hesitate. "You want that crest thingy, right? Since we're already headed to Maltherius's place, we can grab it for you. Easy-peezy."

The staid expression on Finnian's face showed that he knew it was anything but easy. Still, he continued to humor Calina. "You mentioned the solstice?"

She nodded. Calina's words came a little quicker now, telling me we were losing ground in this battle against my old ally and foe. "Yes, that's the deadline he gave Tilda. Does it mean anything to you?"

Finnian shrugged as if none of this really mattered much in the scheme of things. "Possibly. Hmm. Maltherius may have a spell planned. It's a very powerful day, the solstice, at least for us magic types. More than that though, it means we have plenty of time. Yes, yes, more than enough time. I will help you on your rescue mission, but first you four will help me. Your celestial too, so make it five. We still have a good many sunrises left before the solstice. Complete my errand, prove I can trust you, and then you will have my aid for what's next."

Calina took a deep breath and kept the air held high in her chest for several beats before at last she let it go and spoke. "An ally like you is worth having, no matter the cost. We will gladly accept your errand." This didn't sound like the impetuous, strong-headed girl I knew, but it didn't sound like her defeat either.

The game was still being decided.

"Tell us of what we can do for you, Finnian."

My old master smiled. The grin started beneath his nose and crept back along his snout until it had also encircled his ringed eyes. He was all in now, which meant he believed he had won this stand-off with Calina. I still wasn't quite so sure.

"A thief's life is not an easy one, child. Many come and most go, fizzling out like a shooting star. *Zip, flash, boom.* They die off just as quickly as they are born. Understand?"

Calina nodded and gestured for him to continue.

Now I was the one fiddling with my hands. One pulled at the inseam of my pocket, groping and twisting, while the other caressed the soft under flesh of my wrist; it was where the bracelet Brynlee had entrusted to me once lay clasped, but Finnian had taken it along with the rest of our valuables. Half of me was pure anxiety but the other half represented faith. The bracelet was gone, but what it represented was not.

Neither Tulip nor Rurik bothered to speak. They saw, just as I did, that Calina was leading us now. That the more of us got involved in this battle of wits against Finnian Sly, the more opportunities he would have to exploit our weaknesses, to turn us against each other.

That, or they were too tired, too afraid. Perhaps they had finally realized how out of their element they were with this whole adventuring thing. Funny how sometimes we had to learn the same lessons again and again before they finally stuck.

But would it stick this time?

"To truly endure, a thief must not be a star but rather like the sun. He needs a network orbiting around him, each with unique strengths and assets. Moons, if you will. Hmm." Finnian stopped speaking and frowned for a moment before his face lit up again and he continued. "And while I do enjoy a good metaphor, this one is quickly growing thin. So, let me begin again. Most thieves run away or die. Those that endure are truly special. For the longest time, I thought Tilda was special like that... until she disappointed me so greatly that I had to admit I'd been wrong in my estimation of her. I do so hate being wrong."

"What if you weren't wrong though? What if—"

"No, that's not the point. It's never been the point." The tanuki tutted and shook his head. "None of this is about Tilly. It's never been about her. It's about something far more important. It's about me."

Nobody was looking at me, so I rolled my eyes extra hard.

Calina swallowed but kept her voice steady and nonjudgemental. "Go on."

"I am the greatest thief of them all. Perhaps the greatest thief ever. And yet there is always room for improvement. Hmm? My record is nearly flawless. Nearly!" He grabbed one of the bars and tugged at it in a sudden outburst of rage, then recomposed himself by grabbing and stroking his tail.

"Only twice have I been bested, and with your help, I can rewrite both of those past mistakes. I can erase the black marks from my record, if you will."

"We will. What do you need?"

"Finishing the quest for the Genesis Crest will come when the time set forth by Maltherius arrives, but it is not the wrong we must right first. First, we must lay siege to the Mystwood Keep."

"Keep? As in castle?" Calina spat, blinking hard. "You want us to storm an honest-to-goodness castle?"

"Storm? Oh, heavens no. Do you take me for

some General laying siege to an opposing army? No, my sweet, you see, soldiers storm, thieves slink. And today, you are a daughter among thieves. You will not siege, but rather you will infiltrate the castle, and there you will reclaim what has been stolen from me."

"And what's that?"

"Why, it's the most valuable thing any creature can possess."

"Like a crown or scepter or something?"

"My pride, child. You shall reclaim my pride."

"I don't..."

"Tomorrow! At dawn, my henchmen shall outfit you with the necessary gear and then we will form our strategy. You will go, and I shall wait here for the triumphant return of my glory. Dream sweetly tonight, children, for I cannot promise that tomorrow will be without its share of nightmares."

Finnian dropped to the floor in an abrupt shift to his rat form and scurried out of the dungeon, leaving us to ourselves.

"What just happened?" Tulip demanded, but her words didn't hold their usual heat.

"I'm sorry," Calina mumbled. "I thought if I could get into his head, that we—"

"It's fine," I said, refusing to let the girl apologize

for my mistakes. "It's fine. You did good, Calina. Your mother would be proud, and so would your dad."

She sniffed and smiled at me with a fresh swell of unshed tears. "I understand why you didn't tell me, but I still don't like it."

"I know. Just give me the chance to make it up to you?" I hung my head. This was more than I deserved—her friendship, her forgiveness, if not quite her understanding. She was so much like both her parents that it made my heart swell with love for all three of them.

"Oh, I'm counting on it." And then, before I had the chance to dart out of the way, Calina's arms wrapped around me, and she lifted me in a tight hug. "We're going to win this, Tilda. We're going to win," she whispered.

And this time, I'm pretty sure I believed her...

WHAT?!
Don't stop here.
Find out what happens next in *That's The Way The Castle Crumbles*, available now.
Order your copy today!

THAT'S THE WAY THE CASTLE CRUMBLES

The gang is back and at the behest of the tanuki master thief, Finnian Sly. Their original rescue mission must wait as they first work on restoring something far more important--a certain someone's injured pride.

Their new mission is clear: infiltrate Mystwood Keep, depose its regent, and try not to die in the process. Formerly retired halfling rogue Tilda Quick-thatch is, unfortunately, quick to realize they're all in way over their heads with this one.

Can she turn her ragtag group into real-life heroes? *Maybe.* All it will take is:

✔ Teaching would-be-wizard Rurik how to master a level-two cantrip.

✔ Convincing centaur barbarian Tulip to fight even if she's not the "main character."

✔ Ensuring that half-elf ranger Calina doesn't defect to the other side.

✔ And never, ever letting her guard down around the masked bandit she once called "Pa."

That's the Way the Castle Crumbles picks up right where *When Life Gives You Legends* left off, delivering an edgy, edge-of-your seat fantasy adventure where the laughs come just as fast as the punches... Are you ready to roll for initiative?

The party's next adventure is available and ready for you to read! Grab your copy, then turn the page for a sneak peek of the action.

When real life feels a bit too crazy, you can always find comfort in the fantasy realm!

Yup, this feels like the exact right time to send you the first of my monthly slice-of-life stories starring Durgan Stoutbarrel, dwarven tavern owner and everybody's favorite guy.

I hope you'll enjoy learning more about his backstory and witnessing the meet cute with his half-giant husband Pat.

I'll write a new story about Durgan each month and deliver it exclusively to my newsletter subscribers. It's my version of giving you a warm, mead-drenched hug. *Awwww.*

You can sign up at www.LunaRAuthor.com/ subscribe to start reading the first delicious slice-of-life instantly. Enjoy!

WANT EVEN MORE?

If you loved this book and want to go deeper into the world of Verandel (or just collect shiny things), here are two ways to keep the adventure going...

SHOP THE LEGENDARY LOOT

Signed books. Special editions. D&D campaign adventures. Swag fit for a Chosen One (or a tavern wench with good taste).

Find it all at my official shop:
www.LunaRyderBooks.com

JOIN THE SECRET SCROLLS SOCIETY

Want to:

- Read new books *as I write them*
- Unlock exclusive lore and magical backstory
- Vote on plot developments and future projects
- Possibly become a character in a future book?

Then my Patreon is the place for you:
www.patreon.com/LunaRauthor

Your support helps me keep telling stories that are gloriously weird, queer, and chaotic... and I'd love to have you along for the ride.

Thanks for reading. Stay strange. Stay brave. Stay bard to the bone.

— Luna

ACKNOWLEDGMENTS

Oh, gosh. It takes so much to bring a book to life. Basically, whoever's life touches mine helps the process, for better or for worse. Hey, we writers need inspo for our bad guys too, right?

But I count myself very lucky to have so many of the good guys in my corner...

Thanks to my kiddo, a very self-aware 10-year-old whose insight altered my self-awareness and opened up a whole new world, one I already lived in... but just hadn't noticed yet somehow. Vincent, you're the reason great rainbow characters like Tilda, Durgan, and—yes—even Finnian Sly exist in Verandel as their true selves but are also not defined by their labels, no matter how proudly or rightly they claim them.

Everyone deserves to see themselves represented in likable, powerful characters. And it's also of vital importance to me that LGBTQ+ characters be able to exist without needing to be defined by their relationships or some other such pigeonholing plots.

Similarly, a shout-out to my neurodivergent peeps! Who says we can't be the heroes? Given that our big, beautiful brains work differently, how can we be anything but? Our unique problem-solving abilities make for some epic adventures. Entertaining too. Go live your life as the main character and remember that your story doesn't have to be told chapter by chapter. Sometimes it's really freaking fun to skip around.

To my dearest friends and most ardent supporters: Bethany, Mallory, Mallory again (but this time a different one), Jennifer, Russell, Kaitlyn, Becky. I'm so glad to have you in my go-to adventuring party. Cheers!

To SJ Gautreaux and her beautiful cover illustrations and divine title idea, which I happily adopted for book one in this trilogy, thank you very, very much, SJ.

To Crystal and her combined editing and therapeutic guidance. I forgive you for removing so many of my beautiful ellipses. I know you had your reasons... I think.

To my actual therapist, because therapy is life, people.

To my emotional support animal, Sky Princess, three-fourths Chihuahua, one-whole legend. You were there for every single word, just as you are for every single breath. You are a very good dog even if you bark a little too much. It's okay, I bark too much sometimes too.

To Emily, Aaron, and Jacob. You know why, but if I said why, then I might have to change the content rating of this book, and I worked so hard to keep it PG up until this point. Thank you, though, for believing in this project and in me, for serving as a buddy, a muse, and a safe space for my oddities.

Thank you to the readers, past and future, but especially those in the present—and especially those committed enough to actually read through these boring post-credits. I see you; I appreciate you, and I'm so glad you're here.

And last, perhaps most importantly, I must thank Luke Gygax for welcoming me into the world of Dungeons & Dragons during a writer's con in Las Vegas. I didn't feel like I belonged with the group of serious, hardcore gamers. All of whom were a lot smarter than me, but Luke was so very welcoming that I soon found myself letting it all hang out as one centaur barbarian that I just so happened to decide to play like My Little Pony. I had such a great time that I went back and did it again the next year. The second time I played that centaur barbarian like Britney Spears. Both times, Luke gave me a prize for being the most entertaining player. And that was enough to A) show me that maybe I did belong in this fantastical world despite being a bit different than its other denizens, and to B) prove I needed more of this weird diva centaur barbarian in my life.

Yes, I wrote this whole dang book out of a fervent love for Tulip Thunderhoof.

There, now you know.

Sorry, Tilda. But thanks anyway.